THE WILD HUNT SERIES

RISE OF A HUNTRESS

H J REESE

RISE OF A HUNTRESS

THE WILD HUNT
BOOK THREE

H J REESE

Cover designed by MiblArt

Paperback ISBN: 978-1-7390756-4-4

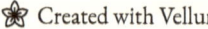 Created with Vellum

CONTENT WARNING

Rise of a huntress is a fantasy romance novel based around the myth of the Wild Hunt. This is book 3 in a 4 book series.

Its content warnings include: sex, violence, and swearing.

For my amazing readers following Kade, Val, Jair and Teal's journey

SUMMER COURT

Angus, God of Love
Gift: His Daggers

I am the water
The river runs through me

AUTUMN COURT

Gael, God of Forging
Gift: His Hammer

Hope lights the fire
Fury fans the flames
Courage carries me through

SPRING COURT

Daina, Goddess of Fertility and Air
Gift: The Berserker

With a song on its wings
And life at its feet
Wind guides us all

WINTER COURT

Bruma, Goddess of Ice
Gift: Frost Witch

Frost quiets my mind
Ice hardens my soul
I will persevere

EADHA ISLAND

BY MAP
MAKER TEAL

WINTER COURT

SPRING COURT

SUMMER COURT

AUTUMN
COURT

THE COURT OF
SHADOWS

GALEAIRY STRAIT

THE COURTLESS

THE MAINLAND

MAP TO THE
SCALE OF A
MERMAID'S TAIL

1

VALENTINA

"She called you a mangy cat?"

"Among other colorful names," Jair answered with a deep laugh as we strolled side by side through Auris' bustling Main street. He nodded to the Shadowfae guard to close and lock the large marble doors behind us on our way out of Shadow Court's capital.

We headed toward the old medicine hut, which now stored dry herbs harvested from Gillies Forest. Teal, the small seething pixie, found herself in need of quite a bit.

"Teal wasn't nearly as unhappy with me when I visited. Even though I deserved her wrath most of all," I said, glancing up toward the black and violet sky.

Kaderyn was out there. Somewhere.

Jair rested his heavy arm around my shoulders. "You took down a baliroq, Valentina. Don't discount yourself."

I thought back to the white-wooded bow and arrow leaning against the tree the day Teal got her arm bit off by a baliroq, a massive four-legged and scaled, snub-nosed beast of the northern plains, in Winter Court. If I were a better shot, if I had *any* shot at all, she'd still have an arm. Instead of that . . . *thing*. "Jair, where can I learn to shoot a bow and arrow?"

"Ah," he scoffed. "We were all there. We were all too slow."

"Yeah," I answered, but I'd live with that guilt for the rest of my life.

The beast only dropped to the ground when my gods' daggers sunk into its back. It died in the same tundra I killed General Mohr in. Both their bodies were now locked in Winter's clutches. And Kaderyn—*my* Kaderyn—dragged Mohr's soul out of his body before shadowfading me to Auris.

Home.

Was Autumn Court going to retaliate against me for killing its general? Unease settled in my gut. I was definitely going to need to learn to shoot a bow.

It had been a week since we got Kaderyn's shadows back, and the Wild Hunt was still out riding across the lands. Occasionally I could hear them, the baying of the hounds and the braying of the horses as the six Hunters scoured the lands for souls destined for the Underworld, the darkness in the next life. Jairek didn't know how long it would take for them to finish. The Hunt had been split for so long. So instead, he had been giving me a tour of The Court of Shadows with quick visits every day to a healing Teal.

Jair and I were on our way to collect more herbs for Oir, Kaderyn's advisor, to make more Virtusa, a pain-relieving tonic for Teal. I struggled to keep down the nausea every time I smelled it. It was the herbs used to drug me in Scarlotta's prisons. But we were moving on past our plights, and I'd already talked Jair into heading to Hawrenthia in Summer Court to make Lord Grigory protect his fae better. Especially since Mohr burned Elaria and my old theater to the ground in an attempt to give me nowhere to go back to—except back to him.

We stopped just outside the doorway of the old hut.

"Mind if I wait out here?" I clamped my mouth shut as the bile rose.

Jair turned to me quickly. "It's the smell again, isn't it?"

And my face must have been green because he gave me a brief nod and went in. I watched from the doorway as Jair gathered the herbs needed for Oir from baskets and drying racks on makeshift tables.

The hut was full of hung roots and drying stalks. Their faded purple petals swayed in the breeze of the open door; their stalks looked crunchy to the touch. Floral and bitter smells escaped the hut. I didn't know what they were all for, but I had an idea some would kill quite quickly. And not nicely.

I turned to the sprawling midnight black forest where all these were harvested. Small lights, maybe fireflies, floated throughout the dewy air. I wandered closer, right to the edge where the grass turned black, but it wasn't any place I was going without Kaderyn by my side. A slow mist crawled along the edge, and though I knew Summer lay on the other side, I also knew all who went in never came back out.

A tingling started in my toes, and I wiggled them in my black calf-high laced linen boots. Shadow boots repelled the rain nicely. But the tingling continued until my body was humming, buzzing with an energy I only associated back to my time at the theater. My heart raced as my vision faded. I turned as best I could for the medicine hut door. For Jairek.

"Jair!" I shouted and watched as he turned to me just as quick.

His face blanched, and his normal calm brown eyes shot wide. The Virtusa herbs dropped to the floor and crunched under his boots as the lionshifter dove for my outstretched hand.

I willed myself forward, I reached for him, but my body

3

wouldn't respond. I tried again, clawing, crawling at the air, but fell.

And fell and fell and fell.

WHEN THE SPINNING, THE ENDLESS CHURNING, stopped, cold marble—not unlike cold cobblestone when I was six—pressed against my cheek. I curled in on myself with the memories it brought with it. I couldn't *stand* the cold. Not then —not now.

I opened my eyes, groggy and dizzy, and peeked through my forearms to see white.

So much white.

"What—" I shielded my eyes as best I could with a hand that felt not my own.

"Welcome, Valentina."

I flipped over, pressing my entire body against the floor, bowing away from that voice. Lord Aborys, in his pristine white and pale blue regalia, stood over top of me with his hands clasped together.

His tongue flicked over his teeth. "Welcome to Winter Court," he said, leaning down as the power of ice, steady and quick, ran through my body. "Siphon."

2

DERYN IRONSIDE

"Teal, sit still. If I fasten this on wrong, the only thing you're going to be good for is a talking paperweight," I said, trying to calm a fidgeting pixie atop the worktable in my iron tower.

The sun was setting low, and only the glow of my forge allowed me any grace to see.

"Oh great, let us talk of its weight
I hate to protest but it's heavier than rock slate.
Don't be surprised if you find this lump of metal at the
bottom of the Galeairy Strait," she seethed, spit flying
through her pointed teeth.

Her 'S's' came out slurred, probably from the Virtusa Tonic Oir was giving her.

With a huff, I blew three coiled strands of my unruly hair out of my eyes and leaned back, glancing up at her, crouched at her side. "First of all, no part of you hates protesting. And second, I've spent four straight nights trying to make you something with the likeness of a pixie arm. The least you can do is pretend to be grateful. Besides," I said, standing to join the last of the ties around her small shoulders, hoping it would hold the metal strands in place until her skin could heal around it, "you haven't seen what it can do yet."

Oir had given her something for pain not long ago, but a pixie—especially one with the metabolism and energy of Teal—was going to burn through it in another hour tops. I had to get the arm on before the skin of Teal's shoulder fully healed—assuming it would work at all. Thankfully, Jair had brought her to me quick enough.

I shifted my own iron leg self-consciously. It scraped against the iron floor of my workshop, a second half-floor in my tower on the Mainland. I hadn't made an iron limb in over a hundred years, but my welds had improved in that time significantly. I'd strung this iron out so thin and molded it before it hardened that the little six-inch arm looked more like a piece of art. Far better than the crude, clunky thing I had strapped just below the knee.

But Teal was already shaking her head. Her pointed hat flopped back and forth.

"It is unnatural in my pixie state
To lug cold iron around
Pulling down my gait.
So, I thank you, Deryn, for your—"

I lifted the iron arm, now fully fastened to her shoulder, and held it out straight. "Fire away, Teal."

Her face contorted briefly before it scrunched up in concentration and fired a blue blast through the newly welded iron arm I spent the last hour attaching to her ripped and shredded —but slowly healing—shoulder blade.

Blue pixie magic shot out through the palm of the iron hand and blasted into my shelves of bottles and broken iron gadgets. I ducked away from spraying glass as things exploded and mangled metal ricocheted to the floor.

I peeked through my forearms. Oops.

But Teal was elated.

"Deryn! You devious iron-magician!
You've recreated a limb from ore composition!"

"So it's not too heavy for ya, Teal?" I hummed as I leaned on my good leg and jutted my hands on my hips.

"Oh, who has the time to complain of the mass
When I have an arm to kick some baliroq's ass."

"Not yet. Oir still needs to heal the skin around the metal, but from what I've learned of pixies in . . . "—I looked to the clock now lying in pieces, broken, on the floor—"the thirty-six hours spent scouring books in Auris' library on pixie healing. We'll know in two days whether your body will reject the metal arm or fuse together as one."

Teal, grinning like a faeling, shot another blast again.

I ducked just in time. "Take it outside, Teal!"

"Oh, sure. Give the annoying pixie a metal arm. What could go wrong?"

I twisted to the familiar voice. The demigod in a navy and silver tunic, one of his many, no doubt, sat sipping his wine on a haggard daybed on the other side of my workshop near the massive floor-to-ceiling window to the east.

I glared at Adrian. "How long have you been here? Hey, get your feet off my table."

He came and went when he pleased.

He pulled his long legs to the floor and took a healthy gulp of red wine. "Long enough to see you almost lose your head."

"Not all of us can sit by while pixies die," I said, stamping on bits of flaming wood chunks littering the floor.

"I've apologized for not telling you about the pixie cage in the mountains already. What more must I do? Grovel?"

"No, but come help me tidy this up, will you?"

Not long later, I sent Teal home on the crude moldy ship we were using to cross the Galeairy Strait to travel from The Court of Shadows to the Mainland. Hoping it was the last time I'd have to strap the metal arm on the healing pixie.

Four brush strokes in, cleaning up the last bits of broken shelving and battered iron bits, a caw stole my attention from the floor I was sweeping. My ears pricked, tuned to the caw of a hawkshifter. A smile turned up my lips, and I rushed to put the dustbin down, cursing when my iron leg snagged on a blanket that loitered on the floor again.

No doubt left there by a chatty demigod who did *not* help me tidy and instead rambled on about god's know-what. I tossed it on his head and hurried up the tightly coiled winding stairs that led to the top of my tower, my bedrooms, and where Rhett was waiting for me.

There he stood on the blankets of Faebric I had draped over this part of my tower. Because Shifterfae, like any other fae, couldn't touch iron and before I met him I'd built an entire sprawling tower out of the damn stuff.

His naked toes lined the edge of the Faebric, desperate for me to come to him. I sunk into his arms and relished his face nuzzling into my neck. It had been a week since he came last.

"You haven't been sleeping?" he asked with a muffled voice and hair that smelled like ocean spray.

"My window for helping Teal was running out." I sighed into his arms.

"You must take care of yourself, Deryn. If you come to Illediff—"

I pulled out of his arms and walked back toward the dresser and fiddled with little iron bowls. My amateurish first creations. Some were hideous, even barely held together and broke when the west wind pushed through my rooms, but I kept them all just the same. "I won't return to Eadha Island. You know I can't."

And there might as well have been a cavern between us instead of the dozen feet from where he could step and a conversation I refused to have.

"Did you do it?" he asked, softening his shoulders. "Did you make Teal an arm?"

I turned to my love, my beautiful hawkshifter from the Courtless with sun-bleached blond hair and a body hardened with muscle. Scars littered his skin, puffy and raised, the body of a warrior created at a young age. "It's up to her now."

I watched Rhett's reaction, but his attention strayed. Running two courts in Jairek and Kaderyn's stead had taken a toll on him. Dark circles made his normal vibrant blue eyes look haunted. *And he lectures me on looking after myself.*

"Please tell me you can stay the night." I nudged the Faebric, pulling it farther along the iron floor.

He cocked his head to the side and listened.

"What is—"

"Shh." The muscle in his arms twitched and he gave me a severe look.

It started as a soft rattle, a vibration. Not unusual for the whipping south wind to shake an iron tower erected thirty feet along the shore of the Galeairy. But before I could ease his mind, it grew into a rhythmical clanking. The tower shook like the earth was crumbling. Iron bolts bounced around inside their metal bowls. "What is it?"

"Come here," Rhett ushered.

My throat was screaming. I wanted to dissolve the ten feet between us, but my feet wouldn't move. Something was coming. I didn't need to be fae to feel it.

"Rhett!" I yelled as darkness roared, strong all-consuming power, shocked my very bones. The cracking of hooves and barking of hounds echoed around the room and into my mind. A thunderous rapture of smoky skies overtook the early evening light.

My nerves lit a fire that panic had suppressed and I stirred to run to him.

"No! It's too late, Deryn. Don't move." He thrust out a hand, urging me to stay.

But I'd not felt something like this in centuries. Death was coming on fast horses and I ran to Rhett.

He dove for me in one swift motion, pulling me under him as the deafening drumming of hooves surrounded us. Then darkness swallowed us entirely as shadows, the Wild Hunt, ran right through my iron tower. Rhett squeezed me to him as I cowered from between his arms. His face a hard stone. Weathered and worn.

I peeked around his flexed arm, watching the six ghostly Hunters with Kaderyn in lead charge through the tower looking for souls destined for his Underworld.

Soon, within seconds, they were off, charging across the southern Mainlands pivoting across the valleys and moors. I tilted my head backward toward the balcony Rhett came in from and saw them moving like smoke filtering across the ground.

"Never run when the Wild Hunt sounds, Deryn." Rhett kissed my upturned throat.

And I knew that, I was old. Really old. But it had been so long since I'd seen them and I wanted to run. Badly. An omen had come, and I wanted to leave its path.

I smelt burning flesh and sizzling skin. Rhett pulled his hand back out of my hair and little pock marks littered his skin. Scorched. I scrambled out from under him. Brushing the flakes of iron out of it from Teal's explosion.

Oh, no. "Adrian?" Panic struck my voice as I called for the demigod I'd left drinking alone down in my shop.

"I spilled my bloody wine," he called back, muffled through layers upon layers of iron flooring. "Damn it, this is my best shirt. You know how to reach me, dearest Deryn."

But before I could say another word, the loudest, harrowing roar cracked the skies. Like a beast in pain. Rhett jutted his head up in answer.

"What is it?" I whispered.

Rhett looked down at me sharply, but an exhaustion coated his eyes. "It's Jairek. Something's wrong. Stay in the tower." And before he could finish the last word, he jumped over the balcony railing and shifted into a tawny hawk with a twelve-foot wingspan before the last of the sun's rays touched his face.

I leaned down and gathered broken chunks of iron—bowls that fell and broke a final time from my tables. Jairek, the heir to the Courtless throne and Rhett's would-be king, was in distress.

Of course, I'd stay in my tower. I'd never leave the safety of my metals.

I returned to my workshop below, where a deep red stain greeted me on the daybed's armrest. And as if Adrian feared I'd forget him, dozens of little iron bowls surrounding my shop were full of brine water. Adrian's calling card.

"Thanks, Adrian," I snipped.

A pulse thudded through the tower, rippling the water in the bowls.

I chucked all the broken iron pieces blown apart by pixie magic into the forge to melt back down into usable metal. Then, using long-handled tongs to pull out a flaming hot shard of iron, I pulled my hammer out of my side satchel and smashed it down, flames sparking. My shoulder muscles screamed and I fell into a comfortable rhythm.

I pounded iron until it chased away the fear I held for the fae, for the ones responsible for my missing leg, and the life I left behind.

Whatever was happening on Eadha Island it would not involve me.

3

VALENTINA

Nausea rolled through my gut, and I turned in time to hurl on the white marble floor. Frost magic crept across my fingertips like it did in Blackwater. Through split vision, I could make out icicles hanging off sprawling, white-frosted chandeliers suspended to vaulted ceilings. From their bows hung purple grapes coated in thin glass-like ice.

I looked up into the sky-blue eyes of Lord Aborys.

"What did you do? How am I here?"

Dropping my aching head against the cold stone, I breathed heavily, blowing hair out of my face.

I was finally safe.

I was finally home.

Soldiers convened, pulling my hands into metal shackles. I fought to find shadow magic, *any* magic.

"Don't touch me." I spit.

But they didn't stop trudging and sliding through vomit, locked onto their single-minded task.

Click.

The last binding snapped closed, and I looked down at my frost-covered fingers.

Ice magic.

"I hoped to find bindings unnecessary, but I can see you need some convincing that you are where you belong."

"You took me from where I belong." I shuddered into my chest.

Two soldiers hefted me to my feet from under my armpits and I heaved again, leaving a trail of vomit as they dragged me behind their lord. Their white hair, eyebrows, and eyelashes so different from my own.

We stopped in front of a large domed window where a busy city alive with movement carried on below. White horses adorned in blue saddle blankets carried white-haired fae through the streets. Faelings ducked behind barricades, and I gasped. But they were . . . laughing?

Suddenly one popped up and threw a spherical ball of snow at the others.

"Welcome to Silvermere City," Lord Aborys said. "Welcome to the most northern city on Eadha Island."

I dropped my chin to my chest, squeezing my eyes, but I just smelled like yesterday's dinner from Auris' tavern. *Please let me wake in Kaderyn's bed.*

But unkind fingers jutted my head up and held. Forcing me to meet Aborys' stare.

"How?" I grit out, trying to pull my head away. "How am I here?"

"I apologize if the way I got you here was . . . uncomfortable. I can assure you, it wasn't pleasant for me either. Afraid I had to give up something I prize deeply in return." Lord Aborys started walking, hands clasped behind his back, and the soldiers dragged me on. "I had to act while the Hunt rode. The first ride since the fall of the Wild Hunt will carry a call so strong that the

Hunter of yours can't pull away. For anything, Valentina. Though I don't underestimate the depth of his ire toward me once he finds out what I've done." He spun around with the energy and grace of a fae half his age. "Tell me, Valentina, as I go to order you clothing more suited for this court, can you feel the chill of Winter? Do you feel the lashing of Bruma on your bare skin? I wouldn't want Summer wilting in Winter. I'm afraid we are all pure fae here. There are never any visiting fae to ask."

"Or faeless?" I chided.

His face drew down into a mask of anger. "*Especially* faeless."

And though I was fearful, a calm pumped through my veins and there was no buffer against it. It sharpened my senses into something pointed, almost single-minded. Ice magic. Obsessive clear thinking ice magic.

My black Shadow Court clothing stood me apart from the room of soldiers. Small faelings huddled in dark corridors and went wide-eyed at the very sight of me. If not my clothes, then my black hair did.

"You'll have to change regardless, unfortunately. Though your shadow clothing resembles my strong-willed daughter, I have to see that she is the exception and not the norm. These castle attendants will help you into something more appropriate."

"I don't plan on staying." I pulled against the shackles now coated in a layer of ice. Ice chips fell to the floor.

Laughter bubbled up from the windows and a quick look told me the faelings were still playing. I blinked and blinked again. Why did I think they'd all be forced into their homes, controlled?

"Time is not on our side," Lord Aborys confessed, pulling me to the present. "Though, it's the first Wild Hunt in centuries and I'd imagine it'll take that Hunter of yours a deal longer than he used to, collecting the souls destined for the Underworld. I do not doubt that he'll come back with a vengeance. I need you prepared before then."

Female castle attendants in long, thick dresses bowed down as they passed their lord.

I didn't like the way this was going. *Kaderyn!* I yelled down a bond so thick I could hear my plea fizzle out well before it reached its mark.

"You were a wrench thrown in the fate of Eadha. Other lords and ladies might not have felt what you are, but Winter knows better." Aborys greeted each of his passing servants individually. "I think no matter any gifts the gods and goddesses bestowed to the courts, you are the greatest gift of all."

Kaderyn! I tried again. Panic struck me, but the magic of ice made me act. I spun quickly, focusing on this court's magic to calm my shaking, and pulled a soldier's bronze sword from his belt. I charged, tugging out of reaching hands, then screamed a sound like cracking ice, of panic and pain as I lifted the weapon aiming for Lord Aborys' neck. But he was quick, and my hands were tied. My sword hit his hilt and vibrated out of my hands to the marble with a ringing *crack*. A splitting pain snapped in the middle of my back, and I dropped to my knees at Lord Aborys' feet.

"Your confidence and bravery are admirable. Nothing worse than weakness." The massive male knelt in front of me, and I recoiled, his magic so strong it stung. "I'll tolerate it once, Valentina."

"You can spew on about gifts from the gods all you want. I am not one of them and I'll never rule at your side," I seethed, staring at an ornate door. An escape. But I turned and faced the brutal lord head-on. "I'll never agree to harm the faeless."

His tongue flicked over his teeth as I glared. "Yes, you will," he promised. "And you'll do it willingly."

"Kaderyn!" I screamed, both out loud and in my mind. Neither seemed to echo past the wide corridor.

"I've prepared a room for you. I want there to be no animosity between us, Valentina. But I confess, I need you up to speed as quickly as possible. Tell me, what do you require? Food, warmer clothes?"

"I want nothing from you. Your general won't be able to protect you from Kaderyn."

"No, Valentina. You will," he said with conviction.

I hurled again down the front of my shadow clothes.

4

DERYN IRONSIDE

A FEW DAYS LATER

The cavernous insides of the Twin Peak Mountains looked like a giant's fist scooped through it in one half-thought-out swipe. Large iron beams lined the crude rock walls with dents of ogre's knuckles lodged into them ten feet high like they smashed them into place with their fists—like they manhandled the metal into submission. I'd installed brackets over the years to keep the boulders now above my head from crashing down, but I always wondered how much magic was at play.

Not that I'd ever ask her.

It was the first of May and I'd just spent the past three hours lugging a heavy bag of bolts and gussets from my tower across the valley to the mountain face on the other side. Sweat ran down my back, soaking through my shirt and into the leather harness straps I permanently wore. Formed for Rhett's hawk feet to pick me up quickly if need be.

Next week I would test out the tracks that ran straight across the valley from the tower to here. Only another thirty feet of iron rails, thrust twenty feet above the slope of the valley, were needed to fasten them into the mountainside and it would be complete. If I had built them right, the trip would take no more than twenty minutes, depending on how fast I wanted to brave the speed of the cart.

"Hello, Deryn."

She saw me before I heard her.

Carmen leaned on her staff—which she often downplayed by calling a cane—and hobbled closer. Her gray hair hung in ripples down her back, frazzled but clean. *Witch magic*, I thought. It was something akin to fae's ability to glamour. The glass ball on the end of the staff glowed and swirled faster as she approached, blending the red and blue into a deep purple that matched her dress. I didn't know the full extent of a witch's magic, and I knew better than to ask.

I swallowed. "I have the bolts you asked for."

"Just put them there." She tossed an aged hand toward the wall. "The ogres have a load of ore ready for you if you want to beckon one of your *friends* to bring it to your tower."

"I'll have them pick it up next month." I was sitting on a pretty pile of ore from last month still.

"Bring Adrian. It's too much for the hawkshifter."

My mouth twitched. Thank my iron ore, Rhett didn't hear her. It was far easier to get Adrian to move large batches of ore back to my tower, but getting him to help me near the mountain was like catching wind with a net. Useless and frustrating.

"Only on the first of the month, as per our agreement," she said. "You know how I feel about unexpected guests."

"Of course."

She looked me over thoughtfully but calculating. "You know, when Adrian pulled you out of his waters two hundred years ago, I thought it'd be the end of my quiet days, but it's been a beautiful partnership."

If it wasn't for Adrian, I had no doubt Carmen would have left me dying at the base of her mountain. I gave a quick smile and edged toward the door.

"I see your tracks are almost done," she said, tapping long fingers on her thigh.

"Close. A few more rails should do it." Then fifty years of working would all be worth it. "The ogres are smelting away?"

"Yes, more than ever," Carmen called back. "But I think I want some archways installed. Really make this mountain a castle. The ogres can do the heavy lifting, but I need you to figure out how to make it hold. The last thing I want is this mountain coming down on me. Right here and here." She pointed.

The growling of an ogre echoed around the room and everything Carmen had said filtered out of my mind as there, around the corner, was a gray, balding, ten-foot ogre peeking around crude rock face.

"Umm..." I mumbled, my words coming out stuttered and stiff. I did not know how she slept with them so near. *What had she wanted built?* "Once I have my rails done. I should be able to travel twice as fast. Then whatever you need built will take me half the time."

The ogre moaned again.

"Dineen!" Carmen snapped. "The horn is hung up for the day. You will not get more rations than the others until all the nights mined ore is smelted down. Now, stop pestering me," Carmen said, shoving her cane toward the ogre in a threat. "Be gone."

Dineen the ogre tried reaching for the brown Horn of Bran on the wall that filled full of whatever liquid its user wanted. In the ogre's case, it was pixie blood. Decades ago, Carmen was feeding pixies to the ogres to get them to smelt and mine our iron. I was able to put a halt to it by asking the Lord of Shadows for help. He needed a way to touch iron, which I had already made to allow Rhett into my tower, and I needed a way to keep the ogres mining my ore. But my conscious wouldn't let it be at the expense of the pixies. His solution was to retrieve the Horn of Bran, a horn that allowed its beholder whatever drink they desired. And now that ogre named Dineen was on its tippytoes trying to flip the horn off the wall with a fat-pointed finger.

I tried to talk again, but a whimpering growl came from the tardy ogre again.

"Oh, just wait one second. I cannot possibly think with all this racket," Carmen said. "Dineen, I warned you." She pointed her staff at the grumbling ogre and mumbled words only witches knew.

The next thing I saw was a creature not too discernable from a shrew in the ogre's place. Its chin tucked into its throat and buck teeth came out of a pointed nose as it chattered into the dirt. No bigger than my shoe.

She straightened out her long-layered dress and pointed her nose in the air. "He was on my last nerve."

I blinked, frozen in place. Transfiguration was a new one for me, even loving a hawkshifter for as long as I have. The staff swirled with a myriad of colors and pulsed again with witch's magic.

"Oh, don't look like such a little mouse, Deryn. I can control a bunch of blubbering ogres."

I stole a glance at the now dusty cage that once held two dozen blue-skinned pixies. Traded off for the Horn that now hung on a bolt—one of mine—by the stairs going up to Carmen's loft.

Just then, a caw of a hawk came from above.

"I suppose the hawkshifter can try to carry the ore now. Don't say I didn't warn the bird, though."

"I'm sure he just needs me," I mumbled, and half ran for the opening out of the mountain, feeling her follow close behind.

And we both watched Rhett land off to the side of a large red boulder, sweaty and out of breath. I hadn't seen him since the night the Wild Hunt ran through my tower for the first time in centuries. And he positively *never* came to Carmen unless it was pre-planned to help me.

"What's wrong?" I stepped forward out of instinct.

"It's time, Deryn. You have to come to Eadha." His eyes flicked distrustfully to Carmen.

I was already shaking my head and turning sharply on a heel to start the long walk back to my tower—to my safety. My pace was as quick as one iron leg would let it go. "I can't Rhett, you know why. Stop aski—"

"Damn it, Deryn!" he said to my back. "It's your sister."

My heart stopped and my vision tunneled into nothing but black dots, but I whipped toward his voice, nonetheless. My world spun on its axis, and I had nothing but his voice and words I didn't want to hear to ground me.

"Deryn." Rhett puffed out a breath, his eyes hard.

But my stomach was in my throat.

"It's Avika."

5

VALENTINA

I spent the next half a day horror struck in a room of light gold and white. There was nothing behind the wallpaper, no pixie vents to crawl into, nothing sharp to use as a weapon. I practiced ice magic when I could, tried barricading the door like I'd seen done to Jair's door in Scarlotta. But I was untrained and a swift kick from a soldier on the other side broke down any progress I made.

Two castle attendants came to help me get dressed at one point and I growled and thrashed like a wild thing that they ran out with my hair undone. I shoved the dresses they brought into a long-dead fireplace. Winterfae surrounded me, yet not a single whip of frozen wind through an open door chilled me. Which was a reminder of how far away from . . . *any* other fae I was. A deep longing stretched through me. I missed Kade.

When finally, the door unlatched, and behind the guards appeared a short female with a nervous smile. She led us down winding corridors. The guards shoved me ahead of them toward a grand doorway where the wafting of food made my stomach betray me and it now growled like the wild thing from earlier. They sat and chained me to the table with barely enough room for a spoon to reach my mouth. I had to huddle down—cower. Ice magic sharpened my senses, pulling out every object that was or could be a weapon.

Once crowds of fae piled into the room, I thought of thrashing again, gnarling bared teeth like a nuckelavee. Winterfae threw me sideway glances, perhaps fearful, but all I felt was otherness again.

That I didn't belong.

And just when I went to gnash my teeth at some pointing males in impeccable clothing, Lord Aborys strode into the room with direct sights on me.

"Still not in Winter's wear?" he frowned at my puke-covered shirt. "I was sure I sent something suitable."

"Alas, it was not." It was suitably stuffed up a fireplace, though.

Almost forty round tables filled the dining hall with just under a dozen fae at each. Aborys and I sat with others who weren't of the same social standing as him. It didn't help my social standing any that I was the only one in metal bindings.

Dinner arrived in the form of rolls smelling of yeast, baked desserts, and roasted animal. The Winter lord greeted each food attendant personally and pleasantly.

I ripped into a bun and watched him out of the corner of my eye. "What am I here for? I am not the best fighter and you're delusional if you think I'd harm Kade—" I stopped at his name. If you're strong enough, why not wipe out the other courts?"

"Winter is not the absence of life," he said between mouthfuls. Someone invaded my court and took what didn't belong to them. Which solidifies their cowardice and the state of the island."

A wind whipped through the room, and for the first time, I felt it. A shiver ran down my spine, racking me through. *Oh gods, not the cold again.*

Briefly aware of a dish of butter being placed before me, I tried to ignore the tingling in my scalp and my fingers as winter's cold assaulted me. Why was it affecting me all of a sudden? Unless someone here wasn't as pure winter fae as Aborys suggested. Or an outsider was here. I gasped. Someone other than Winterfae. Hope rose in my veins as my teeth audibly chattered.

I leaned down, cringing because it looked like I was cowering again, and glared at anyone who dared point, but I pulled my filthy shirt up higher around my neck, blocking the air that ran down my back.

That's when I saw it.

The knife in the butter.

A slick film coated my palms, but I thought back to what Lord Aborys said. Someone took something from him. "Are you talking about the missing fae? What reason would the faeless have for taking a fae?"

"It was not the faeless's actions but inaction. They are weak and vulnerable."

"Whatever your reason for murdering faeless, you'll never have my sympathy."

He wiped the corners of his mouth with a napkin. "Tell me, Valentina. Do you love your Hunter?"

I pressed my lips into a line and turned away. This monster didn't know the meaning.

"If he was taken from you, don't you think you'd do anything to get him back?"

And when I kept quiet, when the only sound was my chattering teeth, he said, "I think you would. And I know your Hunter will. Which is why you have exactly two days to concede; to decide Winter is not such a terrible place, decide to rise to your full potential as Siphon, and help me repair Eadha Island into the isle it was supposed to be before the faeless came along like a blight across nightshades. Kade can offer you darkness, eternal rain, and an Underworld of pain. While no court on Eadha dares turn down my trades. I can offer you better food, tundras to explore, and freedom to take whose pain you want. I'll never force you."

"There's a blight all right, but it's sitting next to me. You're asking me to murder innocent magicless fae, which is immensely worse than taking the pain of entire battlefields. I am not like you. I will *never* be like you. And lastly, there is no world where I *enjoy* the cold." I turned to the fae who had the displeasure of sitting next to me, because I sure as the depths wasn't asking Lord Aborys to do it, and said, "Hey, *psst*, you. You're not the blight I mentioned. Can you pull my hood up? I'm freezing."

The fae gave a nervous glance to Lord Aborys as my breath fogged before me when suddenly a chair scratched out like nails on slate and a beautiful fae the next table over stood up with her eyes wide, locked on me.

"*Lord*." She bowed, moving around the tables with her hands bunched in her skirts. "Perhaps *I* can convince our guests to wear the appropriate winter attire."

Lord Aborys looked at her for a moment, then flicked his eyes toward me. "You think, Freyell? She seems as ruly as Helle. There's a reason I've left the court in your daughters' hands and not my own."

I locked my jaw shut, but the chattering then moved through my entire body.

"Valentina, this is Freyell. She and her husband are my most trusted advisories. She will help you get into clothing more suitable."

And I wanted to protest, but I'd seen many die by ice magic. And my memories of it were almost worse than the chill. I needed the cold gone from my bones. I needed out of this room. Now.

I stood, my feet numb in their shadow boots, and followed her out. She hooked an arm through mine, yet no heat came off her like fae from any of the other courts. "I saw you shaking. You will not survive the north in that clothing."

"Why do you care?" I said, shoving the knife further up my sleeve.

"You, shaking like a leaf, gives away things you know nothing about. More is at stake than you losing your toes," she whispered, avoiding the sound of carrying to the female guard. She led us to what looked like a guest room in the castle, but one recently used.

"Any chance we can do this without the binds?" As nice as Freyell was and as noble her ulterior motive in getting me warmer clothes, I longed to run for an escape and weighed my luck and skill against these two.

"Ha," the guard grunted and, with a click of her tongue and rough hands, chained me to a hook in the wall.

"Greta, will you please go inform the kitchen to have hot broth brought up to Valentina's dining table?"

The hearty guard shifted from foot to foot—lumbered, really, like she was unaware of her body. "And leave you alone with her?"

"She's no different in size to my daughters. I can handle one unruly fae. But don't be long now."

My spirits fell, but already the chill had disappeared.

"Don't touch me. I'm fine already. Bruma's chill has left me. Must have just been memories of your horrid court."

"You'll freeze every time we have dinner." Freyell ignored my taunting and quickly pulled out clothing from a chest under the bed. She bent down at my feet. "Take it all off. Especially the soiled shirt. I could smell you as soon as I walked into the castle."

"I'm not stripping bare in front of a fae from Winter Court," I snapped. "You fae are wicked."

"Oh, so wicked that we'd get you into woolen leggings and spoon warm liquids into your mouth. Step into these . . . quickly now, before she comes back. The sheep's wool is the warmest across Eadha. Take those off. Oh, don't be shy. We don't have time for that."

But I wasn't the same fae from a dusty theater in Elaria. "First, turn around."

She sighed but did as I asked, and I shoved the butter knife up the edge of the duvet cover before sitting on it. The ease of pulling my clothes off and being locked to a chain on the wall was another matter entirely.

Eventually, with ushering from Freyell, I dropped my clothes to the floor and left my shadow shirt to hang on the chain between the wall and me. Frowning at how much it reminded me of the Caterina del Aamod ties with Kaderyn.

Soft wool brushed against my skin as the Winterfae shucked leggings on. This motherly fae was the perfect height for kneeing in the head, but the look in her eye had me pointing my toe so she could edge them on faster.

"Do not change in anyone's presence," she said, snapping them around my waist. "Can you lie like the faeless?"

I shook my head slowly. How does she know this in a court without any?

"If anyone asks where you got them from, you'll say, Mother."

"I don't have one."

"Then let's hope no one asks *whose* mother." A thick white dress exploded out of the chest. "Put your pants back on.

They're thin, they can fit on under this dress." She kicked the chest back under. "It's four layers or so. It should do."

Once it was on, she slid an overcoat over my arms that covered my neck and a rabbit-furred hand warmer in the shape of a tube over my free hand.

Since when are leggings a secret, unless you're planning to lace me with a weapon next?" I asked.

"Winterfae do not feel the cold. If you're not wearing the wool, then wear two dresses at all times. That fur shawl will keep your heart warm. With all of this, it should be manageable."

"If you think you're changing my hair or eyes, think again," I growled. I'd changed my eyes once for Autumn's Fortress, but I was quite done with the demands of the courts. Even if Shadowfae clothing wasn't meant for Winter.

"Fine, but do not shiver in front of my lord again."

"What court are you hiding fae from?" I felt the ice magic running through her veins. I narrowed my gaze. "Who're you protecting?"

That hit a nerve. She turned suddenly, and I took advantage of it and gathered the knife under the large sleeve of the dress.

"I'll have warmer dresses sent to your rooms. Tell Aborys nothing and I'll do what I can to try to have you released."

I gasped, stepping forward. "When?"

"When I can," she said. "He went through a great deal of trouble to get you."

I pulled the dress sleeve down in time as Greta, the guard, rounded the doorway. Freyell busied herself across the room as Greta unchained me from the wall.

I squinted at the metal on my wrist. "These are not bronze?" But they also weren't heavy like the iron key we lugged halfway across the island.

Freyell barely gave them a glance. "I know about dresses,

proper attire, and court etiquette, not locks and things of combat. Is any part cold? Uncomfortable? Pinching?" she asked, but a plea was in her eye. She was depending on my secrecy.

Better to have leverage now, so I shook my head once and within minutes they chauffeured me back to the hall for dinner.

Lord Aborys' chair slid out upon seeing us. "Ah, much better, Valentina. How kind of Freyell to offer one of her daughter's dresses." And to Freyell, he said, "I'll see that I've had it replaced."

"No need, my lord. I have them ordered in myself. You know how I like my patterns and whatnot." Freyell smoothed her hands down her own dress and took her seat.

Why did I feel like someone here was not as pure as it seemed? I peeked at her table where two almost identical females sat, one perhaps a bit older than the other, but both white-haired. A book slid up between the older one and me, blocking my view of her face, but from around the edges of the pages, I saw her tugging at the collar of her dress.

Identical to *mine*.

"What have you decided?" Lord Aborys slurped another morsel from a sea crustacean. "Will you willingly rule at my side or am I going to have to prove just how far Winter will go to wipe the faeless from the earth?"

"I've decided . . ."

Death by butter knife.

"Neither." And slid the knife out of the sleeve and lashed out, jabbing for his exposed neck. But before the smooth tip reached his skin, the double doors split open like glaciers cracking and ice magic pummeled my hand faster than my eyes could track, freezing my hand still in a block of ice. The weight of it crashed to the table. Bronze shimmering metal gleamed through the chunk of solid ice, with my Summer-tanned hand

RISE OF A HUNTRESS

locked inside. But memories of my father dying the same way choked me and I cried out.

"What, pray tell, the fuck, Father?"

There in the doorway entrance was a harsh white-haired female I wished to never see again. Hair wild, eyes fierce, hand outstretched from where she just thwarted my attempt to kill her father.

General Helle.

6

VALENTINA

Deep red blood congealed on Helle's skin and parallel lines tore through the armored clothing on her chest.

Lord Aborys glanced over at his daughter once before thrusting his fist in the air and smashing it down on mine, almost crushing my hand between shattering ice and the hard table. I swallowed the pain. Quickly he plucked the knife away and his soldiers pried my hands back in seconds.

"Helle," Lord Aborys said, tossing the knife across the table. "It pleases me to see you well. But for the love of Bruma, cover your face. This is court."

"And this is my face," she snapped. "Generals have scars."

"You're fae, not a beast. Act like it." But he muttered 'stupid female' under his breath.

"Are you sure, Father? I'm feeling kind of beastlike. I haven't eaten in two days."

Out of the corner of my eye double-swinging doors whipped back and forth as Freyell led her daughters out of it, hands locked together, half-running. Though they weren't the only ones, Helle's appearance marked the end of the meal whether anyone wanted to or not. But I've also always found meals tense when someone is bleeding out across the floor.

Helle limped over to the nearest table and plucked an abandoned charred bird's leg off the table. "One minute I'm in Winter's tundras training with my soldiers, the next I'm flat on my back under black skies looking up at a—" Though she had captured our attention, Helle stopped abruptly. She pulled her shoulders back painfully and her lips stretched into a thin line. "A little warning next time would have been nice. Maybe enough time to grab a fucking weapon." She spit blood onto the polished marble, matching the dripping blood trails that followed her in here. "Had to make some bargains I'd rather not talk about in an attempt to get home. And there's some dead Spring soldiers north of the Yegevani Mountains half-buried in Winters glaciers I'll have to go back and take care of later."

"Ah," Lord Aborys scoffed. "You're being so dramatic. You're a soldier. You did what you were supposed to do. Go get cleaned up. Consider a dress this time."

She tossed the leg and stared at her father. "Generals don't wear dresses. I'll save them all for next in line to the ladyship." She nudged her head toward the doors Freyell and her daughters retreated from.

Aborys let out a sigh and pinched the bridge of his nose. "Perhaps if you were more in tune with ruling a court instead of gallivanting with the army—"

"Pretty pleased with my gallivanting, Father," she said, limping back to the door she came in from. "No dress would have saved my neck as I trekked across the island to get back to you." She rapped her knuckles against the wooden doorframe, pausing once before looking back at us. "They have the demigod on their side, Father. I saw him myself."

Lord Aborys shoved out from the table and snapped his

fingers. "Adrian's loyalty changes like a chinook wind on an ice lake. We'll see where he goes when he realizes I have her. When he knows I have the Siphon."

The guards hoisted me up again and I went for their hands with my teeth. There was some finality in the air. I'd disobeyed him twice. There laid a risk in staying docile. My foot met the table, and I pushed back, smacking my head into the nose of a guard. A snap echoed and swearing roared after it until a sword pressed against the curve of my neck.

Kaderyn, I called through our bond, tangled in guards and dresses as they carried me off the ground through a half-finished meal. But he was so far away. Some place dark.

"That's the second time you've tried to kill me, Valentina. It pains me to say, I don't have the time to convince you that you're on the right side."

"What do you want me for?" I screamed, placing a kick to the belly of a guard. "You're the north! You have an army. You have *her*." I thrust my chin to Helle as we passed. Closer now, I saw the claw marks etched into her chest. Claw marks of a lion-shifter. "There's hardly any faeless left because of you."

"There are places I cannot get to. Small outposts deep in Autumn. Strongholds in Spring. Shadow Court, perhaps?" He held open the door and the soldiers pushed me through. When he rounded up beside me again, he said, "Thank Bruma for our strength, but unfortunately, a Winterfae can be spotted a mile away."

The white hair was a giveaway, even if they glamoured themselves to blend in.

" . . . you can pass through Autumn *and* wield firefae magic. You go to Spring and same with air magic, and Adrian's rain did not shrivel your flesh in Blackwater Junction. You're going to be my spy, infiltrate these towns and take them out. Convince these wayward courts of my strength and to side with me in the

War of Many. Helle crushes like a hammer, but you're going to slip in and out like a needle."

I'd never met someone with so much conviction. Mohr from Autumn Court knew he was wrong in using me for my pain abilities, but the lord before me now had no idea his morals were six feet under.

I writhed and ripped an arm free. "I will never kill faeless."

"They are not what the gods intended," Lord Aborys roared.

But neither was I. I looked at my ice-covered hands and whispered, "How do you know?"

"The gods do not value weaknesses. Faeless die easily, they cannot protect themselves, let alone . . ." he trailed off. His tongue flicked against his teeth.

"Spring doesn't care about the faeless." I thought about Spring's games and sending faeless like Jassa through their Hunt.

"No, but that damn demigod, for whatever backward reason does."

"And Summer?" I scoffed. Lord Grigory will hardly do anything. "You've been going in and out as your please for centuries. You don't need me in that helpless court."

He stopped then, near my rooms from before while a guard unlocked the door. "Seems a stone in the form of a scared fae from Summer Court has sent ripples across Eadha. You have two days to change your mind and help me rid the island of the faeless."

"I'll never."

"Two days," he repeated, "before I take matters into my own hands. Sleep well, Valentina."

I NEEDED OUT OF HERE, BUT CARVING THROUGH ICE with fingertips was impossible and I didn't give off body heat to melt it. I'd been shut in my rooms for half a day. A beautiful large bed sat along the back wall and a curved wooden dresser and mirror sat directly opposite it, intricately inlaid with golden patterns of snowflakes. A snow globe and a vase of snowdrop flowers sat on top and a narrow window above a window bench showed the street below. Soft cushions piled high on top, but I quickly dragged them off in my earlier search for a weapon. I heaved on the sconces along the walls, but this new metal was different, stronger.

Kaderyn! I tried calling through to him, but he felt farther than before. When that didn't work, I tried ice magic but any icicle I made broke when I tried to pick the lock. So I curled up on the window seat and watched the outside world of Silvermere as they went about their evening.

It was a long street lit up on both sides by tall lanterns half covered in banks of snow. I wondered how much snow had to fall to reach their square glass cages. Ice sculptures of Bruma, Winter's goddess, in different poses stood at street corners.

A faeling stooped down and bundled snow into his hands and packed it down tight. I touched the glass with my nose, trying to get a better look. He stood then, reached back his arm and whipped it at a group of faelings across the narrow snow-covered street.

It pinged off the tallest's head.

I stopped breathing. Was this a battle like I saw earlier? Did the faelings train young?

I lifted to my knees and pressed my hands to the glass. But the taller one wiped snow off his face and . . . laughed. Like before. The group split instantly, diving behind snow piles or behind store corners. They created their own balls of snow and launched it back.

It was a *game*.

Suddenly, the door lock clicked, and I leapt up ready to defend myself.

"I'm not going to hurt you," General Helle said, showing me her hands as she moved inside the room slowly, like entering that of a caged animal. She had changed into new clothing; these were not a beast's skin but dark blue and she'd been recently patched. White cloth peeked out from the neckline.

"Did you kill Jairek?" I asked, my voice hoarse, giving a nod toward her wounds.

She looked down at herself briefly before moving to the dresser and hopped up onto its surface. "Oh, the King of the Courtless is alive and well. I don't think he expected to see me flat on my back in your stead any more than I was."

Relief fluttered through me.

"He chased me off your court lines, too."

But talking about my family with the enemy was raking my soul. I knelt to the bed's surface and held my stomach that threatened to hurl. "Why are you here, Helle?"

She stared for too long. Far too long. Enough that I thought I could slip out the door without her noticing. So, when she finally spoke, the words were too loud for the room. "I saw you floating down a swift, wide-mouthed river as a faeling. I saw what you did for the male shouting your name in that hot, sticky courtyard. I knew something was different about you back then. And the farther you drifted down that damn river, the further I felt you as fae. Then there you were again in Blackwater—blue eyes, dark hair, petrified. I never forgot." She paused and chewed her lip. "I've always worried what fate I brought to myself by letting you live."

I sobbed into white and gold bedding, shaking my head. "No. Don't say this. Don't make me remember."

"It was me watching from the shore, Valentina."

My memories were back, and I wanted to stuff them away, bury them in the glaciers outside. Sky-blue eyes had tracked me down the river.

It was Helle.

"You killed my father," I whispered. My body went limp, and I couldn't focus on any one thing but the memory of frozen limbs winding down a river.

She winced. "It wasn't my magic, but, yes, it was my command."

The words were stuck, lodged in my throat, and they came out broken and jumbled. "Just because you spared me as a faeling doesn't mean your soul isn't meant any less for the Underworld."

"I know," she said so confirming that I recoiled. She picked up a snow globe at the back of the dresser and shook it. "Did he tell you what happened? Do you know why we hunt the faeless?"

I turned away from her. "It doesn't matter."

"He didn't always hate the faeless, you know. My mother adored them. She was gentle and kind and Winterfae loved her. A few hundred years ago, when I was a faeling, my mother went out collecting pine needles and mistletoe during Yule. She'd taken a dozen faeless with her. Some were her friends from neighboring houses, some were attendants from the castle. Others needed something to do for the festival. Feel useful, as the castle's fae took care of most—or all—other aspects," Helle said, pausing. "Well, days eventually passed and every last faeless came back, but Mother did not. They said she disappeared. One moment there and the next. Gone."

"Carried off by an Aileen, no doubt." But I chided myself because I was snide, and her mother didn't deserve it.

"There was nothing in the skies," Helle said as if she'd considered it, and placed the snow globe back to the dresser.

I swallowed, feeling like I was being pulled into something I had no business in, and I urged myself to stay silent but couldn't. "Why didn't you ask the faeless that went with her?"

"Father doesn't value weakness. Whatever happened, they were not strong enough to protect her. He did not let them live long after."

Repulsion bloomed in my belly, and I curled my lip at her. "Maybe she left you and him of her own freewill." But as soon as the words left my mouth, I could tell they hit a nerve in the general. Ice started webbing out along the surface of the dresser below her, consuming the fine wood drawers and curved mirror until she sat on a throne of ice.

I berated myself again before settling the cause of my ferocity on ice magic. It made me bold, unafraid.

"My father wasn't always like this," she muttered. "At first, he blamed everyone, but at the end of the day, that ire settled on the faeless who had no magic to protect her. It's been his personal vendetta ever since." She jumped off the dresser and headed for the door. "Exactly one fae has ever been taken from Winter, Valentina. They chose my mother, and it nearly destroyed him."

I focused on controlling the severe ice magic flowing off her and tried to stick to what I, Valentina would say, but I couldn't give her the sympathy I wanted to.

"This will not end well for you. If you get out of here, find a corner of Eadha Island and hide. Disappear. Go to the Underworld and don't come back."

"I cannot unsee the horrors of the island, Helle. I cannot sit by while helpless faeless die. Not because they are evil, but because you and your father are."

She spun, arms wide. "Damn it, Valentina. How was I supposed to know you couldn't shoot a bow and arrow? If I'd have known that, I'd have left a fucking sword in Winter's tundras."

I gasped. "It was you who left the white wooded bow and arrows?"

"I could have left a sword, an axe, *fuck*, a butter knife if I knew you preferred it. Baliroqs are not to be messed with."

"Is that why your armor is made of their skin?" I knew I'd seen it before.

She said nothing.

"He's going to come for me," I said when she cracked the door open to leave.

"For your sake, I hope Kaderyn does," she said with certainty. "You will not like what's coming."

The white-wooded door clicked shut, followed by the clank of a lock.

I pried the snow globe out of Helle's webbed throne and shook it in my fist. Soft white snowflakes danced down across a crystalline castle.

Kaderyn! I called through our bond again. The connection felt stiff, like bones locked from ill-posture, like shouting underwater.

Nothing came back.

I heaved the snow globe with all my might against the thick-paned window. It shattered into shards of glass and sparkling liquid spewed down the wall.

"HELLE TELLS ME WE ARE RESPONSIBLE FOR YOUR father's death. What was your town's name?" Lord Aborys asked the next day as I was led to a part of the castle I'd never been before.

"Willowspeak," I choked on the word.

His eyes flicked over my face. "You must have been young."

I was.

I sniffed once. The same way Helle did as I pulled hard on her ice magic. Numbing me to her father.

"Did she tell you they took my love, Embee?"

"Fae from across Eadha have been going missing for centuries." I cursed. "Your court was no exception."

"But only one from Winter, Valentina. And I do not know if she was put to rest. Has her soul returned safely to the Other-world? Was she properly sent off with a Winter's funeral? I've begged Bruma to come down and give me any peace of mind, but she feels quite strongly to ignore my requests." He clasped his hands behind his back.

"I'd like to return to my room."

"I'm afraid we can't." He looked at me and there was no fooling him. He was full of intellect and grace, not like hot-headed Ohrem or conniving Fede.

Fear ran its claws down my back, and I stopped. "I have one more day." *One more day to hope Kade finished up the Wild Hunt and came to find me,* I thought.

A soldier prodded me in the back, and I bared my teeth at him, but we were moving again.

"Unfortunately, I've had to expedite my timeline. I should

have hidden you in the cellars. Seems you scared some faelings, and my court is unhappy."

"They're unhappy I scared some faelings?"

"No, they are unhappy I have you in chains and locked rooms. They are good fae, Valentina. It's unfortunate that you hate them so."

"Just you, Lord Aborys. It's just you."

"Give me an hour and all that will change."

I tried to keep my bearings as we twisted down sets of stairs until I lost count.

"Do you know the history of the gods' gifts, Valentina?" he asked down a particularly long hallway.

Six, I think we went down six staircases and took two right turns. It didn't matter what Lord Aborys was saying. I was getting out of here. I hoped Helle would go easy on me. She'd helped me once. I was counting on that again.

"When the gods left us fae to our own devices, they graced each court with, hmm... some help. Autumn was given Gael's hammer, a mighty thing to forge all Eadha's metal. Summer, as I'm sure you know, was given Angus' daggers."

My back seared hot from where his eyes searched for my daggers. I dropped my head in regret. I'd never step another foot out of Kade's bedrooms without them again. Lord Aborys' tongue flicked over his teeth and his eyes narrowed. "Mmhm," was all he said.

We turned another corner. Left this time.

"Spring was given a beast, that Berserker."

I wanted to roll my eyes. Did I ever know that.

"And Winter," he said as we reached a nondescript door too short for a fae to walk through without bending over.

"Father!" Helle's thumping steps echoed as she charged down the hallway, dressed back in her baliroq armor. "What are you doing?"

"Change in plans. I want it done."

"What done?" I asked. *Oh gods. Six staircases. Two right turns. One left.* I pulled on ice magic and instantly my heart stopped rattling against my ribs. *I had to run.*

Lord Aborys ducked and pushed the door open. The guard behind shoved me with his palm to the center of my back.

"Ouch." I stumbled through the short door and fell to my knees in front of a river running straight through the underground of Silvermere's Castle.

On the far bank stood two guards above a female creature stuck in dark metal chains looping around her entire body. She clung to the edge of a softly flowing river. Her hair, like all of Winter's, was white, but she had a scowl on her face and did not possess any sharp ice magic. Crystalline features peered up at me and her clothes, completely iridescent, made her shimmer like the reflections on the river. The silks of her dress flowed with the ripples of the river, blending in entirely. If the chains didn't hold her, she'd slip into the current like a silver fish and be gone like she was born from the very river she clung to the edge of.

But as I stared, she bled from both corners of her mouth.

I wanted to help her.

"Winter was given the Frost Witches," Lord Aborys continued, hovering over me.

My mouth fell open. *This was Winter's gift?*

"They are incredibly hard to find and even harder to catch. But once you have a Frost Witch, they are bound by a magic running through their bones to grant three wishes to its captor."

My voice felt not my own, like I was asking for a cup of nightale tea and not asking about the power of the creature in Lord Aborys' thick-muscled grasp. "What do you mean wishes?"

"I wished for you to come to Silvermere. Quickly. And immediately."

"You sacrificed your own daughter for nothing. I will not kill the faeless for you," I said, surprised it was a witch's magic that pulled me across the island.

"Hardly," he said, "Helle is strong. She can survive anyplace I throw her."

I looked at his daughter, who didn't so much as flinch.

"Frost Witches are unique. Not like other witches across Eadha. But there are rules for wishes, as I've learned." His words came quickly, like he was frustrated. "I cannot wish someone alive. Nor can I wish someone, or *many* someone's, dead. It cannot kill nor grant life. The two very things I am looking for.

"It took years, but I carved through the base of Silvermere Castle. Diverted a stream to rush through for the Frost Witch to live."

"Don't fool yourself. She's as captive as I am."

"If Bruma feels it as wrong, she has yet to tell me. I'm afraid Winter's goddess is not as meddling as the others. I wonder if you'll bring Eadha to its knees for me, Valentina. If I will get justice for Winter's plights."

"Is this your second wish? To know the future?" The Frost Witch asked. Her voice sounded like water bubbling under thin ice. Hollow, broken, and cracked.

"Tempting." He hesitated. "But catching you has taken a lifetime. Bruma was not kind in keeping such few numbers of you."

She smiled now, baring her teeth, leaning her head against the frozen bank.

"No, I know my second wish. I've had time to think it through. You are tied to me, Frost Witch. You must obey."

"What is your wish, Lord of Winter?" Her throat barely bobbed, but the sound echoed through the room.

Lord Aborys was harsh as he said, "I wish for Valentina's memory to be gone."

"Father, no!" Helle shouted, stepping forward.

"I want all she knows of is of me and my rule." Stronger, he said, "I wish the Siphon on Winter's side."

"No." I shook my head, stumbling back, crawling on hands and knees. "I'd never hurt the faeless. It's not their fault, you monster."

"I told you once, they are a blight against this land. They are magicless. They are not one of the gods. They are a mistake!"

"So am I!" I bawled. "Please don't do this." I was begging, to the witch in the water, to Aborys, to Helle—whose resolve cracked with parted lips.

But Lord Aborys didn't stop. "I want her bowing to my every heed. I want her only concern is of my wellbeing and the good of Winter Court. Wipe everything else out. Summer Court, Shadow Court. *Kaderyn*," he spit. "All of it gone. She will be enamored, indebted, and loyal only to me. No one else. I want all past memories of her life wiped clear."

"Father, this is too far. The Hunter will come for her." Helle grabbed for her father, but the guards turned on her.

I looked to the Frost Witch's blood-shot eyes, but she was half alive. She couldn't save me. I tried using spotty ice magic on the guards, and when that didn't work, I resorted to scratching at any bare skin I found. And when their skin hardened like ice, I switched to trying to flee. Clawing at the ground, crawling for the bitter sting of the river. I'd rather drown in waters than be Winter's puppet.

But my mind was already turning fuzzy like fog rolling in, like ice creeping. I writhed on the ice floor until snow and ice clung to my cheeks. My head felt heavy, like someone crawled inside and was scrubbing it clean with a fork.

I fought . . .

Until peace.

"Your wish is granted." The voice sounded far away, and I craned my neck to see the floating thing in the river speak.

I feared nothing. I sucked in a deep breath. Of ice. Of calm surrender. I clenched my fist, willing ice into my hands. I focused on it and nothing else. My fear dissolved; my mind rationalized. I couldn't remember why I was in bindings, but it didn't matter.

"Unlock me," I demanded. Nothing was going to hold me back again.

Lord Aborys gave the nod and a guard with shaky hands put the key in the lock, reaching, keeping his distance.

And when freedom was mine, when the door lay open to the castle beyond, I strode up to Lord Aborys and eyed his daughter once. I couldn't think of her name now, but she seemed on edge.

"My Lord." I ducked my head low and kissed his white knuckles. He was my savior. My ruler. He was all I knew. And I would kill for him.

A cruel bubbling laugh started behind me, but I did not fear it. I could hear the half dead soul in the creature in the water. It couldn't hurt me or my lord.

"I see her memories, Winter Lord," the creature continued, cackling. "I see what you took out of her."

I urged my lord out of the dark cavern first, keeping this wild thing between me and him.

Glancing over my shoulder, she continued, "He will carve out your heart for doing this to her."

My hackles rose and I froze. *Who was going to hurt my lord?*

"Come along, Valentina. Let us get started," Lord Aborys said. His tongue flicked over his glorious teeth, and I followed him out the small door.

The watery voice slipped through the cracks. "The shadows will string you from the moon for this!"

Then an awful screeching echoed before it died into a soft whimper.

Shadows? I was sure to be on guard for them.

Something fizzled in my mind, something haunting, like hands reaching up from dark waters toward me. We rounded the corner to the throne room where I'd be standing guard from now on and I shot ice magic through my veins to close whatever it was off.

My attention was needed here.

With my lord.

7

DERYN IRONSIDE

There was no time, Rhett said, to get to the Sinking Albatross, the half-sunken and moldy ship I had wedged between rocks lower down on the Mainland's shoreline. So I tried to ignore the wind whipping my face as Rhett's talons curled into the harness on my back and carried me across the Galeairy to the shadowed docks of Inkravere Port in the Court of Shadows.

I thought the last time I'd be on Eadha Island when I gave Kaderyn the Faebric, was going to be the last of these shores I was at now. But as my feet hit the hollow wooden docks, I wasn't so sure I'd be calling these marshes' strangers any longer. Worst of all, the one staring back at me was no stranger at all.

Avika Sardona.

My sister.

And she looked positively deranged.

"Deryn?" Her nostrils flared as her hands fell to her sides. No doubt she saw us fly in. She shook her head, and I wanted to hide. "I thought you died. I thought—"

"She cannot stay here." Interrupted Oir, Auris' general, though I didn't think they called her that. Appointed out of necessity when Lord Kaderyn drank more than ruled. At least that's what I'd gathered from the rumors Rhett would fly over. But now, the shadows cackled the air around the small but plump elderly Shadowfae.

"Long ago the faeless shunned to these lands were turned Shadowfae," Avika said, her chest rising and falling as she spoke loud enough for the entire port and lower half of Auris to hear. "You all found a home here. A place to belong. Why can't we?"

Oir charged at her, the skirts of her black dress in her fists. "Never before, Avika, have I met such an abrasive fae. Especially one with no magic, and now, no home." Her cheeks turned vibrant red.

"I'm defending Blackwater's faeless," Avika shot back, standing her ground. "We have a right to safety, just like you. We were doing fine until your lord and that . . . that other . . . decided to come in and disturb things. There's room west of here, I've seen it, near the shores of Summer. But you won't let us stay because we aren't like you, is that right?"

"No, it's because you're crass and rude and I'll haunt your nightmares if you stay," Oir raged, her small plump hands curled into fists. Shadows charged off her, licking the air. "Take them to the Mainland, Deryn. I have no room for them here." Shadows snapped like whips as Oir turned and walked away.

But under her breath, right before the door to the tavern closed fully, we all heard her mutter, "Lady Fede threw the wrong damn Ironside off the cliffs."

"Wrong Ironside?" Avika's voice shattered the air and my skin flushed from my hair to my knees. "What does that mean?"

I couldn't speak, I couldn't find my tongue at all. Sweat soaked down my back and a voice piped up from Auris' docks.

"An Ironside? Well, you're looking at her. That's Deryn Ironside."

Did he point? Oh, by my iron ore, why was this happening?

I cleared my throat. I think. "Avika. I'm so glad to see—"

"You forsake our parents' name?" Avika, still so small and mighty, bellowed across the docks and I wished the sea, the treacherous thing, would swallow me whole.

Everyone looked at me. I was going to hurl.

But Avika didn't stop. "Too embarrassed to be one of us? I've been struggling to survive every day in our home city of Blackwater Junction. Meanwhile, you've been sleeping comfortably here with Shadowfae and shifters flying you around on every whim." She shook her head. "What would our parents rest their souls in the Otherworld, say? We are Sardona's." She shoved a finger into my chest. "Don't you dare forget it."

If she hadn't poked me, I might have thought I'd fallen out of bed again. That this was all a horrible dream, and I'd wake with an aching back from sleeping on wrought iron. But she might as well have stabbed me with a sword where her finger had touched.

My sister was very real. And she was very mad.

Rhett stepped between us both, and I thought he would kill her. I ducked under his arm, just not sure who I would be saving.

"Rhett!" Oir shouted back through the doors. There's news of panthershifters approaching from the Sidina Mountains pass. We're on edge already. Please intercept."

My love let out an exasperated sigh so softly I was surely the only one to hear. I wanted to beg him not to go. Not to leave me with her.

He ran his hands up my arms and glared back at Avika. "Valentina was taken, and Oir is on edge. The Wild Hunt rides on, and no one knows how to reach Kaderyn. You going to be all right?"

"I'll be fine," I lied.

"I'll come back to you as soon as I can." And he kissed my lips quickly before passing through hordes of onlookers, heading for Oir.

But Oir continued from where she held the door open for him, "What is *she* still doing on my soil?"

"Come to the Mainland." I found myself saying to Avika, but by all my iron ore, it wasn't because I wanted to. I wanted to kill the guilt that seeing my faeless sister brought up. Because I should have gone back to her in Blackwater. The faeless' curse was living just as long as fae but without magic and for two hundred years, I held myself in an iron tower away from it all. I abandoned her. "There is space in the valley."

Her eyes, so much like mine, lit up. "Is it safe?"

I winced. "It's your only option."

NOT LONG LATER, A CROWD OF FAELESS TRAILED behind me, gathered with carts and chests and faelings running between them all. Though they might as well have been the worst of Eadha's monsters, and I tried to stifle my limp as much as possible. Inkravere Port wasn't big enough to support them all and the docks creaked under the weight.

Avika quickly organized the faelings to safety on the shores and loaded supplies first.

But even just hearing her voice sent my body into spasms of anxiety. She wasn't going to understand why I didn't come back, my fear of the fae, and I didn't know how to tell her. I cursed myself for not bringing the ship over because now I was going to have to commandeer one from Oir.

Avika stopped bossing her faeless around and stood beside me with her hands on her hips, waiting.

I couldn't swallow. I couldn't breathe. "I'll—I'll just need to borrow—"

"What's that?" she asked, a curved hand blocked the sun on her forehead as she scanned the waters.

I trailed her gaze, fearing more bad news. No doubt at this point that a mythical monster, long dead and bones water-logged, was rising from the depths to make this day as worse as it could possibly get. But instead, three blue-skinned pixies buzzed around a familiar ship heading this way from the Main-land. The very ship I had wedged between boulders. They dove into the moldy ship's interior and back out. One pixie in partic-ular had an intricately welded iron arm.

"Teal!" I shouted when she tossed a tow rope onto the heads of three faeless. "You're not fully healed. You should be in bed." I used my hands to help lift my iron leg onto the swaying bridge between the rocking ship and docks as I stormed toward her. The last thing I needed was Teal's shoulder healing wrong and her screaming at me, too. And before I could say much else, the other two pixies shuttled the faeless aboard. "And who is this?"

"Bean and Scout," Teal said through needle-pointed teeth. One was dressed in a dirty white sock and the other looked posi-tively menacing.

"I've taken control of the Sinking Albatross.
We've commandeered it to get the faeless across.
This port side is rank with opportunities amiss
Adrian has raised another; the Meandering Sea
Mollusk."

I ignored her declaration that she had stolen my ship. What a losing battle to fight the pixie on. "Fine. But then to bed," I urged. "Or I'll tell Oir."

Her eyes narrowed. "You wouldn't."

I winced. "It takes a toll, Teal, having a missing limb. Let it heal properly. Rule the seas once you're no longer in pain."

She grumbled but nodded and I spent the rest of the ride over on the hull watching red-bellied salmon ride in the ship's wake. A stray thought wondered what Adrian was up to.

The ship hit a plank of wood near the base of the Twin Peak Mountains that I didn't remember being there before. And sure enough, another ship just as moldy as this one was anchored beside it. Two other pixies in small, marigold flower petal dresses were propping up wood slabs and banging a nail into a chunk of wood.

I ran a hand down my side and into my bag. "Hey! That's my hammer. Give that back."

I huffed at Teal.

Her lips spread wide in a guilty smile.

"You're building a port here on the Mainland?" I asked, jumping to snatch my hammer back from a passing pixie.

Very aware that Avika watched me with critical eyes. My cheeks heated.

"I have a sea to rule
And a port to attend.
I declare this shore land
Fillagree Fen."

As soon as the last faeless' heel left the ship, Teal started sailing the Albatross back across the Galeairy. She'd earned a decent enough fare from them and a sharp warning from me to stop calling her passengers scallywags. Which she felt was a proper travesty. So many rhymes could be thought up with scallywags. The Sinking Albatross now had a flag tied to its mast and a crude drawing of pixie wings smudged in black ink. Like they dunked a pixie in black paint and splatted him starfish-style against the ripped and worn flag.

"To bed, Teal!" I shouted to the retreating ship, wishing Teal would stay with me.

I wished anyone could show Avika where to set up her camp of faeless. Literally anyone else.

Looking down over a sloping gorge, I led the way past the boulders near the shoreline and into the deep, lush valley below. "This way. Mind the rocks." I avoided their gazes.

It wouldn't be a twenty-minute walk from this theoretical port Teal was building.

I helped Glynnera, who it warmed my heart to see, down the steep slope.

"Good to see you, Deryn," she said with a wink, and I almost forgot my sister was on the other side of her.

Almost. But she glared at me.

Ten minutes into the trek, I stopped to lean against a larger rock.

"Are we resting again or are we here?" Avika said from just behind me. Sweat dripped past her temples. It made her look fierce.

I rubbed the sweat off my cheek, and it came back dirty. My iron leg came with challenges, a reason I was now building the track across the valley. "I just need a minute," I huffed, eyes fixed firmly ahead like if I did so I could prevent any in the company from looking to our right where down near the tree line my tracks sat twenty feet high of iron metal. Up high away from all kinds of things, I was planting my sister and her town in the middle of now. Another week or two and I'd have made it across the valley entirely. I cringed. Now the faeless would watch me ironwork.

Familiar embarrassment crept up; others were seeing something I created. It was now freely open to their opinions and scrutiny. And I spent the rest of the climb down the embankment with my stomach in my throat and my heart on my sleeve.

"This is the valley?" Avika asked as she climbed down faster than me. Her gray eyes were as sharp as the mountain range at our backs.

She leaned down and grabbed a handful of dirt. Like our parents taught us when we were little. The memory of them so deeply stuffed down in things I wanted to forget that I winced as if in pain. She closed her fist around the black humus, the most important part of any crop planting—our connection to the earth. With no magic, we had a deep need for fertile land to grow our food. We didn't have the luxury of Springfae magic.

When we moved on to the Otherworld, we'd enrich the humus once more.

Or the Underworld, now that Kaderyn was back.

"It's good," I mumbled. "The valley provides shelter from the winds, and the runoff from the mountain keeps the earth from drying out." But I pursed my lips because it wasn't just *good* soil, it was great here and I wanted her to be pleased. "Leave some trees rooted. The shade will help block the sun when Summer rules."

"What do you mean when Summer rules?" Avika's head snapped up toward the sky.

"I mean, in Spring the wind whips harder on top of those mountains than any magic a fae can do. The summer sun beats down on my iron, heating it as hot as any autumn touch. There are seasons here. It comes and goes in a quarterly rotation with no push or pull from the fae. Don't be surprised in two seasons when it snows. But be prepared, have your gardens dug up and winter seeds planted long before that. Winter perseveres here without the fae all the same."

And I didn't tell her, but I'd stay here for the seasons alone. For the gradual sway of the earth. Like she's showing me her moods. Except I spent three weeks holed up inside my tower when the first strong wind blew through, thinking Lady Fede had come to finish me off.

"And where do *you* live?"

My stomach soured. *Please don't come to the tower.* "There." I vaguely pointed off at the black lumbering tower in the distance. Now looking crude and out of place.

"What is it?" she asked, dusting off her hands. Black soil fell to the earth. But she viewed my creations with critical eyes, and I couldn't turn away from it all.

"An iron tower," I mumbled to my shoes. The water to my left rippled like a stone dropped.

She quickly put two and two together. "So you stay holed up in the very thing fae can't touch?" She paused. "And you'll leave us to our luck out here. I swear, Deryn..."

"The valley has the most fertile land on the Mainland!" I said quickly.

She crossed her arms and her voice raised. "Then why aren't *you* growing on it?"

Because I had made a deal with the mountain witch for privacy and solitude. *Oh*, I rubbed a hand down my face. I was going to need to talk to Carmen about the faeless now inhabiting the valley. But I couldn't say anything now. There was no good solution here. The faeless needed somewhere safe and they had nowhere else to go.

"Don't build past the tree line." I pointed past my iron rails, readying my slow escape from this conversation. "There are HorCains that live farther down in a crumbled city. My iron tracks should keep them from the valley."

"What do you mean, *should*? What in all of Daina's creations are those beams for? Why hasn't your hawkshifter gotten rid of these creatures for us?"

Because I'm pretty sure they keep the other monsters to the west at bay. My cheeks heated, almost two hundred years of separation between us, and Avika could still scold me like a faeling.

But she didn't stop, and I was sinking under her ferocious gaze. "This is *really* where you expect me to set up my town? Honestly, Deryn, you come back from the dead and—"

"The middle of my Galeairy is always an option," came a voice I've heard every day for the last century.

A sigh escaped my lips and my shoulders dropped. *Thank my iron ore*, Adrian was here.

"If that suits you better, Avika," the demigod continued, holding his elbow out for me near my side. "You left my rain cover, I see."

"As brief a disturbance as it was when the Lord of Shadows and his band ran through Blackwater and chased you off—"

Adrian scoffed.

"—it reminded us of the difference between surviving and living. So we packed up and trekked to Shadows' gates and, low and behold, I find my sister who left for Scarlotta almost two centuries ago and never. Came. Back."

"I can explain," I started, but she held up a hand, demanding I stop.

"These creatures you mentioned. HorCains?" She ignored me and turned to face the demigod head-on. *Gods*, she wasn't afraid of anything.

There was no amicable reaction I could get. She wanted a fight, and all I wanted was warm tea and my face heated by my forge. A pang hit my heart. "You know the birchhounds in Lady of the Woods? Like them, but these will definitely hunt you down. And unlike the birchhounds, they eat meat. I haven't seen them since I put up the last two lengths of track," I mumbled. "They seem to have an aversion to iron. I'm not sure."

She wrinkled her nose at my tracks, and the heat of embarrassment flushed through my body.

"What is it?" She looked from one end, near my tower, to the other.

"They are . . . something else I've built. I will finish them through that cleared acreage down there. Please don't build there."

"And if I do?" Her eyes flicked from Adrian to me, and to where our arms linked together, where my friend let me lean half my weight on him because my leg was blistering and swollen. "You feel this is an appropriate place for us?"

This is the only place for you, I thought, but instead, I said, "I'm trying, Avika."

"For once in your life, you're trying. Great. Thanks. While you stay safe up in that forsaken tower. You leave us down here for slaughter."

"That's enough, Avika. I can forgive you for being cantankerous by nature, but to be one to Deryn on purpose makes me want to set your hair on fire." Adrian started pulling me off and away.

Her eyes flashed like she'd won some match to some game I didn't know I was playing. "So *that's* why you protected Blackwater Junction! Because of *her*?"

Adrian whipped us back around, pure vehemence in his voice. "I found your sister laying half dead in Galeairy's reeds, one leg chewed off by my seamutts. She's the only reason Blackwater has survived the miscreants to the north and east. You'll do well to remember this."

I grabbed his arm tighter, the silk of his navy and silver tunic soft under my fingers. It was better to go now before Adrian reminded them what he was capable of. Or before I could see if Avika risked the glance down at my legs, or if she wondered which leg was missing, covered in my thick brown pants and strapped on beaten boots.

We didn't make it ten feet before we heard her again. "And what am I supposed to feed them?"

"I suggest you learn to fish!" Adrian yelled back. "Come along, dearest Deryn. Your tower awaits."

Oh, by my iron ore, I groaned. Avika saw me fly down in the grasp of a hawkshifter and now she was going to watch me mist away with Adrian, a demigod.

"Will your seamutts behave?" she shouted through cupped hands.

"No promises," Adrian volleyed, but his eyes were on me.

Brine water burned my nostrils as he misted us away, and we faded to nothing in front of my sister.

I risked a look back. My stomach churned because I was leaving her once more.

Their voices carried on the breeze.

"Avika, what do we do?" someone asked, looking around at nothing but land.

Avika pulled her gaze from where she last saw us, her voice strong and determined. "We rebuild. Separate into groups. Mal, start a hunting party. Don't go past the tree line." She barked orders. "I saw geese on the shores sailing over here. Set nets in the waters, but don't go too far in. Take the axes and start cutting trees for shelter."

Misting was hard on the senses, but I clung to Adrian's shoulders and felt his very real arms around my waist. It was like tumbling through invisible waves. My head wasn't quite sure which way was up. But he saved me. Again.

"Thanks, Adrian," I whispered through mist and sea spray, not quite whole but in some secret place Adrian only showed me.

"Don't thank the fae, dearest Deryn," he warned with a sly smile.

"I'm thanking a friend." I looked at the iron fortress I'd built.

Adrian and I were going home.

Where it was safe.

8

VALENTINA

There was something on the very edge of my memories. That if I looked too closely, it would surely flee. I lit the lanterns in the night to keep the shadows at bay or else something crawled through them in the darkness. Winter's white wasn't a lack of light. The shadows grew here, too. Moreso in the cracks of my heart.

Guarding my lord was an easy enough task. Tracking down why I felt the chill of cold in the west section of the castle was another thing entirely. But if there was an imposter in his castle, I wanted to be the one to present them to him.

I'd spent two days in the Dahlin Tundras with Helle and her soldiers training. Ice magic came easily, but icicles and ice arrows were hard to make. My fingers didn't feel right with a bow, and I wondered if I had any training at all with it. I couldn't remember. When I asked Helle, she growled at me. So, I stuck to making icicles as daggers.

Later that second night, we returned to Silvermere Castle. "Her sword work is fantastic; you can thank shadows for that.

Her ice magic is spotty, but stronger than most. And don't talk to me about archery. I'm not in the mood." Helle recounted my training to my lord.

"Good." He leaned up from the throne chair. "Valentina, there's something I need you to do."

"Anything for you, my lord," I said, stooping low.

Helle scoffed and dragged her eyeballs so high to her hairline I thought they'd fall out.

"Is something the matter, Helle?" I sniped. Her devotion to her father wasn't as strong as mine, and it bugged me to my core. How could I keep him safe if I had to worry about his general?

"Yes. Your ass-kissing is going to make me hurl."

"You're jealous because he trusts me to guard him as he sleeps. Is that it?"

"You can guard him as he uses the bathroom. You can guard him as he picks his fucking nose, Valentina." She bumped into my chest and lowered her voice. "But you'd stab that sword between your eyes if you could hear yourself now."

"Helle, stand down," Lord Aborys roared. "Keep your stupid mouth shut for once and do as I ask."

Happiness swelled in my chest when my lord's anger settled on Helle and not me.

"I believe someone made you for a purpose," he said, his hand tucked affectionately under my chin. "To help clean the faeless from our island."

"I understand," I said with a nod. He was right. He was always right. "Where should I hunt the faeless first?"

"But first, a test."

The icy air roared into the room with a vengeance. And I was the only one to feel it. Was the infiltrator here? "Lord Aborys, who's here?"

I drew my sword and faced the open doorway, ice magic

ready, but three fae, bound and gagged, tripped over each other as a half-dozen guards shoved them out a side door.

I narrowed in on the blonde one. A soaked and dirty cloth was bound tightly over her eyes. Wet from tears, maybe? I couldn't remember what it was like to cry. Her blubbering now bothered me though, and I sent ice magic to soothe an ache hurting my chest at the sound.

"Must they be here?" I asked, bristling. "They're noisy." It was more than irritation. Something pulled at my insides. Something was clawing, trying to get out. I smothered it.

"They must, Valentina, dear," Lord Aborys said. "Why doesn't she have her mouth gagged?"

"She hyperventilates and passes out," one guard said. "We moved it to her eyes. She seemed to calm down."

"Like we do with the horses," another guard mocked, laughing, and anger bloomed in my veins.

"Do you recognize them?" Helle asked, chewing her thumbnail and fidgeting.

I looked them over; a male and the other female's mouths were gagged, and they were trying to say something beyond it. The two of them stared at me like I surely should have known them. Water dripped off my hands, freezing at my feet into tiny stalagmites. Summerfae. "Should I?"

Lord Aborys folded his hands behind his back. "I had them taken from Summer Court. Does that bother you?"

I glanced up at him, refusing to answer my lord with another question. I looked them over again. *Should it bother me?* This unease sent my spine stiff and irritated my nerves. I needed the blonde one to stop crying. "I haven't finished patrolling the west side of the castle. There's a chill that reaches my bones more so over there and I'm close to figuring out what it is. I'd rather not be listening to this."

"Valentina," my lord said with conviction. "I want you to kill these three fae."

"Father!" Helle burst from her edgy position.

I put myself between her and Lord Aborys as she marched forward.

"I want you to kill them like Helle has been teaching you."

I stood tall and pulled a dagger when Helle got too close.

She looked beyond me. "This is too far."

I frowned. "Have they threatened you, my lord? Are you in danger from these three?"

The blonde one was heaving now, chest shaking. "Valentina? Is that you? Oh Angus, I'm so glad it's you. Please save us, Val. It's so cold here."

The tall male with a shaved head stared like I'd killed someone he loved. And maybe I had. But the middle one. The female with long brown hair and expensive dresses, though now wrinkled, stained and unkept, just looked at me with derision. And I didn't know why, but it *bothered* me. My scalp itched and fingers turned shaky. There was something about her I wanted to please, if even just a fraction of the amount of desire I had to please Lord Aborys. I don't know why I did it, but I walked up to her with brief steps as she mumbled through the cloth in her mouth. *What was she saying?* I needed to know.

My fingertips touched the soft skin of her cheeks, and I pried the cloth out of her mouth. Strings of saliva coated her chin.

"You naive female, aligning yourself with this tyrant," she spat. "I thought you too stupid to know right from wrong for yourself but this—"

Her mouth fell open, gaping. Her eyes turned saucer sized and slowly blood curled out of her mouth until it flowed in gurgling gasps. I pulled the icicle out from where I stabbed it between her rib bones. *How dare she call Lord Aborys a tyrant.*

Water magic suddenly spewed from my mouth, choking my lungs as she grabbed my hands and we stumbled to the floor. I was gasping, but also *comforted*. I pulled on the water magic that felt as natural as ice and cleared my lungs of water.

Reaching up a finger, I brushed hair away from the side of her face and sent ice across her mouth and nose. Streams of water pooled around us.

Rosy dusty theaters. Honey. Golden ties.

What was this? I froze. My mind betrayed me, filling with nonsense.

Sunshine. Warm courtyards. A chair with a broken leg.

And when I hesitated, Lord Aborys said, "Don't make me regret bringing Summerfae here, Valentina. Kill the others. Don't think of anything but my voice. Kill them."

I blinked back to the white crystalline castle of my home.

Frost quiets my mind
Ice hardens my soul
I will persevere

The two other Summerfae tried to clamber out of the guards' hands, and I let the dead Summerfae on my lap flop to the floor as I stood. I wondered if this was why I kept feeling the chill of Bruma, unlike normal Winterfae, but the prisoner cells were kept in the north wing of the castle. The library, to the west.

"Kill for me, Valentina. Show me you can take out the faeless settlements without remorse. That you can protect yourself to come back to me."

"Father, stop this!" Helle raged over top the crying.

The gag slipped out of the male's mouth. "Please don't do this! Val! Don't, please. Please look at me, it's me, Petri. That's Sisaria. Why don't you remember us?"

And without thinking twice about it, I created an icicle with my magic and threw it straight at the belly of the squealing one. She collapsed to the floor gracefully, perhaps like a dancer might have. I sent more ice to soothe something inside that wanted to cry with her. Must be Summerfae magic. Weak.

"Sisaria, no," the one who called himself Petri whispered, tears running down his cheeks.

More magic. Damn it, I sent more ice magic to the recessing pit inside me.

Petri's lips were blue and tears froze down his cheeks as he said, "You'll be the death of us all."

Which triggered a different need inside me.

I stalked up to him.

"Valentina, stop. Fuck!" Helle screamed, and her small hands tried to pull me back. "Father, you're going to break her."

I wrapped my fingers around the prisoner's lithe shoulder, struggling as Helle fought me every step of the way. I pulled him down to me as I whispered, "But not Lord Aborys'," and stabbed an icicle into his chest.

9

VALENTINA

The ice wall at my back seeped through my white and gold dress, chilling me to the bone. I played hot and cold with whoever thought they could infiltrate my lord's castle.

I warned Lord Aborys that a chill ran through me in certain parts of the castle. In this wing, it was more consistent than others.

I held out the small mirror, peering into the west wing where the library stood. In its reflection, fae bustled in and out, both males and females in elegant wear, not unlike me. And like a baliroq caught on a scent, I was close. Then it was a simple game of cat and mouse.

Wooded bookshelves so white they looked like carved bones of animals vaulted to the ceiling in neat, organized rows.

I felt the cold.

The librarian gave a noiseless laugh over the faelings on their tippytoes, slapping dozens of books down on her counter. Air swooped down my dress as I entered.

Colder, little mouse.

Two fae to my right, sitting in low brown chairs pressed tight against each other, held up a large book *Topography of the Dahlin Tundra's Lakes* between them, covering their faces.

Hiding.

"I can feel you," I hissed, determined to get my mark. I pressed the sharp blade tip of my bronze sword down along the book's spine, revealing their faces.

And frowned.

Two perfect Winterfae startled apart, lips swollen red, and cheeks flushed. They weren't hiding from me, but from everyone else. The male's affection could clearly be seen through his pants.

I dropped my sword and sighed. Erections were not threats to my lord.

By now, everyone gave me a wide berth. The librarians felt erections were a threat to their library, and they quickly shooed the couple apart.

The chill left my bones, and I cursed.

The mouse knew I was coming.

The tail end of someone running caught my eye, and without thinking, I jogged toward it around narrow sky-high bookcases.

Cold, again.

Turning in time, I caught a glimpse of a foot. As I ran again, the damn dress and damn cold tangled around my joints. I'd ask for an outfit like the general's next time I saw my lord.

Colder.

I shot around a shelf. The full bottom half of a female in a thick intricately designed light blue dress caught my eye. Have I seen this before?

Something scratched at my mind, but the chill made me clench my teeth in anger. Why did I have to feel it? I pulled the dress collar higher. If I was from my lord's court, then why did I *hate* the cold?

"Stop!" I yelled, shattering the near silence of the library. Close enough to my prey now to hear her gasping. "By the order of Lord Aborys and the Siphon of Winter, you'll stop."

The footfalls ceased, and I peeked through empty book holes in the shelving to see a large window blocking their escape.

Caught in my trap at last.

A strangled gasp echoed around the corner as I reached the last shelf. Grabbing the side of the bookcase, my fingers numbed, and my breath fogged in front of me. I smiled. Lord Aborys would be so proud of me.

"Valentina!"

Metal clanked together from the front of the library like a threat, and I whipped around to face it, compelled by a desperate urge to defend the castle grounds by any means necessary. There in the doorway stood a dozen guards in full bronze-plated armor.

"Our lord has ordered you to the throne room. It's urgent."

Giving up my mark, I ran, with my entire attention, on the well-being of Lord Aborys. "Is he all right? What's happened?"

Warm.

We exited the library.

Warmer.

Three corridors later, the guard said, "There's been a trespasser."

"I know I'm trying to find—"

"He's in the throne room with Lord Aborys."

He.

My mind filtered his words. That deep internal crying sobbed again like my chest was splitting in two. I rubbed at it.

"Are you well, Siphon?" the guard asked.

I siphoned his magic and sent ice out to kill it, to strangle the blubbering otherness inside. Leading them to the other side of the castle, I grumbled, "Come on."

I wanted to please my lord, and he had no tolerance for weakness. So, neither would I.

I prepared myself before the throne room's azure-coated doors, sending frost out to quiet my mind, and ice to harden my soul. Starve off any filtering magic that might assault my senses.

Biting my lip, I was so sick of the cold, and it was near even now. I was Lord Aborys' Siphon. Despite using magic from all courts on the island, why did I despise my own?

And why were all my memories of Lord Aborys? A shadowy figure appeared in my mind as I blinked, and water pooled in my eyelids. It was happening more frequently now, and when I tried to focus, endless white smudged it out.

The doors thrust open and kneeling on his haunches, golden hair flicked back, with hands locked in thick, muddy-colored chains, was someone not from one of the main four courts.

Something animal-like who made my heart beat steady.

"Ah, here she is. My Valentina," Lord Aborys said, beckoning me to him. He stood on the small, raised platform before the empty throne chairs of solid ice.

Helle flanked his side, though she didn't acknowledge me. She stared down our prisoner with fists clenched.

"I am close to finding the infiltrator, my lord," I said, but the words were toward the Shifterfae I couldn't take my eyes from. "I had it cornered in our libraries."

"And I have no doubt you'll catch them, but Jairek thinks he can waltz into our court and take you out with him. That you'll leave me. Tell me, will you leave me, Valentina?"

Jairek Sanguis.

King of the Courtless.

I dropped to Lord Aborys' feet, my knees smashing on cold white marble, and scooped up his hand in mine. "I will never leave you, my lord."

The lionshifter's deep brown glare bore into the back of my head. "You're one of us, Valentina. Not this frigid place."

"Don't say my name," I seethed, but something inside smashed against my ribs and I heaved. "I don't know you."

This Jairek, this lionshifter, spit bright crimson blood onto the white marble. "The fuck you don't."

"Leave here." I turned to face my lord, trying to keep my face calm. I ran ice through my veins to overpower the steadiness the lionshifter made my heart beat. Why did I have holes in my memory? Why did this one's face remind me of something? Why did I breathe better when he was near? Something in me was screaming, snarling, shrieking and I couldn't figure out where it was coming from.

"Get rid of him," I urged to the guards and considered freezing them where they stood when they didn't act soon enough.

The golden one threw his head back and let out a loud, easy laugh that echoed around the tense cathedral. It was a throaty, warm sound in this sprawling ice room. And in one blink, like a sword to the back of the skull, a flash of him laughing around a fire, of dancing in white-wooded trees, of flutes and of shadows seared through my mind. I blinked sharply. Never. Those weren't my memories.

"I took a holly arrow to the gut for you once," he growled, demanding the room's attention. His eyes flicked to Helle briefly. "You know me better than that. I'll bleed dry on this floor before my feet walk out that throne door." With such conviction and threat in those words, ice trickled down my spine in response.

I turned my face up to my lord, trying to keep my features

calm, but a gaping black shadow-filled hole carved through my memories.

My lord's eyes narrowed. "Do you know him, Valentina?"

And I went to say no. But I couldn't.

He leaned up, flicked his tongue over his teeth, and said quickly, "Get it over with. Jairek, it is unfortunate you've found yourself on my castle doorstep. I greatly respect the Courtless, and it pains me to do this now."

Doors opened, revealing a massive soldier with a long whip.

An executioner.

"Now is not the time to test my patience. I do not fear you, nor the shadows, nor death. My fight is with the faeless, not your court. I could have overlooked your trespassing, but you're filling my lovely Siphon's head with nonsense. Valentina, leave here while I teach this feline how to behave in a dignified court. No hard feelings, King. I'd expect the same on your lines."

My heart raced, but that steady beating calmed it and I looked at the Shifterfae as I spoke. "I'll do it." My feet moved, but it wasn't out the door. "Give me the whip. I'll punish the trespasser."

The lionshifter froze, steady depths-deep brown eyes on me. Like he *knew* me.

Lord Aborys chuckled, deep and loud. "I warned you, King," he said, and I stalked toward the intruder. "She is not who you think she is. The things she's done . . ."

"Valentina," Jairek whispered as I swayed past, "are you with me?"

But I couldn't look him in the eyes again, so I focused on his shoulder, where if I stared long enough, I swore the outline of a little winged creature appeared. I shook my head, rattling the image free as I spoke. "You were right about bleeding on this floor." And I sent a finger out, grazing the tanned skin of his cheek.

The lion's skin was slick with sweat and blood, but he was *warm* like the summer sun. So unlike my castle.

So unlike me.

Two guards ripped the white shirt from his body, and it hung around the chains like the broken wings of a spirit.

"You hate the cold, Valentina. You're not meant for Winter."

I sauntered past, and grabbed the whip, a twisted bundle of leather, from the guard.

Golden ropes of muscle shifted through Jairek's back in anticipation. I hesitated once. This was going to be painful. But I was my lord's Siphon, and I did what I was best at.

I snaked the whip through the air and cracked it once against the lionshifter's bare spine. His head flew back.

I parted my lips. Hissing. Once.

Sucking in a shaky breath, I did it again.

Frost quiets my mind.

Blood soaked down his legs and onto the floor. Again. I snapped the whip out, lacing it deep and thick across his shoulder blades.

My teeth clenched so hard I heard a crack.

Ice hardens my soul.

He hung his head down and leered back at me through thick, sweat-soaked golden strands of hair. Brown eyes fumed furiously, like he wanted to rip out my throat with his teeth. "Stop this, Valentina," he grit, but he wasn't begging or pleading. He was *commanding*.

I considered whipping his face, but he spit blood on the floor again and turned forward toward my lord and his daughter.

A tear ran down my cheek.

I will persevere.

And I whipped him again.

But a cold, small hand gripped mine tightly, halting the whip in midair. "That's enough, Valentina. Stop this!" *It's Helle. And there was screaming. How long had she been screaming? Or was it me?* I was drowning in a sea of white marble I couldn't escape.

A sob left my lips as she pried the whip from my hands before I did it again. Before I gave pain where pain was due.

"Put him in the cellars. Keep him locked with Autumn's new chains. We do not torture the Courtless." Her fury swung to her father. "We are not Autumn," she seethed.

"Come, Valentina, dinner will be served shortly," my lord said as I walked stiffly back to him.

I heard them hauling Jairek up from the ground and looked back once to the sight of blood-stained snow-white marble left in his wake.

"Don't worry yourself about the shifter. Helle will ensure that he is properly punished. Though too stupid to rule in my stead, I taught my daughter to be strong. To do what you must. To persevere. I knew she would make it back to her court safely. She got her mother's magic. Incredibly strong"—he shook his head once—"but far too stubborn to rule a court. Afraid she has more power than brains, that one."

I sucked in a breath before we reached the doors to the dining room. Round tables were set up with white tablecloths. The smell of roasts wafted from the side doors, where fae castle attendants bustled in and out.

"My lord, I apologize." Visions flashed in my mind of dancing in a ball like it, with shadows locked around me. Protecting me. "I am feeling tired. If I could rest for a while? I'll ask Helle to stay by your side."

He brushed a thumb across my cheek. "My Valentina. Of course. Are you sure you are feeling fine?" He squinted, and his tongue flicked over his teeth. "Who is the enemy?"

"The faeless, my lord." I pulled my cheeks into a tight smile. But my head was pounding like someone was clawing their way out.

He lifted his hand out between us, and I scooped it in mine, bowed my mouth, and brought my lips to his skin.

"Retire to your rooms. I'll have the guards bring you a meal shortly."

Ugh, but the thought of company made me want to jump from the balcony into the waters below my rooms in the tallest wing of the castle, and I didn't know why. A vast and empty loneliness spread across my chest, tightening it so hard I couldn't breathe.

Once I was alone, I sent out ice magic to web across the door. Something I'd seen before, though I didn't think it was here. Why was I forgetting?! I slammed a fist into the wall and continued lacing the ice back and forth like a lattice, covering the door, the lock, and the jamb.

But someone was close.

Light footsteps my fae ears picked up stopped outside the door.

"I want to be left alone," I said through wood and frost.

The door jolted once, then exploded into shards of chiseled ice. I ducked and drew my dagger.

"Clever trick," Helle said, standing there, feet crunching on ice chunks. She came in, head tucked, eyes blazing blue, covered in blood I knew wasn't hers.

"You should be with my lord," I snapped. "If I am away, it's your duty to protect him."

She kicked the door shut with her foot and paced in front of me. "If I were you, I would take your dagger and jab it into my jugular. Right here." She pointed to a soft spot on her neck where her black baliroq skin armor didn't reach and moved into me until my blade touched pale skin. It was then I noticed how frantic she was. "Well, you could try at least."

"Go protect our lord."

"Don't tell me what to do." Her lips twitched and her eyebrows drew down. "This isn't your home."

"Don't be defensive," I scoffed. "Our lord has space for us both—"

"No," she snapped. "Valentina, your home is in Auris."

Screaming, hideous screams erupted from my skull. "What are you talking about?"

"You know what I'm talking about. When you sleep, you beg for the shadows. And when you whipped the lionshifter, you didn't take a single breath. Call to him, Valentina."

"No," I whispered.

She raged in desperation. "Call to the Wild Hunt."

"No," I yelled in equal measure, shaking my head. *The Hunt. The darkness and shadows.* I pulled at my hair.

"Damn it, Valentina!" She stepped closer, my outstretched dagger dug into her skin; a trail of blood trickled down her pale skin. "Save the lionshifter dying in my dungeons!" Her voice was a guttural demand. I had to pull ice magic in to quench the slow trickle of fear it produced in my core. Her stare was poignant, an unmovable force locked on me.

And I caved.

"I can't," I whimpered. The knife clattered to the ground between us. I swayed as long-held tears fell from my eyes. *Did Helle ever cry?* "He cannot see me like this."

A deep unending sadness washed over me, crashed into every nerve ending. A loss of missing someone I barely remembered. Only glimpses of him smiling, dimples of a male I couldn't see a full picture of. My head was forever foggy, and it wouldn't clear, no matter how much I tried to shake it clean.

"I have a deep, unrelenting longing for someone I can't remember," I sobbed, falling to the ground.

Helle stayed, arms crossed above me.

"He was my home, wasn't he?"

"Yes," Helle confirmed.

"And something ripped us apart."

Her blue eyes stayed steady with mine, not allowing me pity.

A memory of his familiar hands fitting in mine like we were made for each other threatened to take me out. "He was my understanding of what safety was and he's . . he's *not here*." I wept into the night air. *Why wasn't he here?*

Helle picked the dagger up from the floor and moved to the door. "I'm taking the soldiers out for training in the tundras two days from now. The castle will be as empty as it'll ever be of swords and arrows." She wiped the blood off her neck with the passing brush of a hand. "Might be a fine time to find your courage." Her boots crunched back over shards of shattered ice. "Valentina, I need you to save Jairek before I do something I'm *really* going to regret."

The door clicked shut behind her and I crawled—dragged—my body to the window seat with my heart aching, bleeding for someone I only saw in the shadows.

Who are you?

The moon lit a path across the roaring sea, crashing waves broke over rocks below. The high tide was coming.

High tide . . .

A song murmured through my mind like falling leaves brushing against each other.

Once upon a time, there was a lover on a cliffside.

Tears drenched my cheeks, crying for a love in a life before this one.

"Where are you?" I whispered to the sea.

Who searched the night stars for her Hunter on the high tide.
I begged for him. But he felt so far away.
She waited by the shores for the sea to bring him back.
He was haunting me.
I was haunted.

The name slogged up from the blubbering, crying, heaving thing in my chest. "Kad-er-yn." I worked it over my tongue.

Searching through the darkness for those eyes of shadows, black.

My heart was barren, alone, and shattered. I was lost. Lost in throws of despair. *Why did he leave me here?*

"Kaderyn," I whispered to the crashing murky waves below me as memories stirred into a force stronger than ice magic, stronger than any magic I'd ever felt before. I pulled at the deep bond in my soul and screamed down into the darkness with every ounce of shredded resolve I had.

I need you.

10

DERYN IRONSIDE

I'd shut the windows facing west days ago. Even this far away, I could feel Avika's piercing stare through my fortress and into my bones. So for days, I covered all the windows in the hopes that the tattered and worn window coverings would block out her and the rising sun.

Which meant I slept in.

Warm, calloused fingers trailed down my spine from where I slept on my makeshift bed. Dozens of blankets surrounded me. I flipped over slowly, peeking an eye open to see Rhett, beautiful Rhett leaning over me, his mouth hovering near mine.

"Afternoon, my love." His voice was husky with need and want. I hadn't seen him in a week or more. Not since the pantershifters came asking for him.

I moved to sit up. "What happened? Is the Courtless all right?"

He leaned me down and smothered my mouth with his, desperate and needy. *His memories must be chasing him again.*

His hands pulled me closer. *Not all right,* I thought. Something bad must have happened. I ran my fingertips down his face, brushing away the sadness I saw there.

"Your sister is—"

I pulled away abruptly. "Why? What did she say?"

"Nothing." He ran a thumb over my lips. "But the way she treats you? Awful."

"I left her, Rhett. I didn't send word that I was alive. She thought I was dead."

"And she should be happy to have you back."

"It doesn't work like that."

"If my father came back from the dead, I would rejoice. I would celebrate for 30 days and 30 nights and never blink for fear of him leaving this earth too soon again."

I shook my head. "Her anger overtakes everything else. She's always been like this." But it made her strong. It made her a fighter. And I didn't want to think about it. "What's happened, Rhett?"

"I saw my father's feathers yesterday. After delivering food to Skulhad in the mountains, I returned to the skies. Lord Ohrem was boarding a ship at his docks. It was brief, just a glance before he disappeared into the cabin, but, Deryn, when I tell you it took all my control not to snap the ship's mast with my talons. . . It took everything I had to bank around and return to the Courtless."

Long ago, Lord Ohrem faced Rhett's father in a clashing of fire and talons. It did not end favorably. The Lord of Autumn Court plucked the brown-speckled feathers from his father's lifeless body and had them made into a cloak that Lord Ohrem wore on his back to this day. I never had the nerve to ask Rhett how old he was when it happened, but I had a strong feeling he was young. And a worse feeling that he was present for it.

"I want his feathers back, Deryn. More than anything, I want to bury him properly."

I smoothed his spiked hair back, and he breathed into my wrist. "I know, my love. I know."

"Jair went chasing Valentina across the island. Kade is nowhere to be seen. The panthershifters think because they have teeth, they're the toughest creature out there. I'm just . . ." he sighed. "Come live with me in Illediff. Our time together is too few and far between."

"But that would mean abandoning my iron smelting. My tower. My tracks. My—" I bit my tongue. Shifters were vulnerable around iron same as the fae, even with all the iron surfaces covered with Faebric, a fabric I made with Adrian's help to allow fae to touch iron, it wasn't comfortable for long. "I know you hate my iron, Rhett. But it's taken me a very long time to build this tower and the tracks across the valley." And *she* couldn't get me in this tower.

"You don't need it. Lady Fede never comes to the Courtless."

I froze, and a cold flush dropped through my body. "Don't say her name here."

Fingers stilled on my spine, and I was up in seconds, scouring the cloth strewn about for my thin linen shirt and frayed work pants.

Rhett sighed, but it morphed into disappointment in my gut. He leaned up and crossed his arms on his knees. "I'm sorry, Deryn. Shit, I know better. Please don't go. I can't be with you down there."

"I left the forge burning," I said, tugging the shirt over my chest. This was a battle he'd lose. He'd said *her* name in my tower, and I needed to hammer it out, dislodge the fear it carried. Besides, the faeless were in the valley now, and the only one who knew how to deter the HorCains was me.

"Deryn?" he called as I was halfway down the spiral stairs, fixating on my fear.

I stopped and swallowed gulps of air as the memories raced through me. Lady Fede sucked the air from my lungs on her cliffside almost two centuries ago, then shoved me off as the Flutes sang their song, and. . .

I needed my hammer.

"The stuff you had Jair, Kade, and Teal place around Eadha? Will it work?"

My shoulders tensed. There were a lot of factors I had considered when I gave those three one of my creations, but fae were notoriously tricky, and if others found out what I did—

"Will it?" he asked again, and I realized he was looking for hope.

I wiped the sweat from my brow line. "Yes," I lied. I was *almost* sure it would.

"Just because you can lie doesn't mean you're good at it." I heard him sink back into my Faebric-lined beds.

The flickering light below me of a hot-burning forge stole my attention. Black coal crackled, beckoning me like a warm greeting. I swallowed my panic; I was almost there. "Be happy I'm good at my inventions, then. Trust me, Rhett. It'll work."

"You're *too good* at them. Look at all this iron. It's why I had to keep bending you over the rock outside in the valley below until you made the Faebric."

My mouth creaked into a small smile. I focussed on Rhett's voice and leaned my head against the iron staircase. "I kept getting burs stuck to my pants."

"Your pants? Imagine the state of my wings."

I pumped air into the forge, flaming it into a beast.

He called down the stairs between slams of my cold hammer against the unheated iron brick to be melded. "I'll sleep for an hour, then be gone again. Use your mirror if you need to reach me."

Three flashes toward the sun with the small circular mirror in my pocket would alert Rhett across the Galeairy that I needed him. Two flashes meant come but without urgency. I didn't have the heart to tell him I'd called him after I sorted the faeless on the Mainland and he hadn't come. He was busy.

And angry.

Smack! I hit it again. Pain laced up my arm and settled into my shoulder. I wanted to hobble back up, trace the constellations of scars along his battle-hardened body, soak in the smell of blue skies under his jawbone, sea spray in his hair, and me on his lips.

No amount of force would turn this cold iron ingot into anything but a beating stone to remember why I worked as hard as I did. But I needed something louder than her name still ringing in my ears, and this was a fine substitution.

11

VALENTINA

Winter's cells were carved of ice and stone. My breath fogged in front of me, leading, guiding me to the one I sought.

I rounded the last corner, nodding to the sparse guards clad in gold and azure. General Helle led a band of soldiers walking in lines of five out Silvermere's gates early that morning. My knees locked up suddenly, and a dizziness threatened to send me back to my rooms. *Because what was I doing?*

I smoothed down my equally gold and azure regalia, but this close to him and the chill of Bruma went straight to my bones. But that braveheartedness I felt in the throne room overcame it like an intoxication.

And there he was, kneeling with his arms limp at his sides and his head down in a sludgy puddle, denting the ice floor like a fire lit on a ice lake. A metal stronger than bronze chained him to the stone wall behind.

King of the Courtless.

His nose sniffed the air once. "Took you long enough." But his eyes fluttered closed, and his head dropped lower.

I blinked at him. Ever since that night, whispering for memories to come back to me, I'd been seeing dreams of us traveling the island. But if I thought too hard on any of it, all I could see was the white of Winter.

I grabbed the metal shackles around his wrists. Sweat coated his skin and his mangled back, done by my own hand, looked red and swollen.

"Why haven't you broken the chains?" I scolded as an internal struggle sparked within me. I was going against my lord's wishes.

"And go where?" he snapped. "The metal is different, stronger. Autumn has forged stronger metal, but at least it doesn't burn like iron."

"If it's not iron, why can't you break it?" I wasn't planning on him being weakened. I gave a nervous glance behind me. We were being too loud. Was I doing it on purpose? Did I want to get caught?

"Can't shift in them to find out."

I chewed my lip, ready to shout at the Shifterfae before me. Anger festered inside and I almost backed down the ice and stone hallways, away from the cells.

A part of me hoped he would be half out already, ready to spring free with a gentle prod from me needed. But he shifted his crouch slightly and his face scrunched up into an awful wince. He was weak, pale, and feverish.

Infection set in.

I gave him a wide berth and pulled on the chains against the wall.

"How's your back feeling?" he asked through clenched teeth, and I stiffened.

"I'm going to get you out of the chains, then take the south road out of here. Hey, listen. Don't fall asleep."

He sucked in a deep breath through his nose when I prodded his head. "You shouldn't have taken my pain, Valentina."

I straightened. "Don't say that out loud."

He dropped his head back down, hooded eyes closed again.

"There's . . ." I choked. "There's a Frost Witch in the castle."

"I know, Helle told me."

I scoffed. "Whose side is she on?"

He ducked his head and said nothing.

Noise down the corridor sounded. *How was I going to get him out of these?* "I thought you'd be out of the damn chains already. I wasn't counting on this." Damn it, I needed a weapon. Why didn't I grab a weapon? *Because you weren't even sure you were going to free him*, I berated myself.

But the clanking of soldiers grew closer and instead of pulling on their magic, I pulled on the only other one I could feel.

That of a lionshifter.

The calming, strong-hearted magic of a lionshifter soothed the ice away and pure determination drove on my need to pull the magic from Jair.

"Jairek," I cried out. My voice shook and my insides felt like they were melding together.

The voices grew louder. They were just around the second last corner.

"Keep going, Val, or we're both dead," he urged.

I fell, panting to the slush at his feet, crying out as my spine arched painfully. I couldn't do this. The invasion I felt toward Jairek was overwhelming. But his forehead pressed into mine and memories of a seething pixie yelling at me flushed through my senses.

"You don't belong in Winter, Val." Jair breathed into my face. Warm. Commanding. "Now, get us the fuck out of here."

I pulled again on his magic and drifted away with memories of shadows and home. Shutting all out but the lionshifter before me and the darkness inside me. And when I came to again, I hefted up from the blissfully cool ice against my too-hot fur. Pure animalistic needs surfaced, shutting out any logical thought. Fading any memories of *before*.

I toss my head and snarl at the male attached to the wall before me. A prisoner.

"Easy, Valentina," he commands, his face near mine so close to my teeth. I shake off his authority because someone rounds the corner, shouting. I growl and bask in the way it shakes the ice under my paws.

"Break the chains first. No, Valentina!" the chained one commands again, but I charge at the ones in yellow and blue, swiping at their arms until they fall, then crunch them under my teeth. They scream and I move again. One runs. Oh, I'm so happy he runs. I chase.

Until they all stop moving.

I growl, a deep-ranged thing of fur and fury. Senses turn sharp and instinctual. A desire surges to eat the guard under my claws. The air smells of fear and weakness. I want to pounce.

To rip.

To rule.

"Easy, Valentina. They don't taste good puking them up later. Let's go," he speaks again with such a command I wanted to bow to, but he was in a body of flesh and I of fur and fury and claws. I rage. Growled jaws open in his face.

He doesn't flinch nor fear my teeth but stares me straight in the eyes and dominating authority deep and guttural screams, "Move your ass, Valentina," as he presses his forehead into mine.

He stares me down.

I feel his pull and I swipe at the chains he wants me to with claws outstretched. They break to the floor at our feet. If I do what he says, maybe he'll let me eat one.

He grunts to his feet, wincing. Wounded. I mew into his side, smelling festering flesh.

Another one in yellow and blue rounds the corner and ice shoots out, but I am faster, and he yelps under my claws. These ones with the weapons thought they were predator but under my claws, my paws smearing their blood, they're prey.

"This way," the prisoner says with chains still on his hands.

We turn a corner to a large courtyard. My senses so sharp they have me sniffing the air. There, up top. Arrows, white-wooded arrows, point at us. I growl into the frosty air and smile as the sound carries far across this cooling ice castle.

"Maybe I should have let you eat them," the prisoner says, sighing.

But I stalk in front of him, eyeing the fleshy ones whose fear drifts into my nose. And stare them down. Back and forth, I pace as they wait for something, and I choose which one I'll sink into first.

The next one who moves, I decide.

"Don't move, Val. We're dead."

But I grunt, pacing. What does that one know? If I don't look him in the eyes, he can't make me hesitate.

There's a slip of a foot on ice, shaky hands clank arrow to bow. I narrow in, crouching low.

That one.

I go to pounce to start this off, but a crack shakes the ground and I dig my claws into the ice instead. Black shadows swirl up like the night's sky is striking an attack and I back up, hitting the prisoner's legs. What is this? Why does it smell . . . familiar.

I growl. Swipe at them. Arrows fly, but the shadows hold them still in midair like they pierced the belly of a different kind of beast.

From the shadows emerges a male. Fleshy, like the prisoner. No. Not quite.

He stalks like a predator, and it raises my hackles. Some part, some instinctual part cracks inside me and I growl at it when it waters my eyes. It's time for eating. Fighting. Not wet eyes.

"Easy, Val," he coos, and the demand combs through my fur worse than the prisoner's.

But it's not what I want. I want to stand on the bodies of those before me. Him too. But even the thought makes something inside splinter again. And I swipe at him, now a tail length away, in warning. He was hurting me inside somehow.

He kneels, black shadows sink on white ice.

So close to my teeth.

"Little lion, indeed." He smirks, eyes fully black, unlike anything my feline eyes have seen before. Wide eyed and black like the starless night sky, but I have seen these before. So many times.

Something inside remembers.

But I retreat a step as that ache inside swells and explodes, dropping me to my belly worse than any physical blow or strong-wooded arrow. I growl again and swipe out. At what? Now, I'm not sure.

Shadows slink off him so fast I panic, but they slither past me down corridors I'd already mangled.

Ones in yellow and blue hack at the black wall of shadows but it's too strong.

The darkness, the one with black eyes, is not concerned about anything but me.

Behind him, I see them now, stands five males dressed the same. All with deep black eyes and weapons longer than their arms. I growl at their stoic and stoney faces. How dare they not fear me.

"Took you long enough," the prisoner in chains says from behind me.

"Looking for someone," the familiar one, their leader, growls. His eyes flick behind me to the windows of the castle. "Did she do this?" he asks, seeing the wake of my carnage.

"Least she didn't eat them," the prisoner grunts.

You can relax now, Valentina. I'm here, *he says, but it comes from inside my head, and I flatten my ears and snarl. But his voice soothes, and my insides cry harder. Begging me to close the distance between us. I bow my head and the darkness comes forward. I let him. When he's close enough, I press my nose into his neck. A seductive, dominating caress dances down my spine, and I nuzzle my face in. I drop to his lap and let him carry my strength.*

His hands hold my big, furred head close, and he whispers into my twitching ear, "Let's go home."

And we're spiraling, spinning, fading in shadows and clouds. I cling to the leader.

Kaderyn, the name bubbles up from somewhere and I cry out. A mix of fleshy form and furred. Half in and half out from what I was to what I am until all went dark.

12

DERYN IRONSIDE

Bang! Bang! Bang!

I turned the glowing iron ore with the metal tongs and hit it again. Three times. Same force, same spot.

At this rate, I'd have the tracks done in a few days' time. I'd loaded up the cart the night before, filled it with bolts and brackets to fix the next length of track in place. All I had to do was keep my eyes on my task and avoid the valley and the rapturous anger that waited for me there.

I wasn't going to look, I told myself. I was going to feel my way down the tracks, bring a sharpening tool in case the cart caught on a jagged edge of metal, smooth it out, fix the beams in place, and take the cart back. All without a single glance toward the faeless settlement.

But I was faeless and lying to myself was easy. So I was blindsided when, three-quarters of the way down, with the briefest of peeks that I said I wouldn't do, I saw the valley and its six-foot-tall stalks of corn, growing in a matter of weeks. *How did it grow so fast?*

By my iron ore, I turned fully, mouth dropping, nails scraping the edge of the iron cart, whisking me across twenty feet in the air, half as fast as Rhett could fly.

Avika's stare found me. There she stood, in the middle of a half-built settlement, plowed fields, and faelings playing. She found me.

I must have looked like a buffoon. A gaping buffoon.

I snapped my mouth shut and cranked the hand break forward so fast that the cart's front wheels lifted from the track.

Too fast! I berated myself and leaned forward.

Just what I needed. To topple out in front of her.

Faelings raced near me, waving. Screaming my name "Der-yn! Der-yn!" and I crouched down in the cart, to duck and hide. The cart squeaked an awful noise, drawing more attention. A side effect of spring's rain on iron wheels. Even just hearing my name had my shoulders up to my ears. My name embarrassed me. But how could the faeless have grown crops so fast?

The shade of the Twin Peak Mountains casted over me, bringing with it realization.

Carmen.

Did Avika go to the witch?

I slammed the lever down seconds before the cart toppled off the unfinished track. It squealed to a halt, and I scrambled out. Less graceful than I wanted. Damn broken body.

I climbed down the iron support beams notched out from when I worked on them last. My sister's scrutinizing gaze tracked me like a predator. And when I was not ten feet from her, Avika turned her back and walked away. *Fine*, I grumbled.

Faelings ran up and danced around me. "Metal Magic! Metal Magic!" they chanted, pumping their arms in the air.

"It's not magic," I mumbled, pulling my hair in front of my ears, trying to hide my reddening face. "There's nothing magic about me."

"How did you do it?" I shouted when Avika's stiff back was close enough to hear me, but it became clear she wasn't going to slow down to my gait.

She whipped around, her face scrunched down in anger, but her mouth smirked with a confidence I didn't possess. "Pardon me?" she said, arms crossed like I was the rude one.

"How are your crops so tall?"

"You should be happy for us."

"Avika, stop it. I spread kelp on these lands before you planted, but even then, they shouldn't be this tall." I used the last of my damn kelp to do it. It had plenty of nutrients to grow itself. "This is the use of magic."

She kicked out a foot, and the faelings took the hint that this was not a conversation for them. "The pixies told us of a witch in the mountain that could help."

"The pixies? No." I shook my head. "They fear the ogres inside."

"*They* do, yes." She pointed at the makeshift port Teal was working on, then back at her. "I don't have the luxury of fear. You tell me winter is coming and we need stocks of food to survive that. I can't just take the word of my dead sister."

"I'm not . . ." But I was. She thought I was dead. I'd never sent word. I'd never stepped foot near enough to. "You can't make deals with witches, Avika. What did Carmen ask for in return?"

"How curious that her cavern was filled with the same iron as your tower blocking my eastern view."

I pressed my lips into a fine line.

"Tsk. Tsk. And you sit here demanding I don't protect my town."

But they were encroaching on so much of me. And *I* made deals with Carmen. Not them.

"Why are you so worried? Why can't I trust her? I don't

have the alliance of Shifterfae and demigods." Her nose scrunched, and I didn't know what that meant.

But I also didn't know how to answer that. Was I jealous they made deals without me? Carmen, for so long, fed pixies to the ogres, to get them to do her bidding before Kaderyn got them Bran's Horn.

"Mother," a young female faeling said, walking up to us. She pulled on Avika's tunic.

"Mother?" I gasped, stepping back. Avika had a faeling?

"Go with the others, Breena. I'll be there shortly."

Breena looked back at me with the same skin color as her mom and I. Deep golden brown.

"How many fael—" I stopped. "I'm an aunt? I didn't know." Why didn't she tell me on the ship on the way over? I craned my neck, trying to get another look at her.

"How was I going to tell you? I'd talked to the stars, Deryn. Thinking you were up there with mother and father. Meanwhile, you were here, constructing that gaudy thing."

My cheeks heated and I couldn't look at my tower or her. Digging my heel into the ground, I spun, needing out of there.

"You would have been the first to know, Deryn," she said like a final punch to the gut.

I HOBBLED INTO THE MOUTH OF THE MOUNTAIN, hugging the dark tunnel, damp with the spray of the Galeairy after having limped my way across the valley. But I all but burst into the mountain mouth now, looking for Carmen.

"Carmen!" I shouted into the mountainside but cursed myself when it came out strangled and choked. Some small inkling remembered it was the second week of the month and our agreement only had us meeting on the first. A moan from deep in the cave had me rethinking this entire confrontation. Usually, the ogres slept during the day and mined at night.

"Either you've hit your head with that hammer of yours or you're intentionally trying to irritate me."

I spun and stumbled. The metal tools in my satchel attached to my leg clanked together. And immediately upon seeing her, my eyes hit the cavernous floor. "What have you done to Blackwater's crops?"

"Blackwater?" She raised a brow.

"The faeless in the valley, Carmen!" Sweat dripped down the small of my back like spiders shuffling.

"Watch your tone," she warned as the staff in her hand glowed. "The one who looks like you came to me asking for help. Said she didn't have time to wait for the crops to grow and she didn't trust wading into the god's waters for fish."

"I can help them; you don't need to."

"I'm not quite sure why there are faeless on the Mainland to begin with. There have been faelings skipping near the base of my mountain for days and you're just coming to me now."

"Sorry," I said. "I meant to tell you about it. A large group of faeless had been displaced. They are looking for a new home." I couldn't stand to even look out my westward window facing the settlement of faeless, let alone ride my cart past them.

"And as they multiply and spread and devour resources. What am I to do? Grin and bear it? When you came to me all those years ago, we swore not to mention our plights. I wished to live alone. You wished the same. Now you ask me to let a band of faeless on these lands I've spent ages protecting. For both of us."

"There is room for all of us." My hands shook. "They could

supply food twice as fast as importing it from the Courtless. They could help in the mines—"

"The ogres do the mining," she scolded, "and the mountain remains off-limits. But they will pay their way. Like you have."

"They are not strangers to labor. But Carmen, all dealings go through me."

"All except the one I've already made with Avika and her daughter."

I spun. My world was crashing on its axis. "She brought her daughter?"

"Yes, small faeling. Not . . . normal."

"What did you ask for in return? Carmen, what are they giving you for your help?"

"I simply asked to be left alone. No one is to come near the mountain. Ever. Under any circumstances."

"That's it?" But I knew better than to breathe a sigh of relief.

"I may have suggested that the young one come train with me, hone her magic once she turns a rightful age."

"And Avika agreed?" She would never. At least not the Avika I remembered.

"It was all or nothing, I'm afraid. You know how I am, Deryn. Don't worry, you're still my favorite faeless. How's the smelting coming along? Ready for our next meeting? I want these beams up before the winter snow."

"Yes," I mumbled and headed out of the cave mouth. I needed fresh air.

"Deryn!"

I stopped and placed a hand on the cool rock. I couldn't turn around. My eyes burned with unshed tears.

"I don't know what those pixies think they're doing building so close to my mountainside."

"Our small world is changing, Carmen." I wanted it least of all.

"Well, you'd do well to warn those pixies building shambles near the shores that if they come near my mountain, I will not hesitate to restock the ogre cage."

I said nothing and got out quickly.

It was a threat I believed and I swore I heard a moan again.

First Teal.

13

KADERYN

Valentina slept for days.

I woke her on the third day with a platter of food, but she just blinked up at me and rolled over. I did what I had to do to come back to her, and I didn't regret it, no matter how much Oir threw books at my head about its consequences but, by my hounds, *Valentina please eat*.

"We need to talk about this," Oir said, standing outside my bedroom, her hands on her hips.

"There's nothing to talk about. It is done." I gave the tray to a Shadowfae castle attendant and clicked the door shut. Closing my love off from the world for one more day.

"Much has happened since you took off to find your shadows. You left here broken and you come back whole, but now it's everything *else* that is broken."

Valentina most of all.

Oir trailed me like a hound nipping at my heels and I loved her too much to shadowfade out of this conversation, but when she called me an idiot, I considered it.

"And the faeless from Blackwater have gallivanted across Shadow Court. You're lucky I was here to swat their attempt to plant their roots down near the caves you forbade anyone from visiting. That Avika," Oir scoffed, "she's got more bite than Gal. She'd wilt riddenweed with that mouth."

A weed so tenacious, we'd taken to the tactics of Autumn Court and burned it out of Shadow Court's meadows. It suffocated all that grew nearby.

"Well, how lucky I am to have you to graciously allow them passage across the Galeairy. Please send extra food to the valley for distribution." Valentina would want that.

She snorted, and I tried to take this time to exit the confrontation.

"Kaderyn!" she shouted with so much conviction that I stopped and looked over my shoulder. "You broke apart the fabric of nature. You tore through the veil between this world and the Underworld. That has had consequences."

I stopped; my heart sank. "What's happened up here, Oir?"

"It split a crevice straight down Main street. Shadowfae have reported things going missing."

"What things?"

"Non-important things. Books. Our spice trader's trowel. She's put in four complaints to the castle staff about it. Apparently, it was lucky. But Kade, she nearly fell through it when it happened."

"Did anyone get hurt?""

"Well, no."

"Good," I said, satisfied. But an uneasiness sat in my gut, I was still unsure of the state of the Underworld. Judging by the tension coming from my Hunters, through an internal link I had with them, not unlike the bond I had with Valentina, things down there were messy. Tense. A gut feeling told me I'd be needing to go down there sooner rather than later. "Come, Oir. Let's celebrate my return with a glass of Solanci and plan the immediate demise of Winter fucking Court." I held open the door for her to the tavern, a shortcut to Auris' Main street and if I could grab a glass of Solanci on the way, then so be it.

Did you not find him when you were there?" she asked, and I struggled to keep my shadows under control.

"No," I growled. "I sent shadows through the entire castle. Three dead Summerfae in the dungeons, a faeless female in the library who was quite curious, but no Winter lord. Oh, and a very dead creature in a river running through Silvermere Castle's cellars."

"What do you mean in a river? There's no river under Silvermere Castle." Her eyes went wide. "*Oh by Angus*, describe the creature to me."

"Pointed ears like fae. Skin translucent. Locked in chains on the edge of a frigid river." It grated on me hearing the god's name though and I said, "You're shadows, Oir. Don't be bringing that damn God of Love to my city."

"Old habits. Old habits," she muttered before exclaiming with a smack to the back of my head. "The Frost Witches of the north. Lord Aborys must have caught one! That explains how Valentina disappeared so suddenly. Jairek said she had no memory of him when he went to rescue her. Or you, for that matter."

Did I ever know that. It tormented my soul. I spent our nights quenching her screams for that fucking Lord of Winter. Twice I had to stop her in her groggy state from leaving Shadow Court to return to him.

"Well, someone talked her into remembering because I heard her screaming my name and found and fought my way back to her. Which I would do again if I had to. Nothing stands between me and her. Ever. Save your guilt trips about missing effects. I am not designed to care about Eadha." I was going to keep Valentina drenched in my shadows until she remembered who I was.

And who she was.

"But Valentina is. And she *does* care. And you promised her you'd win a war for her."

Faeless needed saving. Autumn was still slaughtering the Courtless. Summer had a hapless leader and Spring had a damn Berserker struggling with his own internal monsters. The worst kind. "But first I need to know who broke the Hunt. What if they try again? What if they target my brothers? I got by all those centuries on Eadha because I knew they were safe."

"But now?" she asked.

"Things went through the rift and the Hunt's still calling."

"Still?"

"It wasn't enough. We hadn't finished pulling the souls to the Underworld. There were so many, Oir. But if Aborys takes her again while I'm gone . . . " I stopped. I needed the Frost Witches gone. By any means necessary. "I will fight in The War of Many," I reassured Oir, who stared at me as I worked out a plan.

She crossed her arms, edged out a hip and said the only thing that actually made me pause, "Oh ya? And how do your Hunters feel about that?"

I chugged down the glass of inky liquid.

I'd give Valentina one more day of rest. Then I was taking her recovery into my own hands.

I rubbed her back, brushed her beautiful black hair off her shoulders and kissed down her spine.

"Valentina," I whispered. "It's time to—"

"I won't get up," she said, her voice cracked from unuse.

"—talk," I finished.

"You hate talking." She nestled further into the sheets and away from my advances.

To everyone but you, I said through mindspeak and rolled her over, forcing her to look at me.

The minute she did, she burst into tears and tried to hide. "Don't look at me." Wrecked. Destroyed. She pulled the black sheets up, trying to cover her face. Her beautiful face that I longed for during the Wild Hunt.

"It's over now, little lion." I kissed the tears, her wet cheeks, and reddening forehead.

"No, you don't understand what I did. Kade, you won't love me once you find out."

"There's no explanation necessary. There's nothing you could have done to make me love you less." I kissed each finger on a hand trying to push me away. "I went through great lengths to come back to you."

"I'm not . . . whole anymore," she sobbed.

"I'll take whatever pieces you give me. Please don't push me away."

"He's going to win, Kaderyn. He has a gift from the gods . . ."

"I know. But she's dead."

She stilled, wrapped in the covers, contemplating this. "He must have used his last wish to get far away from there. At any moment, if he finds another one, I will be taken again. He wants me to infiltrate the courts and wipe out the faeless."

"I won't let that happen. From now on, you're sticking by my side. Come, see this." I scooped her, black sheets and everything, and brought her to the window. "Look across the Galeairy."

"What . . . who is that?"

"That is Blackwater Junction. They relocated to our backdoor."

"Not really," she said, cracking the faintest of smiles, and as the first glimmer of one since we'd been back, I'd take it. "There's a strait between us."

"Thank my hounds," I grumbled. Oir didn't speak as if things were going well.

"What are they doing here? Did Adrian abandon them again?"

"No, actually. Well, he might of, you know him. But Oir said they came searching for a better way of life. Because of you, Valentina. You helped them."

"After we doomed them to the advances of—"

Winter.

She couldn't say it.

I kissed a trail down her neck, past the waterdrop tattoo on her collarbone. Jagged and broken, I'd ask her about it one day. But this wasn't the right time.

"Will you help them, Kade? Will you protect the faeless until I'm ready to fight for them again?" she asked, and I might as well have just fallen to the Underworld, shadowless and broken because her words smashed every piece of my heart.

She wasn't just hurting. This was something more.

"Deryn Ironside is on the Mainland. She and her sister have been reunited. I'm sure, between the two of them, there isn't anyone else more capable."

She snapped back to me. "Avika and Deryn are sisters?"

"Yes, both incredibly smart. Give them a month tops and they'll have a sprawling city bigger than Auris."

"Oh, thank the gods they are sisters," she said, snuggling back into my neck.

I guess this was as adventurous as she wanted to be today, I thought.

Her eyelashes fluttered against my neck as she said, "It would be incredibly difficult if they didn't get along."

14

VALENTINA

I fiddled with a rough-edged book, worn from use as I languished in Auris' library. The hounds lazily jumped on the sofa and laid at my feet. Gal stayed on the floor near my head. Red ears pulled back, wagging her tail for attention. Fragmented memories plagued me for days and I fought deep compulsions to jump out of Kade's bed and run to the Lord of Winter. I spent my time trying to decipher between genuine memories and one's put there by males who should have known better.

Kade met me with an ultimatum. I didn't have to leave the castle but I had to leave the rooms. And whether Kade made them or they wanted to, the hounds stayed close.

Oir walked in and gave a brief hello. I tried to tip my mouth up into a smile.

She looked over her glasses at the hounds surrounding me. "You pups better stop using my closets as a bathroom or I'll tie you outside for the faelings to assault. They'll fix your hair in bows, Dormar. Mark my words."

Dormar sneezed.

I smiled a true smile then, and the glint of a glass case caught my eye. There on the back wall was a map of Eadha encased in thick glass with a sign below it in cursive, saying,

Map of Eadha Island by Oir
Winnetiren 'Second Edition'
Teal—Don't Touch!!

I remembered back to our traveling days when Kade confessed his accusation that Teal had shredded Auris' map of Eadha. And Teal had declared she was indebted to drawing him a new one as they traveled the island together. Cartographer, she'd said. I don't think she could, or anyone could have known that she'd lose an arm in the process.

"Wait," I said, leaning up, startling the hounds. My eyes snagged on the coast of Spring Court. "Where is the river that runs through to Spring Court's mountains? The one through Kinswood Forest."

We crossed it on our trek into Winter Court, looking for Kade's shadows.

Oir glanced up from her writing. A book about creatures, I think. "I drew that map after Teal shredded my last one. It's an exact replica. And there was no saltwater river running through those trees when I drew the first."

What could cause a river to enter the court now? The nuck-elavees used the river to get inland and then got trapped by the freshwater run-off from Spring's constantly melting mountains."

"Who's making all these damn rivers!" Oir sighed and went back to her book. "Only two can know for sure. Adrian, a demigod of the sea."

"Oh, I know of Adrian," I scoffed.

"Or his father, Rhion, God of the Sea."

I contemplated this. "We never prayed to either in the theater."

"Adrian was cast out of the Otherworld long before your time. But in Hawrenthia we prayed to Rhion. We'd swim in his waters."

I looked at Oir. "You're Summer?"

"I'm shadows," she sniffed. But she pulled the high collar of her black shirt to show the waterdrop mark on her collarbone. "But I wasn't always. I was exiled to Shadow Court from Summer. Back when this area was just a wasteland. There was prejudice toward faeless even before Winter started hunting them down. I was good with herbs, and I think that worried some fae."

"Do you miss Summer?" I asked.

"Kaderyn's saved my life over the years. No less the time his shadows exploded over the south of Eadha, turning me Shadowfae," came her nonanswer.

"As she's saved mine." The thumping of Kade's footsteps echoed in the vaulted library as he sauntered to me and kissed my forehead before nudging Lolo off my feet. "Oir dragged me from the caves the day I fell from the Hunt." He flopped down beside me and pulled my legs on top of his lap.

"You still won't go to them?" I asked, but immediately regretted it.

He rubbed his eyes. "I allow no one to go."

"He keeps it as a reminder," Oir said, moving books around.

"Of my stupidity," Kade huffed.

"That even the gods can fall," Oir corrected with a stern eye.

But where would I be without him if he hadn't?

I blinked the thought away as Oir went on, "Kaderyn, is now a good enough time to talk about the dealings of your court?"

Kade ran his hands against my calves. "Mmhm."

"Our caravans have returned from Summer Court's borders. It was our second attempt this month at a trade with them. It seems they have a new lord."

We both snapped our attention to her then. Because . . . *what*?

"You're saying Lord Grigory is dead?" Kade asked.

"I do not know for sure. But this new lord . . ." she paused. "They call him *The Star*. Like some divine being that's come to save them."

That's a dumb name, Kade grumbled via mindspeak.

You're not worried? I asked the same way.

"Even had the nerve to demand one hundred dimas more for apples from us," Oir continued.

"Pay it," Kade said, after seeing my face. "Just pay it. But I might need to make a trip to see this . . . *Star*, if things continue to get out of hand."

She shrugged. "A ripple has been set off, changing not just our court."

"I'm coming with you," I blurted. Something about it felt familiar. Maybe because it was Summer Court. Was I missing it? I didn't know.

"Before you go sending welcome baskets in the form of threats to our neighbor's new lord, you need to sort out business here," Oir berated, with the needle tip of her pen pointing his way.

Why is she so mad? I asked, mind to mind.

"I broke apart the worlds. I stopped the Hunt to get back to you. It shattered the veil between my Underworld and here. Briefly, at least."

"And I'm still cleaning up your mess. Still getting complaints about missing items when you blew a hole through Auris' Main street. Where did it all go Kaderyn? Hmm? Hate to think Ms. Lethara's undergarments are just waving about somewhere between time and space. Juniper Hatch has put in *another* complaint to the castle over that damn shovel. Quite obsessive about the thing."

"Buy her a new one. She supplies Auris with spices from all over Eadha. I'd hate to try your cooking without her at her best," Kade pestered Oir.

I squealed a laugh into Dormar's side as she launched a book at his head. His shadows caught it right before impact. "Fool me once . . ." he said, giving me a wink.

Jair's voice came from the doorway. "Sorry to interrupt."

I jumped up, startling the hounds. It was the first time I'd seen Jair since I'd siphoned his shifter magic in Winter. I ran to him and placed my hands on his shoulders, shaking my head, so unbelievably sorry that I whipped him.

But he spoke first. "Don't you ever take my pain again. I knew what I was getting myself into when I tracked you into Winter Court. You didn't ask for that pain." He wrapped me in the biggest, warmest hug ever.

"Oh, by my fucking hounds, Valentina. What did you do?" Kade grumbled.

"What I deserved," I said into Jair's shoulder, but I was crashing on memories again.

Go to our rooms, Kade mindspoke, *I'll be right there.* But out loud to Jairek, he asked, "Did you need me? Can it wait until tomorrow?"

"I wish it could," Jair answered, and I watched his eyes turn dark. "But Autumn wants a meeting."

15

KADERYN

A mangled tree marked where the court lines between the four most southern courts met. It was a patch of land no bigger than one of Teal's ships, but it carried a heavy importance.

Meetings could be conducted here without inviting enemies to your shores. But it also meant no immunity from hosting laws. Meetings could turn to slaughters and there weren't any damn laws broken, meaning retaliation and reparations became messy.

So we waited for Lord Ohrem beside the twisted tree. Deathmarch sniffed the tree's bark, then violently pulled her head away and shook it back and forth.

"Reeks of death, doesn't it, girl?" I stroked her head.

"It's thick in the air with it." Jair scrubbed his face with the bottom of his shirt.

"Let's get this over with quickly, then. Did Lord Ohrem tell you what he wants? The least he could do calling a meeting was make sure he'd be on time."

"I'm sure he planned that, too. Fuck, it's hot near the desert." Jair scrubbed the sweat off his face again.

"We won't have to wait long. Look, here he comes now. Keep Gillies to your back."

The Lord of Autumn Court stopped thirty feet away. His horse's hooves stomped the last bit of heather on his court lines.

"What's wrong, Lord Ohrem? Don't trust us out here in mutual territory?" *I shouldn't be taunting him*, I berated myself. *I need him against Winter*.

"Another one of my soldiers went missing, Kaderyn! That's the second one since you've rejoined your Hunt."

"The fuck do I want with your soldiers?" I scoffed.

This was going well. If I could just rein in this mouth.

"We know what your bitch of a female can do. She steals our essence. She takes what makes us Autumnfae."

My shadows freeze, my fucking heart stops beating and I am utterly consumed by a rage to rival the assholes before me now. I'm going to kill them all.

The lionshifter let out a soft chuckle, and it pulled me back to the importance of trying to negotiate Autumn's help.

"You insult me by bringing the beast with you. What negotiations were you hoping to have by bringing my prey? I won't ride beside any animal from the Courtless. They're called the Courtless for a reason. Beasts, creatures, animals, not dignified fae."

Oh, I'm going to kill him.

"You won't negotiate a truce for the good of both courts?" Jair asked.

And I really applauded his approach. Thank my hounds I brought him.

"Winter wants to rule. He'll take over whatever throne chair you sit pissing yourself in," Jair finished.

So much for tactical, I thought.

Fire licked the air, and I swirled shadows to quench it. "I took your brother's skins, Jairek Sanguis, King of the Courtless. They lie as a rug for our fucking boots in the Fortress. But with you, I'll have your head. If the War of Many crashes, Autumn will slaughter your species and then stand against the rule of the north. Mark my words, Kaderyn, you've chosen the wrong alliance when you fell to the earth and your court will pay for it."

Deathmarch reared up in fury and I spit to the ground. It sizzled. "I look forward to running my Hunters through your army."

"Don't threaten me, Hunter. You're not on your court lines."

Jairek shifted in seconds, becoming the massive roaring lion. The trees of Gillies Forest clattered together, sounding like bones of the dead. Shadowanimals, tigers, beasts without forms, creatures without names snarled at my back, crossing to the tree that smelt like the dead.

"Then come for me, Ohrem. We'll see how this ends."

Jair's claws cut through the earth, inches deep. There was no retreating. Something was changing in the king at my side. Lines were being drawn. I had a feeling I was going to be seeing the power of the king before this war ended.

Ohrem and his soldiers' attention stayed on the moving forest behind us. "Save it for the war, soldiers. I'm not getting blood on my feathers in a skirmish of whose cock is bigger."

A screech of a hawk marked Autumn's retreat, back to their forests of blood-red trees.

Rhett looped around, banking fast, and shifted before his feet hit the ground. "Go after them, Kade! Pull them into your Underworld. They've crossed our borders. A group of pantershifters were found slaughtered at their camp south of the mountains, barely past faeling age."

"Fuck's sake," I grumbled. Their souls were no older than eighteen, nineteen, tops.

Rhett was inconsolable. "Why are we standing here? They're getting away. Let me hunt them down. Kade, he wears my father's feathers on his back. Let me get my vengeance."

"We can't," I grimaced. "He has his entire army waiting beyond the trees. I know you can see them better than I even."

Rhett stood down for half a second, confirming he saw the rows of soldiers wanting in the forests. "I don't care if I die, Kade, as long as we kill some of them. It's better than standing around doing nothing!"

Jair growled a low command.

"Don't you dare ask me to submit. You're supposed to be leading the Courtless and instead, you cower, forgetting your role. No more useful than teeth on a gazelle."

Jair charged, shoving Rhett to the ground. Teeth circled his neck, snarling into his skin.

Rhett lay panting, face wet. "Rise and lead us against them. If not for your brother and my father, then for those of us who don't want to be hunted anymore. Please, Jair. I beg you. Please."

Jair backed away, releasing his long teeth from the hawk-shifter's neck. He turned his back on both of us, tucked his head low, and sauntered down the mountain pass.

He'd have the pantershifter's family to console. If they were even still alive.

"Did they get past Skulhad?" I asked. He was an ogre we moved from the mines to the mountains to deter Autumn's attacks like these.

"I have to go check on him. I've been busy since the two of you have been away."

I saw it now, the exhaustion. The frustration. Rhett was being pulled too far. It was too much. He was suffering.

"Thank you, Rhett. For all you've done."

"I want Ohrem," he seethed. "I want to be the one to send him to your halls. Promise me that, and I'll keep eyes on whatever you need me to."

What could I say? What wouldn't I do for Valentina? I understood that need inside to kill all who hurt her. So I turned Deathmarch and headed straight for those shadows clawing at the air from the forest and growled, "Find Skulhad. Find out what the fuck happened and Ohrem's death is yours."

16

DERYN IRONSIDE

Fillagree Fen really was in shambles. I was too worried to step, even with an iron leg, onto the dock should my foot go right through it. But it stretched thirty-five feet in both directions now, with dozens of shops set up along the narrow-boarded docks.

A store next to me was comprised of seven rectangular boxes stacked every which way and held piles of stinking fish pooling in trays on top of them. The shop beside it sold beetle carcasses on toothpicks. And for three dimas he said he'd lift a black cloth in the back and show me contraband utensils from Spring Court's castle. No doubt this pixie used to work for Lady Fede.

I hurried along, dodging flying pixies pacing the corridor screaming in broken rhymes about their merchandise of ogre teeth necklaces.

They weren't all morbid though and I passed at least two booths selling beautiful flower petals preserved in tree sap.

Teal waved me down, little metal arm maniacally flying through the air toward me.

"Where are all these pixies coming from?" I asked, incredulously.

"I've sent word of my venture
To friends in Spring's center
That here they can find a nice home.
They won't fear Fede's censor
I'm in need of more vendors
To declare this a pixie-ruled zone."

"Mmhm," I mumbled, skeptical. Nothing good would come of allowing pixies to rule unattended. Though mostly good-natured, they often led with their basic needs at the fore-front. And I feared that for this lot, it was dimas. "Watch your new friends, Teal. Carmen is not feeling entirely amicable toward your enterprise."

"We've built a strong port
Among stone and young reeds
Besides, I'm made of metal and might." Her arm cocked into the air; a blue glow lit up the alleyway.
"The ogres can come when they please," she growled.

And just when the corners of my mouth tilted into a smile and a calm thought ran through me that this might be okay, a squealing voice broke over the noise of the docks.

"Empty your pockets
Pull out the dimas.
It's time to pay the toll.
This ain't a nonprofit

We need a deposit.
Nay?" The seething male pixie angled a brown eyebrow
at a group of faeless when none of them moved.
"Walk the plank for a stroll."

"Scout!" Teal shrieked, and she shook her head and
faked a laugh.
"That is . . . what one would say
If one was forcing others to pay."

I tilted my chin at her and crossed my arms. "Tell me you're
not!"

"We're just doing what pirates do." A needle-toothed
smile spread from one side of her face to the other.
Guilty as anything.

"No charging the faeless, Teal." I pointed a stern finger at
her. I needed Oir to handle them. I was in no position to be
overseeing this propped-up dock. And yet I felt responsible for
the faeless downstream and their wellbeing.

"Oh, Deryn!" Her face scrunched up, and she balled her
one fist tightly.
"How will we make ends meet?
The cost of pirate business
Does not decrease."

I bit my lip. "Fine. Two dimas for a round trip across the
Galeairy. And start selling things the faeless would eat and use,
not rotten fish and bug casings."

"Those are delicious," she grumbled.

I maneuvered around a gaping hole in the dock where it looked like someone had fallen through. "You'll make dimas by being a real port, Teal. Not by threatening your customers."

And she might have mumbled a 'fine' at me and zipped toward a newly departing group of faeless coming off a teetering ship. But if I was going to make it back to the tower before sunset, I needed to finish my last task of the day.

The valley.

And Avika.

There were steps now, down from the edge of Fillagree Fen port to a worn dirt path through the rocky base of the Twin Peak Mountains. Occasionally, I came across wooden planks, acting like steps down over the worst of the pass and a wobbly bridge of wood and rope allowed passage over a swampy patch of water. It was brilliant and much more manageable. But as I drew closer to the settlement of faeless, I wasn't expecting to hear sobbing.

My fingers brushed against the forging hammer in the satchel on my thigh and I lumbered quicker to a small group of young faeless, brushing tears off their faces. "What happened?"

One short, skinny female turned toward me, and we both froze. She had Avika's and my skin coloring, but eyes as green as sea glass. It was Breena. My niece.

And she recovered quicker than I did. "Brendan died."

My voice broke, but I thought it insensitive to ask who Brendan was. "From what?" I looked at the forest. I hadn't seen HorCains down here in over a month. Even after I went to where they lived in the ruins and took what I needed to make the Faebric, they rarely came past the tree line.

"Time," Breena said so solemnly and with so much empathy I felt her ages older than she was.

But her answer threw me off, and I slid past onlookers to see the male lying in the middle of an unlit pyre. Daisies from the fields lined his head and cut irises from the river bloomed around him. His skin was gray and wrinkled and his hair as white as Winter's snow. Oh, by all my iron ore, though death clung to the air, it was beautiful to see Spring's traditions here.

"How old?" I asked to my sister's back.

She didn't turn around. "Less than half our age," Avika answered. "Eighty-two."

I'd never heard of this. Faeless lived almost as long as fae. I scanned the valley. Did it have to do with the Mainland? That couldn't be right, or I'd be long gone by now.

"Breena, go wash up."

"Ok, mother," she said with a last glance at me.

"Immortality has lost its former glory. The faeless are not living as long," Glynnera said, weaving strips of Spring's fabric through the base of the wooden pyre. "I wish it was me covered in flowers and lilies."

Avika turned to her. "Don't say that, Glynnera."

"Well, it's an awful long time to feel alone. How long have you been gone, Deryn? A hundred years?"

Avika's head ducked down, away from the pyre, away from me. Away from everything.

"Almost two," I answered.

With that, Avika stalked off, heading for the edge of town.

"Avika, wait!" I still had to warn her about the dangers of witches.

She didn't turn, didn't so much as acknowledge me, and I was forced to hobble behind as fast as I could go.

"Avika, stop!" Something was moving near the tree line. Something as silver as the moon tracked my sister. "Avika, stop! You're too close to the trees. Don't—"

But she was already grimacing as she passed under my metal tracks. Stomping through meadowgrasses.

The HorCain leapt just as I did, but I caught its teeth in my hammer before it could make contact. Someone was screaming, bossing orders around, but I stared the beast down. Green eyes full of fury stared back. It snapped up and away and I braced my stance between the valley of faeless and it.

"Deryn, get back," Avika snapped a few feet behind me.

"You're going to leave the faeless alone, you hear?"

The beast snarled, and I knew it understood me. I'd had a run-in with them before. Specifically, this silver-backed, green-eyed one.

"Don't forget, I know where your den is. You stay to your side of the Mainland and we'll stay to ours."

It didn't like my threat at all and swiped the air between us.

"See these tracks? I have something coming you're really not going to like. Don't tempt me. I told you once before, I don't want to hurt you."

"You don't reason with beasts, Deryn. I've called for the hunters."

"Do you understand?" I snarled back, but my voice shook. The muscles in my arms were tense and waiting.

And much to my relief, the beast dipped its head low. Once.

"Back up," I commanded.

Its haunting growl shook the ground, rumbling through me to my core. I still didn't know the history of these creatures; except they'd had a run-in with the gods before.

It slinked back into the trees and left Avika and me panting beside each other.

I dropped to my butt, slammed my hammer back into my bag, and adjusted the iron leg that half slipped off in my run to my sister. "Call off the hunters."

"They can hunt that one down," she protested.

"And then what? There's an entire den of them. Plus, I think that one's their leader."

"And if they attack again?" She dropped to the ground beside me.

"Then I make good on my promise."

She scrunched up her face. "Like these things?" She pointed to my tracks and, damn if it still didn't irritate me the way she looked at them.

"Something bigger." I sniffed, brushing an ant off my arm. "Louder."

She swatted at ants on her toes.

"You can't send Breena to Carmen," I said finally. "I don't care if she promises you an entire field of corn. You can't trust witches." I wanted to absolve Breena and Avika of their debt, but I was shaking. My voice vibrated, and I knew she heard it, which made staying strong so much worse.

"I'm faeless, Deryn. I lied. My daughter will go nowhere near that cave mouth again." She swiped at more ants crawling up her arms. "But funny how you sit here warning me when your tracks seem to start at your tower and end at her mountain."

"Please stop trying to pick fights with me." An ant bit my leg.

We were fighting on an anthill. Just. Perfect.

She shot to her feet. "How can I not! Every time I look at you, I see a ghost! A ghost who left me in the middle of Spring to defend a town of faeless by myself!" She wiped angry tears off her face. For me or for Brendan, I did not know.

And guilt threatened to spill my own, and I tied my leg on faster. "You don't understand."

"No, *you* don't understand!" Her finger stabbed the air between us, and I wished she wasn't standing over me. "All you had to do was come back to your family."

I lumbered to my feet, finding my anger. "I left Blackwater that spring to petition to Lady Fede and Lord Brexton to allow the faeless into the main city, just as I said I would. I went to ask for help, just as I said I would. But when I got there, Lady Fede would hear none of it. She did not care about Blackwater, a city of faeless, no matter what I said. And when I requested to speak to Lord Brexton instead, she had me cuffed and dragged to the Aeolian Cliffs and within seconds I was soaring through Daina's winds, air sucked out of my lungs, and into the western seas. And the rest"—I slapped my leg above my thigh—"you know."

She stared at my leg and her voice became meek. "You could have sent notice of your survival. You could have come back."

I thrusted down my pant leg, covering the iron. "Not all of us are as brave as you, Avika. Lest a visit to Auris' docks for a quarter of an hour, I'll never return to Eadha. I'll never return to the fae." My hands shook, and the anger had my vision tunneling. I turned before she could see my wet face and headed for the cart lodged near the edges of the track.

We didn't all have a lion's heart like my sister.

We couldn't all fight with words and spit.

17

DERYN IRONSIDE

Bashing my hammer through blurry eyes, I sobbed.

"Dearest Deryn, what happened?" A voice grew dark in my ear. "Tell me who hurt you."

"Adrian, why did you protect Blackwater for all those years?"

"Oh, Deryn, I like my gam—"

But I wasn't letting him get away with that answer this time. "Adrian," I warned.

His eyes flicked to me, but guarded and almost shy. "She's not like you, your sister. I'm starting to think I should have sunk Blackwater Junction into the sea." Intuitively he looked down at what I was doing and handed me my next tool—a pair of tongs to pull a red-hot ingot out of the forge.

"No," I said, turning back to the anvil, smashing my hammer down on the angry metal, thinking of how she just marched a town of faeless across two courts searching for safety. "She's strong."

"She's sightless," he scoffed between the crashes of my banging. "I've seen nothing stronger than the might of a one-legged faeless and her hammer."

I poured a cup of river salt across a blade I knew I'd never be brave enough to use, and it sent me spiraling. I tossed the tongs into the bucket at my feet, and the half-finished sword went in after it. "Why do you sit with me, Adrian?" I sobbed; snot ran down my face as I crumpled to the floor, balling my knees to my chest. "Why do you spend your days passing me tools in my tower?"

I kicked out my leg, sore from walking to the damn port, the damn valley, then the damn HorCains that I untied it in a rush and threw the stupid iron limb across the workroom. It crashed into a dozen small bowls across a small table before whipping into the broom I had on the other side of the shop. The handle snapped with a *crack*.

Adrian was beside me in an instant. "What did that ogress-ass of a sister say?" His voice grew hard.

I wept as my forge crackled behind me, heating my back. How was I going to keep the faeless safe? My sister couldn't stand to be near me. Every time she reminded me of my faults, my failures, I felt less and less like myself. The Mainland was feeling less and less like home. Rhett was so desperate for a war that his home in Illediff, in the Courtless, would never be a home for me, either.

"Why did you save me, Adrian?" I cried into his shirt. "It was your beast's tearing my flesh."

"Little diabolical mutts. Not on my command. And they were punished thoroughly. You can trust me on that."

"For eating a faeless?" I asked. So many didn't care what happened to us.

With a single finger, Adrian raised my chin, urging me to lock eyes with him. "For stealing your bravery."

"Will the gods intervene? Why haven't they done something about the massacres against the faeless?"

He brushed the curls off my shoulder. "They, perhaps, have not found a reason to come."

Did I want to ask it? "And you have?" I whispered.

Adrian stilled, his adam's apple bobbed, but his dark eyes held me still. A thousand emotions flicked through his normally stagnant eyes. Until, suddenly, Adrian's strong arms laced under my legs and back, scooped me off the floor, and carried me up the winding stairs to my bedroom above. A place Adrian never came.

All you need to do now is breathe. With me. Lean against my chest. I'm here, dearest Deryn. Like I was yesterday. Like I will be tomorrow. I can light afire whoever it is you need me to. Just say the word."

"Adrian, stop," I whispered into his neck, and we stilled so fast I thought he ran into something. "Why do you do it, Adrian? Why do you sit with a blubbering faeless?"

"I'm a god shunned from the Otherworld. Where else am I going to go?" he said with a half laugh and sunk to the floor with me in his lap.

I looked away. Right. Of course.

His fingers and thumb slipped under my chin and dragged my gaze back to his. "In all the millennia I've scoured the Earth, I've never seen anything like this." He waved vaguely to my room.

To the creations of metal boxes and tools, some containers filled to the brim with a powder I couldn't keep near my forge. Faebric coated every floor space, so Rhett didn't burn his feet. He was gesturing to my entire world.

"The fae squabble about court lines and spend their days consumed with bygones, but you—" He picked up one of my first functioning iron boxes, a small metal trinket box I kept on my nightstand, and its contents rattled.

I scooped it out of his hands quickly.

"You *create* with these metals. Deryn, you're magnificent. Don't let anyone make you think different."

Curled in his lap, his brown eyes held a weight I was scared to carry. Unsaid words hung in the air as his stare flicked from my eyes to my lips and back again. The temperature in the room pumped hotter than my forge downstairs.

Abruptly, he pulled away and rested his head on the bedside dresser. "Hold tight, dearest Deryn . . . we have company."

Confusion raced through me, and I looked to the balcony, expecting to see wings on the horizon. Instead, inky shadows swirled into the form of a fae.

"Kaderyn?" I said, awkwardly untangling from Adrian's limbs.

"Deryn, it's time," Kaderyn huffed.

"Right now?" My heart shattered. "I didn't think I needed to go there. Can't I deton—"

"Rhett will meet us in Auris with Jairek and Teal," he said. His voice commanded the room, and I had forgotten how powerful Kaderyn once was. "He's coming with something he wants us to see. Let's finish what we started."

I could smell the concentrate I gave him once; something very long ago I'd given Kade, Teal, and Jairek for their travels. For protection. And the very stuff I threatened the HorCains with. A container of it still sat on the far shelf. But now it was time to see it in action.

"Ready?" Kaderyn asked, holding out a hand. Shadows swirled down the stairs past us and returned with my iron leg wrapped in their shadowy clutches.

I glanced at Kade's hand and then Adrian. There was no getting out of it. Slowly, I strapped the leg on and hobbled to the Hunter. But I turned back because . . . it was *Adrian*. "Will you come?" I asked the demigod.

His dark eyes flashed wide as he stood and gave a slight nod of his head. "Always."

Relief poured through me, but Kade furrowed his brows over pitch-black eyes as they stared each other down. Almost daring the other to speak. Something shifted in the air. A tense standoff between Underworld leader and demigod.

"Lord of Shadows?" I breathed.

He cleared his throat, and in moments we swirled in shadows.

Fading to Auris.

To Eadha Island.

To the fae.

18

DERYN IRONSIDE

We materialized from Kaderyn's shadowfade in time to see Teal on the finishing end of a backflip. She had dark markings around her eyes now like smudged charcoal. Truly like a pirate indeed. But I'd spent days looking after her following the baliroq battle and I'd always remember her small and meek tucked into a shirt in Jairek's arms.

"Is it time?" Oir asked, shuffling down the path to where we stood in a clearing on the far side of Auris' castle, away from prying eyes. Whatever Rhett was bringing, it was not for the daily hustle and bustle of Shadow Court's city.

Oir and Kaderyn gravitated toward the bright blue-eyed fae Teal'd told me about.

Valentina.

She was dressed fully in shadow clothing with strips of cloth as armor. And I tried not to stare. She guarded herself, perhaps the only one more scared to be there than me. I'd never heard of a fae being able to use everyone's magic and I bristled as I stood there with none of it.

I could see just the tips of my love's wings on the horizon. He carried something big and gray in his talons.

I sucked in a breath. *Oh, by all my iron ore, it was happening.*

Jairek stood off to the side. He had a worn look to him. Not that time was unkind, but that experience graced him with the likeness of one of my old track ties that'd been fixed in its socket more times than I could count. A hardness-coated exhaustion, like a film of algae on a dead lake. But the little pixie landed on his shoulder, nonetheless.

"Teal, the waterways are a little close to the ogres. You're free to anchor at the Courtless docks," Jair fussed.

Adrian misted beside me. "Do you want to be the one to tell her that most of her recruits are quite . . . unhinged? I mean, what self-preserving pixie would agree to live near a mountain of ogres?"

"Young ones," Oir said. "Ones who forget that they're prey to ogres or one's quite—" she paused. "You know, I once watched the one named Ratt stab the waves with a knitting needle."

"Don't speak to me of unhinged
I've seen better morals in a nuckelavee den," Teal spit at Adrian.

Who probably deserved it.

Rhett banked and soared down; tawny wings stretched wide, and I tried to make out what he carried. Something lumpy. He dropped it ten feet from us and it thudded to the ground with a *thump*. Bile rose in my mouth, and I couldn't comprehend what I was seeing.

It was an ogre.

I think.

It was hard to tell because it was missing its head.

Rhett shifted into fae form as I covered my mouth and backed up. But I didn't miss the off-colored sword sticking out of the ogre's bulging back.

"Found him along the mountain pass," Rhett announced, wiping the sweat from his brow. Ogres were heavy. "Skulhad killed at least six of them before they took his head."

"You don't have any good sense to spare her from your obsessive desire for battle, do you?" Adrian fumed.

Rhett ignored him. "Jair, here." He unsheathed a sword from his side and threw it hilt first to Jairek.

He caught it easily, twirling it once in his hands.

"Turn away, Deryn," Adrian said as Rhett went for the hilt of the sword in the ogre's back.

I focussed on a navy and silver tunic, moving in and out with Adrian's breathing, but the sickening squelch echoed around the clearing, and I winced.

I turned back in time to watch Rhett take two leaping steps, rush the lionshifter, and slash the ogres-blood-covered sword down. Jair lifted and danced back, but the blow of Rhett's sword broke Jair's bronze one.

I gasped, ignored Adrian's warning, and stepped closer. Because it didn't just break in half, it smashed it into shards.

"This one has lost his bird feathers," Oir grumbled, but I saw what Rhett wanted us to see.

"The metal is stronger," I said. But how? What could Lord Ohrem have gotten a hold of in the past few months that would change the metal?

Everyone looked at me, and my cheeks heated.

Rhett nodded along. "Autumn has found a way to create stronger bronze." He tossed the sword to the ground like it disgusted him. "We thought as much from the chains Jair brought back from Winter, but now we know they're making weapons with it, too. And keeping it all for themselves.

"We go to war and I fear we'll be at a disadvantage more than ever. We can't even think of preparing for war when Autumn climbs farther up into the Anduats. Without an offensive strike, the Courtless will constantly have fire at their backs. It's time, Deryn."

Worry spread out across my gut like a wild thing ready to leap. Could I do it? Finally give in to the war Rhett so desired? We were trauma-bonded. One in search of a war and one running from it. We hid our pain in each other's arms.

He couldn't let go of his father's death and I couldn't shake the vulnerability I felt flying over the edge of sea-torn cliffs from a fae meant to lead. But it didn't matter, his pain and mine felt the same. Helplessness. I'd never be stronger than the fae. He'd never avenge his father's death. Not with them hunting Shifterfae. And Jairek . . . near abdicating his kingship.

But the very thought of facing Lady Fede made my stomach lodge in my throat. My role here was merely a supplier. I wasn't joining any war.

"We need Spring on our side. Someone needs to get Lady Fede to—" Oir tried.

"Spring is with Winter," Valentina said, voice stronger than I expected. At least hers didn't shake.

"What?" Kade spun to her, and I wanted to turn into Adrian's chest again.

Watching them together felt invading, personal.

But her words were to her toes as she said, "Winter's lord keeps tulips at his bedside."

Shadows froze in thin air, and the hair on my neck rose as we all gawked at her. Kaderyn was deathly still, his black eyes not leaving her down-turned face. My body screamed for me to run as the clouds above us rumbled and shook. His shadows slunk close, and I eased away.

Adrian sauntered between Kade and me as he pretended to look toward the sky like he was birdwatching or something else innocuous. But Adrian's aura stifled the anger radiating off Kade. I peeked around to look at Valentina, nonetheless.

What did Valentina go through?

Never had I felt so weak. Cowering in my tower while all kinds of horrors happened to the fae before me. And here I was, sitting on a weapon of mass destruction. I could help and all I wanted to do was run back to my safety.

I took a deep breath and tried to speak. "It's going to cause quite a deep crevice—"

"Do it now," Rhett urged, interrupting my warning.

"Your own grief of the things you've lost blinds you to the battles of others," Adrian seethed, defending me. Always defending me.

"You don't want to warn Summer first?" Oir piped up. "This new lord may have something to say about it."

"Do it, Deryn!" Rhett stepped forward, and it startled me to my core. "Lord Ohrem was there. With my father's feathers on his back. He was right there. We should be busy attacking, not still worried about defending our right to live."

His ogre was dead. They paid Skulhad to intercept the firefae in the Anduat Mountains, and now he was dead. More than dead. In pieces.

"What's happening, Kade?" Valentina asked.

Kade hadn't taken his pitch-black eyes off her since her declaration about Winter's tulips. "Remember our travels when we went back to the Fortress? Teal, Jair, and I were in Autumn for a different purpose. Before you and I took to the stage with Jairek in the crowd to buy you back, I sent him to plant something at Autumn's docks. We had an ulterior motive in bringing you back to the Fortress in Autumn, little lion," he said affectionately. "I'm sorry I didn't tell you sooner. By the time I got you back—"

She seemed in contemplation before she said, "You'd said, 'We needed the coast'."

Kade nodded. "Deryn has created something." He looked at me. "For protection."

I sucked in a breath and hoped I didn't look as terrified as I felt. "Might want to hold on to something."

Jairek pierced the broken edge of the blade into the earth and knelt, holding the hilt.

"Are fae going to get hurt?" Valentina asked.

Rhett hefted the new muddy-colored sword to his shoulder and gave her a half smile full of malice I couldn't replicate. "The island is going to scream."

I nodded once to Kade, giving the signal. Shadows, like they were cooped up waiting, perhaps even as impatient as Rhett, immediately shot from him straight through Gillies Forest. Then they would swarm out beyond down the other side of the Anduats. As long as they placed the Faemech where I told them to.

One singular strand of swirling shadows laced back around to the detonator in Teal's small hands, pulled from wherever it was pixies kept such things. Kade was deep in concentration, but said, "Some of it has washed away near their tavern."

"It'll work." I hoped.

"There, I've connected it all. Uh oh, they see my shadows in Autumn. There's no turning back. Teal, do the honors," Kade commanded.

"I am honored
As your most capable companion
To be bestowed with quite a big task—" Teal started.

"She's lying. She begged me to give it to her," Jair jut in. She blew him a raspberry.

"*Ka-boom*," Teal squeaked before slamming an entire fist into the lever.

And my creation detonated. The spark shot through his shadows like a wick to my Faemech on the other side.

Oh, did it ever detonate.

It started as a crack, almost like wood snapping, then deep guttural booming sounded like the earth was raging at me. Rhett faced the mountains while Adrian and I held onto each other for stability. The ground quaked beneath our feet so fast that I almost dropped to my knees.

But there, above the tree line on the peaks of the Anduats, just visible over the mountains that separated the Courtless from the Court of Shadows, crumbled like folding parchment. Clouds of dust and debris bloomed above. Trees behind us crashed and snapped farther down near Summer's borders like a hoard of mythical oxen were ramming them down in a line.

"There," I whispered as the rumbling ceased, leaving behind only the echoing cries of Shadowfae and a spreading gray cloud above the divided court lines of Shadows and the Courtless.

"By my parents, Deryn!" Adrian exclaimed. "You are brilliant. What absolute mayhem you just created!"

All eyes looked wide at me, but I didn't even try to feign surprise at the destruction my Faemech just caused. "If I planned it right, then I destroyed a path right along the peaks of the Anduat Mountains. Autumn will have no access to the Courtless. Did you manage to get some powder near their docks?"

Jairek nodded.

"Then expect their fleet to be crippled too. And you went as far west between Summer and your court?" I asked Kaderyn.

He nodded. "Right along on the far side of Gillies Forest. From one coast to the other. Like you said."

I dusted off my hands. "Then congratulations. We've successfully put a canyon between your two courts and the rest of Eadha. If it's all the same to you, I'll be heading back to my tower now."

"Wait, how'd you make this . . . Faemech?" Valentina asked, blue eyes staring. She didn't look like she'd been sleeping. Dark circles marked her eyes.

I rubbed the back of my neck. "Mixing two metals together." And bat guano, but this wasn't the time for a full recipe.

"A single speck, the size of a grain of sand, blew out the back of her forge," Rhett offered, and I grimaced.

"How much did you give Kaderyn?" she asked, and all attention was on me.

Oh, by my iron ore, why did they all have to look at me?

I side-eyed Kaderyn. "Quite a bit more than that." Ten pounds in a leather satchel, to be exact.

"Someone better make sure Teal dusts out her pockets," Valentina said with a nervous smile.

They may have stayed and conferred what to do next, what the next plan of action was now that a deep canyon gave them breathing room from fae that wanted to put them under. But my job was done and that was long enough away from my forge.

I shot Rhett a smile and a small wave as I started the trek to Inkravere Port to grab a ride across. Not ideal, as I'd have to walk through scores of scared Shadowfae who'd look at me as I passed, deal with pixie scoundrels, and go around the scrutinizing death stare of my sister . . .

"Come along, dearest Deryn," Adrian said, catching up,

linking his arm in mine. "There's no time to limp back to your tower. You've lit a fire in me, and I must be off to see what ruckus I can add to your destruction," Adrian squealed. "The pixie could have blown herself to the moon!"

He started to mist us away, and I peeked back under his arm at the new metal sword in Rhett's hand.

I positively wasn't getting involved in the war.

But . . . what was this new metal?

19

VALENTINA

"Wake up, little lion."

I rolled over to the view of pitch-black eyes and a stony face next to mine. I blinked quickly, but Kaderyn was devoid of emotion.

And I shot up so fast the blood rushed to my feet. "What's happening, Kade?" My nostrils flared, holding back tears.

It had been days since we split the island with Deryn's invention, but I'd returned to Kade's bed where it was safest. Nights were the worst. I couldn't trust my own mind.

"When I cracked the fabric between worlds to get back to you, I stalled the remainder of the Hunt. I've put it off as long as I can, but I need to return to the Underworld and finish the Wild Hunt. But, get ready—"

I blinked at him.

"—because you're coming, too."

My pulse exploded, and I pulled the covers up across my chest as I knelt on the bed. "I *can't* go."

But he moved like a soldier, a Hunter stuck on a scent, and ripped the sheets off with precision before stalking to the dual chairs by the fireplace. An outfit, identical to his black hunting gear, had been laid out on them. I fumbled off the bed and trailed behind. Naked or not, he was crazy, and I couldn't go.

His firm, calloused hands were cupping my face in seconds, scooping my gaze up to his. "The Hunt is calling, Valentina. Put it on."

Will I be able to come back, Kade?" I was puffy-eyed, confused, and my memories were spotty. Did I want to come back?

He dropped his hands and roughly started shucking me in layers and layers of black linen. "If you want to be clothed, I suggest you hurry. Naked or not, we leave in ten."

And I pulled my shirts out of his hands and quickly tossed them over my head.

What exactly did he do on the Hunt? Would I go to the Underworld? Would I be stuck? Could Aborys get me?

Not long later, in fact, exactly nine minutes later, I faced the front of Auris' sprawling castle. Oir held Deathmarch's reins in her hands. But two Oir's stacked on top of each other still couldn't reach Deathmarch's mane. Hooves clopping on the cool marble thudded in time with my heartbeat.

Teal squished Kade's face in her hands and bopped her forehead into his with her famous goodbye.

She turned to me:

"The Hunt rides when days and nights are equal
The transition for nights to linger and day begins to lengthen.
Twice a year encapsulating winter
The Hunt rides in Autumn and Spring."

"Except when it hasn't ridden in hundreds of years. Then the call of the Hunt comes on so strong the Hunters can't resist," Oir said, handing Kade the reins. "And Kade's not letting you out of his sight."

She gave me a hug, and I whispered into her ear, "Will I be able to return?" My throat choked. There were still things I wanted to do here. Even in my misery and fear, there was a screaming echo inside my head telling me I wasn't done here.

Scared as I was of Lord Aborys and the Frost Witches, not coming back and helping with the War of Many caused stabbing pains in my chest.

"I think it's fair to say Kaderyn will do whatever you ask. Break my city even," she scoffed. Without blame, she softly suggested, "You can stay there, if you need to."

I pulled away.

"Fine enough time to tell you, Kade, that Summer is requesting our presence. Most likely to talk about the narrow canyon we just placed between our court and theirs." Oir paused. "But mostly theirs."

"This '*Star*' can wait," was his only answer as the wind swirled and the air crackled like static.

Looking at Kaderyn purpose-filled swelled my lungs. I'd pulled him away from his Hunters once and the time had come for him to join them again. Kade hoisted me on the impossibly tall Deathmarch. Power coiled in every stomp of her legs.

She wanted this more than him.

Kade leapt on behind and, with no warning at all, Deathmarch took off, charging down the castle's walkway. The marble crumbled beneath her hooves. I may have heard Oir cursing, or it was me screaming.

So impossibly fast, she charged over the meadow of shadowlands before wolves snarling, bears growling, and beasts that flew overhead drowned out her hooves. I looked through Kade's solid arms and to the Hunters flanked on either side before they dropped back into the same formation across Winter's tundra.

Pull the shadows to you, little lion, Kade said, soaking me in shadows and I clung to them. He'd said we were tricking the fabric of nature, that if I was enough of his shadows, I could move with the Hunt.

And right before we crashed into the tree line of Gillies Forest, shadows swirled around us, thick and heavy like apparitions, like fog misting atop a lake, and we moved through the trees like ghosts. Kade held me on tight to Deathmarch. Pulling me back against his chest, his thighs locked me in, and arms strung tight across my body.

I didn't dare breathe.

My gods, the energy was intoxicating; the snarling shadowanimals, the male heat radiating from Kade, the family at his back, and the safety I felt atop the tallest mare in this world. I was awake and asleep at the same time. Nothing could touch me here.

The roaring was steady and thunderous enough to pull up the souls from the ground at Deathmarch's feet and across Summer's edge into our wailing cacophony.

They screamed, but their fate had been sealed long ago.

Kade gave a loud yell, rallying his Hunters to his sides. They answered back with a wild roar of their own. The wind slapped my face as the seductive call consumed me and I roared with them, reaching out my arms to the snarling instinctual motion of the Hunt. A crazed smile spread across my face.

A dazed part of me saw the canyon we'd created with the Faemech. I could see the fear in the eyes of the soldiers of Summer sent to investigate its deep, cavernous edges as we rode on through them. I pretended to reach for them, to take their souls. Like I had the authority.

Like they were Aborys.

I blinked and pulled my shaking hands in as my senses came back to me. I wanted no part in pulling the helpless into the Hunt. Not every fae across our path was the Lord of Winter no matter how much I wished it was. But I could feel it. We were cleansing the spirits from the earth, beginning anew. Kade's purpose here was so much bigger than me, than a fae who started as a dishwasher in a dark theater being used. His purpose seemed even bigger than this role I had as Siphon.

Without me, the island would keep on turning. Without him, experience told us the earth would grow thick and polluted with lost souls. What was I doing asking him to fight in this war when his place in this world affected the turning of days?

Shadowanimals carved out space in the air beside us as we dipped low to the valley, through wooded forests and snow crystal tundras. Any soul destined for the Underworld became sucked up into our orbit. Nothing stopped us.

A smell like soot and metal, like earth and fire, stole my attention and I realized we were charging across Autumn Court.

And there wasn't a single fucking thing any firefae soldier could do about it.

I gave a crazed laugh. No one could ask Kade for a tithe for the female. No one would paint my lips blood red; there was no Typhina, that awful sour drink in Iradown Tavern. No Mohr. Kade had pulled his soul in the Winter tundras. I was invincible here atop Deathmarch with my lover at my back, leading the Wild Hunt on its raid.

We charged north across the heather-strewn fields and up past the Yegevani Mountains. Souls that joined the raid either trailed along behind, distraught and caught in Hunt's clutches, or joined in on the screaming.

But ahead, down a dark snowy roadway, a figure in a pale

dress blowing in the breeze froze in our path. Her dress brushed the street lined with crystal-covered trees, and a castle loomed in the distance.

Alive.

Was it day? I didn't know.

But she made the worst possible decision when an innocent soul was faced with the screaming, raging Wild Hunt:

She ran.

"No! Don't move!" I yelled, trying to be heard above the charging hooves of six horses and the Hunters they carried.

Their shadowanimals, like Kade's hounds, Lolo, Dormar, and Gal, charged at our heels in midair. An innocent soul, even the living, would get caught up in the Wild Hunt and be forced to reside in the Underworld for eternity.

"Don't move!" I shouted again, leaning over Deathmarch's mane. Could they hear me over the onslaught of growling and barking?

She looked back. Stark-white hair flew over her shoulder, and her terrified face mirrored my own. A face I'd seen before in Winter's halls. A book covered it once in the dining hall. But it was too late now.

Nothing outruns the Wild Hunt.

A Hunter swiftly swept her up and took her into his arms with one last piercing scream. His hood pulled so low over his face, I only saw his grimacing mouth. A shadowdragon swooped down, threatening the weapons-drawn soldiers motionless in the roadway below.

But they knew better. They didn't dare move.

I snarled. Because I wished to pull them all up with us.

I reached for them, almost falling off Deathmarch, but *oh gods*, I stretched for them. Kade shuffled me back on, and when my butt slipped off the saddle in my desperation, strong arms locked me back against his chest. Injustice lied in wielding power to entrap innocent fae, while the soldiers responsible for countless faeless deaths went untouched.

I sat the rest of the Hunt watching the shadowanimals as they flanked my sides, ignoring who we rode through. Defeated. Despite Kade leading Deathmarch, the raven above seemed aware of souls to be taken. It cawed just west of us and we pivoted slightly. When it did the same thing south of us, we doubled back around.

The shadowdragon was tardy and seemed to take pleasure in taunting the living. The bear roared the loudest but stayed the closest to the Hunt, fading in and out of form time and time again. The wolf twisted back and captured the souls that tried to escape our call. And the snake snapped its fangs at the air but stayed coiled around its Hunter's arm.

I watched them for what felt like hours, until eventually, Kade's lips brushed my ear. "Hold on tight. We're going down."

And suddenly, without a second thought, it was as though Deathmarch tripped and ripped straight down into the soil and beyond, through things I didn't know. I closed my eyes and clung to Kade's arm, listening to the steady beating of his heart. The same beating he hated so much. Until a castle showed through the darkness before us, with expansive wide gates and tall stockades surrounding it.

Deathmarch charged down the path, panting and braying, through gates that opened for us, until she stopped at a sprawling fountain and stamped her hooves.

Windswept and worn, Kade tugged me off her back. But the screaming wasn't over. Behind us, the souls swept in the Hunt were shrieking, wailing, sobbing, and snarling in a pile, moving between utter despair and righteous anger toward their new home. Their chains rattled the ground as the Hunter with the hood shuffled them all down a separate path and to the detached wing beyond. Some fae, some fae-like creatures, and some beasts were pulled altogether along behind him, and herded like one by the shadowdragon behind them.

Powerless.

"Welcome to Castle Mors." Kaderyn's voice was deep and guttural, his eyes blacker than ever, and he pulsed with a strength that captivated me. Drawn to him, I pulled his waiting hands onto my body. Longing for that power to consume me once more. Forgetting we weren't alone.

"About fucking time, eh," roared a Hunter behind me and I moved to Kade's side as this Hunter's shadowbear licked my hand.

"Artos." Kade embraced him. "Rode close enough through Spring I thought you'd be joining us on Deathmarch."

"Well, it looked awfully cozy up there." Artos' fully black eyes, from corner to corner, swept over to me. His black shirt bared open his chest and a thick layer of hair covered his lower face. Scruffy. Ragged.

"Hunters, this is Valentina."

"What is this, Kaderyn?" a Hunter said as the shadowraven landed on his shoulder. "We've just got you back. I can sense the pull she has across the veil."

"Never again will we be separated, Zedekiel. I am home. And so is she."

Artos wrapped me in a rib-crushing hug. "Welcome, Valentina. I'm Artos. Hunter, most good-looking, and responsible for keeping our humble shacks orderly."

"Except the library," the Hunter with the snake on his arm said. "He seems to forget that part."

"Well, how lucky I am to have mother-fucking-hen Gavriel here to be a fucking tattle," Artos roared.

Good-natured.

I think.

"They'll be here all night. Come to Castle Mors," Kade

said, but he walked up to Zedekiel and held him by the shoulders. "We'll talk later, Zedekiel. It is good to see you, brother."

Their sentences to each other were short, and I wondered how much of it was still from the Hunt's dominance roaring through them.

Kade greeted the last one I didn't know the name of. He and his shadowwolf gave me a wide berth but stared until my skin started to sweat.

What did I get in the middle of here? But I wasn't giving up on Kade, so I let him stare all he wanted.

Lolo, Dormar, and Gal disappeared with Deathmarch and a ghostly figure who led the horses down around the corner.

The sky turned in on itself the same way it did in Shadow Court, with clouds of purple and black. I gasped. Kade mimicked Shadow Court off his home. I whipped around. From the fountain, pathways led off into forked directions to different parts of the grounds. Artos sauntered into the one closest. Zedekiel and the one I didn't know the name of went around the far side.

Kade grabbed my hand and pulled me to the sprawling, black, peaked castle in the middle. Light glowed golden from within, flickering, welcoming like the hearth of a fire.

"No female Hunters?"

He searched my face, and I felt a soft but demanding caress against my mind. *What are you asking, my love?*

"It's a very tidy castle, considering." But I didn't much care about the tidiness of the castle with the smoldering need running through my body.

He laughed. "We have help."

Kade's castle stood like a lantern on a stormy night. Warmth poured from the doorway as we entered. Its onyx sides bled of power, strength, and safety. Garden beds of plants I'd seen in

Shadow Court lined its edges and a sea was somewhere near. I could smell it.

A skinny female poked her head out from a hallway to our right. Her wispy mouse brown hair was half hidden by a newspaper folded into a hat on her head.

Was that . . . *Teal's* name written across the brim? I blinked a few times.

"This is Santi. She works in our kitchens. I like your hat, Santi. Is it new?" Kade asked.

"It is. It flew out of the hole in the House of Mythros when the sky was falling. It's good to have you back, Kaderyn," she peeped, hiding behind a planter. "Are there pirates up there?"

Kade sighed and scratched his head. "Of a fashion, sure."

What's Teal been up to?! I asked through mindspeak. In my selfishness, I hadn't checked on her since coming back from Winter Court.

Nothing to worry about here. Come on. "Good to see you, Santi," he said, and her brown vest and too-short pants flapped out of sight as she ran around the corner.

Is she all right? I asked mind to mind, lest she heard me.

"Santi was once faeless, and she ran under our hooves. She was sent to Malek's dungeons for eons until Zed released her to help around the castle."

He turned and angled my face toward his. In the middle of a sprawling foyer, Kaderyn wrapped me into his arms, smelling like Shadow Court, male, and fresh air. Burning with desire, I longed to be embraced by the seductive power once more, nestled between Kade's legs as he led the Hunt. His cheeks were rosy, chest puffed, and muscles strained, and I sensed he needed the same thing as me.

I urged him to take me to his rooms. Ever impatient, he started to shadowfade us. And when we were neither here nor there, Kade devoured me, mind, body, and soul, consuming me in a blissful place with no thought to time and space.

"Kade," I moaned as we materialized in a bedroom of black silk sheets. But it didn't smell like the sheets I'd been wrapped up in at Shadow Court for days. And I froze at the unknown bed and frowned. "It doesn't smell like us."

"I've been away for a long time, Valentina. Let's change that." His chest heaved as he yanked off his shirt, out of breath —consumed by the same fire I that had me in its thralls. His forearms flexed as he tugged at his pants, and I was sure they were ripping down the side.

My hands roamed my love's body, passing over his heart where I knew scars lay, dipping into muscles on his arms and chest as he undressed me before those same arms lifted me onto him. My teeth grazed his neck, and he sunk me onto him in one fluid motion that made me cry out against the darkness.

I basked in him taking me in the middle of the room, clothes strewn at his whim. I could hand Kade my mind and body, and I knew he would look after it.

Even if I couldn't.

I leaned my head back, eyes closed to his mercy, pounding leftover adrenaline from the Hunt into me. And like a transfer of energies, I dug my nails into his shoulder blades and arched my back, deepening the angle.

He let out a growl before my back hit the silky sheets like sinking into living shadows. But this gave me more leverage, and I pulled him close before rolling us over.

I wanted *more*.

I straddled his thighs, mounted his hips, and twirled shadows around like a cocoon. And if I over-thought them, worried they were too much, he instantly grew them thicker. Swirling, they brushed my body in places my hands had never touched and moved in strokes, teasing nerves where we joined.

His thick, calloused hands gripped my hips, and he hissed as he pulled me down on him further.

Within minutes, my mind was gone, drifting into some peaceful place of black meadows, warm waters, and Kade. And like waves crashing upon a shore, I fell apart, clinging to him like a lifeline and Kade proving he's as every bit a leader he needed to be.

20

DERYN IRONSIDE

The sky over Rhett's shoulder was mottled soft purple, like bruises as he stood, breathless on my iron balcony. He looked tattered and torn, like he'd been flying for hours. The sheer fierce in his eyes and his shaking hands froze me solid. What did he have to do? How much did he think he could handle? I turned and, like a storm, faced him head-on. I was scared; scared of Avika coming here with the faeless, the people I couldn't save all those years ago, and terrified that Lady Fede would find me again.

But by my iron ore, I would be there for him now and always. And I didn't know if that was worth anything, the love of a one-legged faeless holed up in a tower he couldn't rightly or easily step foot in.

He dropped to his knees on navy and silver Faebric and buried his face into my navel, breathing deeply, rushing away the horrors he had to face defending the Courtless and the Shadow Court.

"Here's the metal." He dropped a pair of metal hand shackles and the sword found lodged in Skulhad to my feet. "Winter had the hand bindings. I'm not sure Autumn wanted Aborys to get his hands on them. But he did. And now so do we."

I leaned down and grabbed them. I'd been eager for these for a while. "I've never seen a metal like it." I flipped over the muddy-colored cuffs.

"Jairek couldn't break out of them, but he was tortured pretty badly. The infection might have had something to do with it. Or the ice, I don't know. He's brooding about everything lately. And I can touch the metal so it's not *this*." Rhett waved a hand and gave a pained look at all the iron that surrounded him. If I had known I'd fall in love with a hawk-shifter, I never would have built my tower of it.

"It's still bronze," I said, looking at it closer. . . "But there's something else."

"Well, it was bound to happen eventually. Just look at what you're capable of without a god's hammer."

"I wish I could see what Marcus has done to forge it." I shrugged. "You know, forger to forger."

"The day you go to Autumn Court is the day I failed as your lover. I beg you, please don't say things like this again."

"Do they still only trade Summer and Spring in their old bronze?" I asked, comparing the look of the metal to my older iron.

Rhett laughed, half asleep. "Of course they do. Why would they give their enemies stronger weapons than them?"

I whipped back around to him. "Does Autumn know what I've been up to? Do they know the Faemech came from my tower?"

"No," I'm careful about you." He flopped onto my bed. "And I'm pretty sure Adrian keeps all ships from the strait except for Teal's new venture."

"I need to keep these." I paced the bedroom, looking for better light that didn't face the town in the valley. "But they likely won't be in the same form you see them now."

I needed to see how it responded to fire.

"I'm just resting a minute," Rhett said, his voice muffled by my sheets. "You do what you need to do."

I dropped everything. "You're exhausted." I was too focused on the metal to pay attention.

"I thought I relinquished matters at Shadow Court, but Kade's been in the Underworld doing god knows what. And Jairek is sporadic."

"I wish they'd stop leaving you in charge."

"I look after both courts so that when it's time to retaliate against Autumn, they'll listen to what I have to say."

"Sleep, Rhett. Don't worry about Autumn now." I kissed him, tucking Faebric around my hawk lover so he wouldn't get burned.

His thumb turned my head toward him. Flecks of iron chiseled off from my grinding fell from my hair to his cheeks, sizzling as it burned. He grimaced, but didn't brush them off. I ran a thumb across, knocking the flecks off his burnt skin. His pain drove him, constantly looking for retribution against Autumn Court and those who slaughtered his kind.

It was why I created Faemech to begin with. To separate his lands from theirs.

Not long later, I left a sleeping Rhett and descended to the workshop. I tossed the hand bindings into a ceramic bowl and placed them in the roaring forge. I needed to melt them down and see what the metals showed me. What had Marcus found in the mines? What changed between then and now to allow him to create a stronger metal? Or maybe it was something powerful of Kade's, left behind during their time in Autumn? Did Gael give him a different tool of the gods? I grumbled, waiting for them to melt. It was going to bug me.

But more importantly, could I ignore the war brewing between the courts?

I smashed my hammer down against an old piece of iron and waited.

How long could I avoid Avika and the faeless I left so long ago?

21

KADERYN

I could lie beside her until the castle crumbled from decay. I could run my fingers through her hair until it was gray and brittle and never love her any less.

But there were my Hunters to face, and they deserved an explanation. From my absence, my return, and the destruction I caused both worlds getting Valentina back from Aborys' clutches. But half of that would require explaining how I felt about Valentina.

And there was no way these Hunters, born from responsibility and duty, were ever going to understand that. So I started with their onus to me, their leader.

"What has Earth ever done for you?" Orion spit in the large dining hall big enough for an entire court and not just my five Hunter's and a handful of castle servants.

"You'll pull us from our duties? You'll risk the Hunt? And so soon after being reunited?" Zedekiel looked me dead in the eye.

I rubbed the scruff on my chin before placing my arm back

on the table in front of Valentina. Not trapping her in but providing a buffer between my Hunters, their words, and her. Tack was not commonplace down here. "I will."

"Because we don't have enough problems down here?" Artos spoke in the only way he knew how. Loudly. "Larnwich encroaches closer. Monsters born of the soil are rising in numbers. Mythros tells of them setting sights on Castle Mors every day."

"Since when has fear settled in your heart, brother?" I questioned, easing into the conversation before I enacted my role as leader of the Wild Hunt, and begrudgingly made my brothers obey.

"Since love settled in yours." He leaned over the table, fists clenched, and I froze. "You cracked the veil. Shredded the very fabric of nature between our worlds. Zedekiel contained the turmoil in the aether rod, but while you were up on earth doing whatever it was, we . . ." he trailed off.

What's wrong? Valentina asked through mindspeak, and I felt her fingers slide into the hand I had tucked around my back. Her spine was stiff and, just as I guessed, she was ready to run. *Why has he stopped?*

He feels, I answered.

I shoved down the predatory nature that wanted a chase. That'll go well if I take her right here and now on the tables.

She peeked at my Hunters briefly to avoid catching their eye. Malek, shrouded in thick shadows and a black hood, some things never changed, was still as a statue near the doorway where he'd come in from. Artos was fuming. Orion stood, sword tip piercing the oak floor of my banquet room. Gavriel sat with his head hanging back, eyes closed, and Zed stood away, no doubt uncomfortable away from his orrery.

Something happened down here when I split the veil between the Earth and the Underworld to return to Valentina in Winter. I could feel it now. The unease in their stances, in their gazes.

What do they now feel? she asked.

Everything.

"I'm sorry, brothers." But to her I said, *I do not regret it.*

Gavriel, ever the optimist, rubbed his chin and lifted a shoulder. "We cannot die by their means. A war is a wonderful way to spend an afternoon."

"They invent every day, that could change," Artos sniped.

"Their bronze crumbles under my shadowblade." Orion's deep voice bounced off the walls as he reached for a cup of Solanci.

Having the warrior's confidence was important. Though, it wasn't the right time to tell them of the new metal pouring from the Yegevani mines. Deryn hadn't had a chance to investigate the hand bindings Jair brought back yet.

"Agh! Enough of this. I am Castle Mor's protector! I cannot leave." Artos slammed a fist down on the table with such force that the half-dozen cups jittered on their bottoms before toppling to their sides.

"You're such a homebody, Artos, I swear." Gavriel laughed, and it eased the tension in Valentina's shoulders.

"Ah," Artos grumbled and thumped into the hallway, smashing a fist into some piece of furniture I'd fix with shadows later.

"Does this mean you won't ride by our sides in Kaderyn's ask?" Zedekiel shouted, closing his ledger.

"Oh!" Artos grunted, pounding back around the corner, eyes raging. "Of course I'm fucking joining, but I'm not fucking happy about it!" He disappeared once more to the sound of a door opening and closing. Through the castle walls, we heard him bellow, "You'll get yourselves slaughtered without Rook and my axe!"

Zed turned back to me, ever the logical one. "And this is of importance? This . . . defending the faeless."

I looked at Valentina. I'd made a promise, and her soul wouldn't rest until it was done, whether she knew it or not. "It is."

He met me with a nod.

"So, we're joining a war?" Orion asked, hefting his shadow-blade onto his shoulder.

"We're going to lead it." I rubbed my fingertips against my lips.

Orion rubbed his chest. "When?"

I looked at my love; nerves strung tighter than Artos anger. "As soon as we're ready."

"I DON'T WANT TO COME BETWEEN YOU AND YOUR brothers," Valentina said later that night as she leaned against our headboard sipping nightale tea.

"Artos, even before, was hot-headed. It seems that when I broke the rift between worlds, it caused a fissure so deep that earth's emotions and desires flooded Castle Mors."

"I'm sorry—"

"I would do it all again, Valentina. You hold the morals for both of us." I kissed down her neck. My selfishness wanted to keep her in the Underworld in my castle where I rule. Where I was strongest. "So I can crash and smash things until I get what I want."

That brought a smile from her, but I could feel the tension in her body, so I clarified, "Before, we depended on duty and honor. Our sacrifice was only for each other. Hate and rage grow in the Underworld like weeds in fertile soil. We kept it under control with the control we kept."

"And now?"

"Now they watch when I kiss you." I pressed my lips to her knuckles, warm from the tea. "Their eyes linger on your hand in mine. Curiosity flows from them in waves I try not to laugh at."

"They've never known love?"

"They are the Hunters in the Wild Hunt, Val. They've only ever had a desire for order, responsibility, and brotherhood." I stood, cracked my neck, and leaned against the bedpost. If I didn't get up now, I'd never leave her warmth.

"Will they fight for Eadha?"

"They will," I promised.

My love for Teal and Jair, my court, and my Hunters—a brotherhood built on duty and honor—drove me on, carried my weariness across those treks, but my love, my *need* for her was different. It felt selfish, because she was mine. Something I didn't do for honor but because she made me want to live in this world. And I only wanted to experience it with her.

"I love you, Kade," she whispered into the darkness, setting her tea on the nightstand and wormed her way under the covers. "Are you coming to sleep? I'm tired."

But I didn't know if she meant body or soul. "Sleep, love." I returned to her and drew my lips to her forehead. "I'll be up again shortly."

Some things deserved my attention now that I was back.

ZEDEKIEL'S HOUSE OF MYTHROS SAT SQUARE IN THE southwest corner of the Underworld's compound. A thick-walled blockade around the entire castle kept miscreants born of the darkness out. Whatever got close, Artos and Rook, his shadowbear, sent packing back into the abyss. Anything bigger, and Orion and his shadowwolf went out and met them head-on.

I left Valentina sleeping safely in my beds as I went to go visit my most strict brother. Zed's house was always in orderly fashion, even though it seemed to be packed the most with oddities. The massive orrery spun in slow concentric circles, suspended in the middle of his sprawling foyer. Planets swooped in and around others, stars blinked in and out on their own track. But even farther to the ceiling, a very notable recently patched crevice split through the entire thing.

I swallowed thickly.

"Looking at your handiwork?" came Zed's voice from the far bookshelf wall.

"You've patched it up nicely." I moved to his sitting chairs but stalled on a purple-handled hand trowel half embedded into the wooden worktable. A glass cloche covered it. "What is Juniper Hatch's hand shovel doing in the Underworld? And why is it covered in glass?" I went to move the cloche off the still-dirty spice runner's hand tool.

"Don't touch the aether rod," Zed slapped down the book he was holding with an audible smack.

I scrubbed at my cheek with my thumbnail, trying not to laugh at the naivety of my Hunter. "An aeth—"

"When we charged across the far side of that planet there." He pointed up to a spinning orb. "And you had a fine idea to listen to voices in your head screaming your name and stop the Hunt mid-ride, tearing the curtain between worlds, it severed a crack so deep between the two that by the time I got back to my house, things were flooding, falling from the skies into these very rooms. All kinds of contraptions I haven't a need or use for. But the rift was split and to contain it, I had to control it. That aether rod whipped the side of my head and in a moment of desperation I empaled it into my desk to draw the energies to it like a lightning rod while the five of us knitted the worlds back together."

"Fuck. I'm sorry, Zed." What a fucking mess I made. *I'm going to find out who broke the Hunt and I'm going to kill them all,* I thought.

"You were up there for centuries. It is understandable you'd grow attached to something. But I'll warn you, the other Hunters are not as understanding as I."

Which was why I sought Zedekiel first. Far more level-headed than fist-smashing Artos. I'd probably have to duel Orion for forgiveness. He'd want a chance to kick my ass.

I'd be lucky to get two words out of Malek about it.

"So, what happens when you touch it?" I tried reaching for it again, but shadows snapped at my hand, and I glared at Zed.

"It's become a wishing well. Very odd. Very strange. Grab the aether rod's handle and whatever you wish for comes down to the Underworld."

"Huh," I said incredulously.

We stared at each other for a moment.

But quickly and with a dopey half-smile, I said, "We both know I'm going to touch it."

He scoffed, tossed up his hands, and walked away.

"Sorry Zedekiel, but you're using my spice runner's root digger as some mystical energy rod. I need to see what danger it can pose. So I just . . . grab the handle?"

He appeared around the corner. "I beg you not to wish for anything large. I just finished reorganizing the bookshelf for the third time. And nothing alive, for the love of Mythros! Artos learned that the hard way. The little beasts are still ripping through the roots in the ground's forests. Rook is having a blasted time catching them."

"Nothing alive. Got it." I lifted the glass cloche and set it aside.

I owed Juniper Hatch a great big shovel when all this was done, because there was no giving her this one back.

22

VALENTINA

I peeled open my eyes to the sight of the reddest apples I'd ever seen on the pillow next to me.

My mouth watered.

"You can eat them, but you must do so outside of the bedrooms," came Kade's voice from the chairs near the large window.

My spirits faltered. I floated from our rooms to the kitchens and back again, sometimes only leaving once a day. Something was still nipping at my mind, and it exhausted me. I pushed the pillow, and the apples rolled off, disappearing into the sheets.

Suddenly I was tugged, pulled through my cozy warm den I'd arranged, and thrust to cold sheets and nippy air. I growled at Kade's hands, but they stayed like vices around me.

"Ready to tell me about this?" He traced the rudely tattooed waterdrop mark along my collarbone with his fingertip.

I frowned. "Will you let me eat the apples after I do?"

"Maybe."

I sighed, and my mouth watered again. "Fine. I carved it into my skin myself, hiding in the dusty rafters of Elaria's Otti Theater when I was ten. I wanted to fit in. To be like the rest of Summerfae."

"It must have hurt."

"Being alone—feeling different—hurt more."

He was quiet for so long that I thought he'd fallen asleep. I reached for an apple.

"I'm proud of you."

I turned to him, then. Blinking into dark eyes, swallowing me whole. "For what?"

"For surviving, by any means necessary. But, Valentina, I'm going to need you to do it again."

I grumbled and turned back around, pulling the sheets that held the apples closer.

"You can lie in bed and stay in my Underworld. But you cannot lie in your despair forever. We must move on. Keep going. Come, brush your teeth, wash this hair, get food outside our room. Santi will come in and clean."

But the thought of someone else cleaning my messes bugged me to my core. "I'll clean the room."

"Santi will be thoroughly insulted. Come," he urged.

And we spent the day eating and drinking in the banquet room. I learned Malek liked to keep an orderly library and Artos often destroyed it. Orion was their warrior. He came back during dinner covered in a black slime. His shadowwolf at his side was panting with its tongue out. Zedekiel held the knowledge of knowing where souls go, either the Underworld or the Otherworld, a burden I didn't think I could bear. Gavriel was by far the friendliest, often laughing at the others' expense. He was also the best at the card game they played.

Do you want to play? Kade asked through mindspeak as he saw me smiling at Artos, who flipped the table when he lost.

Oh, definitely not. I didn't know how to tell him that I wasn't the same Valentina he fell in love with. I hadn't resolved this undertow of turmoil in my gut. This sweeping feeling like at any given point something was going to kick out my legs, and I'd fall and fall and fall. There was a sudden unsteadiness in everything I'd ever held solid.

He was *home here.*

With them.

I stumbled from the roaring room to the castle foyer, holding my stomach as the world spun. It wasn't the food or drink. Though I'd had enough of the burning Solanci Ipsum.

I was a cliffside crashing into dark stormy waters and I was taking Kaderyn and his Hunt with me. Who was I to demand this of them? Little me. Faeless even, in the right company.

The heavy steps of Kade followed and, *gods,* I just wanted to be alone in my misery. *How could I face him?* They were together. Their purpose was in the form of thundering hooves and baying hounds, not fighting for a war in a world they didn't live in. How selfish was I to ask for it?

"Valentina," Kade snapped, his voice a command to stop but laced with worry.

I kept going. Trudging on through dark skies of the Underworld. I should have killed Aborys when I had the chance. I should have found a bigger knife and stronger courage and rid the island of his cruelty.

Three steps to the wing south of the main castle and I roared, screamed to the purple clouds, loud and strong, full of rage I had nowhere to expel.

Something in the dark night, beyond the fields of shadow meadows and slinking inky things I saw in my peripherals, something howled back, and I lowered my gaze.

Come get me, I urged it.

Kade may have called for me. A lingering trail of orders

tingled down my spine, but I was too far gone. I was trying to run from him, hide this rage I had bundled up under my ribs. Dreadful, awful things lived in the Underworld and I was beginning to wonder if it was inside me too. I thrust open doors before me marked with crossed swords and a golden wolf's head door knocker that smashed against itself when it swung shut behind.

Black-on-black and endless weapons greeted me like violence sought me out, too.

"Valentina!" Kade roared into the echoing chamber of the weapons room, and I froze as sheer power locked every muscle, daring me to disobey.

"You're trying to push me away," he said, defeated as he stalked closer like a hunter chasing a deer ready to run.

"I'm trying to—! I'm trying to feel nothing, Kaderyn. I killed them. Sisaria, Petri, Daria. I murdered them because a mad lord said so and there wasn't anything I could do to stop it. Everything is broken." I dropped my head back against my neck. It read *House of Lonan* above the far wall. *Oh gods, where did I run off into?* A shadowwolf with eyes bright and head low stalked the weapon's wall. A formless creature that solidified and dissipated in equal measure.

"Not us." Kade shook his head. "We're not broken."

"Stop it!" My fingers laced through my hair, ripping. "Find someone else to love." I threw my arms out, sending shadows swirling toward him in threat. "*I am broken!*"

"I can wait."

"I don't want your patience, Kaderyn. I want your hatred."

But he thickened the bonds between us, shadows built upon shadows, until I could feel every part of him in my mind and soul. Deep, reassuring, and powerful. He tugged at the shadows in the room that I held, standing defiantly in my plea.

A hiss rose from my throat. "I swear to the gods, Kaderyn. Put me in your cells. Let me die in my misery."

"I will not leave you," he growled, but his eyes, *those damn eyes*, stayed vulnerable and wide and it tore me to fucking pieces.

I screamed a guttural sound and lashed out, slashing shadows at him. "I am not worth this!"

He deflected them with ease before flicking his hair out of his face and widening his stance. "That the best you got?"

I struck out again. Fueled by this self-hating anger.

He absorbed my siphoned shadows into him, then in the next breath exploded them out, swallowing the room, pitching us in darkness so thick I couldn't breathe. Every crevice of the training room screamed of him and everything Kaderyn was. His footfalls thudded against the marble, but it came in at all sides and I whipped around trying to find him.

"I severed the Hunt to return to you. I almost crumpled the Underworld and my Hunters entirely. You'll have to try a lot harder than that."

I pulled his shadows to me again and sent them to the wall of daggers on the south training room wall. I used shadows to flick them out and, in a recess of clear air, I saw one narrowly miss his thigh.

Kade moved just in time. "Okay, that was a little dirty." He held up a hand toward a Hunter in the doorway, commanding him not to intervene. Artos. The one with the shadowbear.

I gave him my best death stare. I was not in the mood.

"On me, Valentina," Kaderyn whispered so deadly I instantly whipped my attention back to him.

"I am so . . . so angry." I looked down at my hands, my traitorous hands, and the shadows I called to me licked the air, charged. More Hunters filed into the room until all five of them found a place to observe the chaos between Kade and me. And by the gods, if they tried to calm me . . .

Kade gave a brief nod. "Show me."

And I raged.

I pulled all the shadows to me until the room grew bright and clear. Until the only darkness in the room was me. "I. Am. Broken."

Then I will flow shadows into all your cracks and hold you together until you can do it yourself, Kade mindspoke to me, and my heart shattered.

I unleashed them in a hostile rage, like arrows firing, hammers smashing, like the anger I had at an island that felt more broken than when I started.

With an echoing boom, a deep crevice cracked down the center of Orion's training room. It carved down the floor and broke apart the wall on the other side, exposing the swirling shadow clouds of the Underworld.

"There is a darkness inside me, Kaderyn. It's consuming me," I confessed, dropping to my knees.

Within three strides, Kaderyn slumped to his knees before me and laid his hands out in surrender on mine. His voice was but a whisper against the wind howling through the crack. "There is no darkness I haven't seen." His hand laced out and pushed the hair off my sweaty face, drawing me toward him. "Come back to me, little lion."

"Eadha Island will never get better." I closed my eyes at what I had seen. At what I had done. "The faeless will never be safe. The fae will never stop fighting."

"I told you," he said, "I will join the War of Many for you. And I will finish it. For *you.*"

"Not anymore, Kade. You're back with your brothers. Your Hunters."

They all leaned up from where they'd been and came to

stand behind their leader and my love. Artos was the only brave one to look away from me, the danger, to let out a low whistle through parted lips at the crack in the room's foundation.

"You're home," I said, gesturing to the Hunters lined behind him. "Your quest is done."

"Valentina, I am Kaderyn. Lord of the Court of Shadows." But he still winced at that particular declaration. "Leader of the Wild Hunt and ruler of the Underworld." He looked up at his brothers. "And we are the Hunters in the Wild Hunt."

The one farthest to the outside, Zedekiel with the shadowraven overhead, pulled back his shoulders. His voice was solid and determined as he said, "We pass fair judgment on those deemed for these halls."

Artos crossed his arms over his enormous chest. His voice had a lick of an accent as he said, "We safeguard our fortress and fortitude these walls."

"We hold steadfast to the bonds of our brothers," Gavriel said as a deadly shadowsnake slithered up his leg.

Orion, the ruler of the House of Lonan, sent shadows out to mend the crack in the training room's foundation. "We fend off those trying to get in."

Slowly, the wind ceased.

And the quietest Hunter, the one with the hood always tucked low over his face, the one with the hardest job of all, moved out from the shadows. Malek. "We hold captive those trying to get out."

Kaderyn leaned down and brushed my lips with his. "We are the Hunters your elders warned you about." And he pressed his face into mine so hard my tears soaked his skin. "And we'll end the War of many. For you, Valentina."

NOT MINUTES LATER, MY BACK HIT THE DOOR AS Kade crashed us up to his rooms, shadowfading us quickly away from an audience. I was consumed by the seductive push and pull of shadows between us. It charged us like a magnet.

His lips fell on mine, and I wrapped my arms around his neck, squeezing tight. *Fine, He thought he could love me like this?* I ripped apart his shadow shirt, feeding off the power cascading off him and kissed him hard, trying to press myself into his body, willing to not be in my own anymore. Willing the demons inside to go away, to take the goodness of Kaderyn back with me when I pulled back from him. But I was a Siphon of magic and pain, a Siphon of happiness, and it was never clearer at that moment when Kade looked at me. His blank expression was hiding the pity in his eyes.

"Don't look at me like that." I frowned.

"Then stop thinking you don't belong here. I've told you before, you belong with me."

Kaderyn bore the scars of being fae. The fingernail marks down his chest where he tried to claw out his beating heart. The iron imprint in his hand from an iron key. He bore the scars of the island like me. The silence between us became electrifying, like one spark would ignite the entire room.

"I'm trying to fix this eternal decay. Destroy me, Kade. Make me anew."

And strong arms placed me on my knees. His hardness pressed into my back. Kaderyn's breath was heavy in my ear as he lined himself up behind me. "I told you I'd break apart the stars to get back to you, little lion." His thumbs tipped up under my chin, holding me hostage.

I arched encouragingly and gasped as he thrust in. His stomach was warm against my back. "At the end of everything, when everything is dead and gone, when we've turned to dust, they will speak of my love for you."

I trailed kisses up his throat until I met the soft parting of his lips then he devoured me.

His pace quickened, but I was greedy, and I wanted Kaderyn to feel all I felt. I placed my hand on his as it gripped my breast and squeezed. His hand moved to between my thighs and worked in unison. I leaned my head back against the thick muscles in his shoulder.

He kissed my neck as he said, "When cities fall, when stars collide, when there isn't a sound to be heard. A whisper will begin on the western breeze."

And here, surrounded by shadows that never made me feel anything but myself. I peaked with half-slitted eyes. The shadows cascaded around us, dancing us in and out of darkness, in an ecstasy of their own because Kaderyn's control was gone. And when his breathing grew ragged on my neck, I grabbed his thigh, pulling him close. Never wanting to let go. Which was enough to send him over the edge. He gripped me tight, thrusting one last time before roaring into the night air. We fell to the damp sheets, tangled together.

"At the end of it all, Valentina, I will still be heard whispering your name. To come back to me."

23

KADERYN

Getting her back from wherever her mind had gone, from that internal dark abyss, was proving futile in Eadha. Saving her from Winter's castle was one thing. This unseen enemy . . . another entirely. I couldn't drag my sword through regret. I couldn't pull the soul from her own mind. The loss of anatomy she'd felt with Mohr—him deciding when she ate, what she ate, where she went, was one thing. But what that fucking Winter lord did was something completely different. Losing her entire ability to trust herself, her thoughts, and her own mind was another. She lost her courage and I feared it was stuck frozen in Winters tundras.

My love had brought me back to my brothers, and I'd make good on my promise to her to fight for a better Eadha. If she was losing hope, I'd hold it.

For her.

24

VALENTINA

Gavriel threw down four matching cards of a shadowwolf.

"Ah ha! I win again," he exclaimed.

"You're a cheat," Orion yelled from where he sat sharpening his blade.

"There's no cheating at these cards."

Out of the six ones I held, only two matched. Those of shadowdragons. Talos. I peeked up over them at Gavriel, who smiled wide, baring straight white teeth.

"It's normal to lose. It's only your... thirteenth time playing."

"And my thirteenth time losing," I grumbled. I scowled and tossed the cards to the table.

One flipped over of Lolo, Dormar, and Gal, Kaderyn's hounds. One of which, Gal, lay snoring on my feet.

The cards had six suits based on each Hunter's shadowanimal; Rook, a massive shadowbear with claws as long as my thumb snarled on one; Mythros, the stark black raven who circled the dining hall and fluttered in and out from an open window near the ceiling; Lonan the shadowwolf who had little patience for doorways and preferred to sift through walls; Talos, a shadowdragon curled up in the corner with his Hunter; and Soren, a long slithering viper often attached to the Hunter now picking up my tossed cards with a smile.

Kade stalked through the open doors, greeting his Hunters with nods, but his attention was on me.

Gal stretched across my feet.

"I've been looking for you." He chided her before sitting down, legs draped on either side of the bench, enveloping me as he's done since we've been down here.

"What's wrong?" I asked.

"There's someone here I need to visit. But I'm afraid it's not a pleasant place to go." Kaderyn kissed my face.

The stares of his Hunters made my skin heat.

"She has information about the fall of the Hunt. About the day I was turned fae and my shadows were split. Before I drag my Hunters up to Eadha, I need to make sure it doesn't happen again. That it *can't* happen again."

"Why would someone want to stop the Wild Hunt?" I asked.

"They're afraid of him." Kaderyn softly nodded to Malek in the corner perched at a table by himself, shrouded in darkness.

I felt . . . sad seeing him. Even in my own misery.

"My best guess is to prevent their souls from coming here. Languishing between worlds is painless. Here? It is excruciating. I would not hold it against you if you didn't want to come. This place is not like the rest of Castle Mors. You can stay here; Santi can bring you more food. Gavriel can keep teaching you cards."

I'm not ready to be alone, I told him honestly, mind to mind.

Very well. "Come, let's go see Bivanna. The vampfae that bit me all those years ago."

Upon Kade's declaration, Malek's chair scuffed out from the table, and he stalked out the large double doors and into Castle Mor's main foyer. We followed with my hand tucked in Kade's. And if Malek looked back at us because of it, I couldn't tell with his low-slung hood.

Once outside, the slow and steady rumble of black and purple clouds churned in on themselves, just like in Shadow Court. Malek's heavy black coat skimmed the cobblestone that led us to a sprawling detached wing of the castle.

The words *House of Talos* were etched above onyx doors with gold dragonhead door knockers. We followed through a short, wide, empty hallway and turned left to a nondescript door. Directly behind us, double doors were open to a dim-lit but welcoming lavish library.

I stopped. Involuntarily. Everything in me screamed not to move forward.

"Kade?" I asked. Because through this door was wretched-ness and I wanted to leave immediately. An ache in the back of my throat took hold and I couldn't voice this deepening anguish that seemed to want to smother me. And though, I thought I'd felt the worst of what living had to offer. This door was a passage to something wicked.

I've got you, little lion. We are just passing through, Kade mindspoke. *These hallways are not meant for you.*

"Is this why they fear him?" My voice shook.

Malek's fingers stilled on the doorknob, and I cursed myself for not speaking through to Kade's mind.

"They fear him"—the doors opened and the screaming started—"because he brings the nightmares," Kade answered, stalking behind Malek, tucking me in close to his back.

Painful wailing, screeching, unfaelike or even unlike any

beast I knew of poured around us. I couldn't think straight. I wanted to hide. Growls turned to whimpers, then back again. First raging, then cowering. Like their fears were winning. Kade collected me to him when he thought I would run.

Down the very end of the hallway was a cell that lay empty. *Cell 362* it said, etched in the black marble above it. But we moved the other way, near a small, raised platform. On it were two sparkling onyx orbs arm lengths apart on pedestals. Fingerprints smudged their glass surface.

"In here," Kade said when I hesitated at the end of the hallway in front of a large dark box at what looked like a dead-end.

I turned toward him, but he stood, soldierlike. Malek stood just inside the container holding the gold metal sliding gates open, waiting for me. Malek and Kade moved as one, and they stood the same. Patient but ready.

In that moment, and the ones since entering the Underworld, I realized that they were a part of something so much bigger than Kade and I. So much bigger than Eadha Island even. The Hunter's had jobs to do here. They had responsibilities I couldn't even comprehend. And I was begging them to help me liberate the faeless. It seemed trivial here. Though I didn't think the faeless like Avika and Jassa and Sloane would think so.

"What is it?" I asked, trying not to feel outside of it all.

"It'll take us down," Kade answered.

"To Bivanna?" I asked. Did I want to go? Maybe I didn't need to be here.

"That's right. When souls are destined for the Underworld, they are locked up here. Malek reminds them why every single night by driving their worst fears through them." Kade reached out for my hand and briefly, so momentarily brief that I thought I was imagining it. His eyes flicked wide and vulnerable. My love was uneasy.

I grabbed for his hand. Holding one of his in both of mine. I'd do this for him. "They relive it?"

"For eternity."

I risked a glance back at Malek as the container we were in descended vertically through a tunnel in a shaky dance. He didn't move, didn't speak. The hood over his face didn't so much as twitch. I wondered what that was like being responsible for that. I wondered if he cared what he had to do at all.

"Sometimes Zedekiel will release one or two to help around Castle Mors. But only after a millennium or so. Like Santi in the kitchens or Clementine in the library." Kade leaned his head back against the container wall and focussed on the ceiling.

We seemed to go on forever. But the wailing grew loud again, and I knew we were close.

The container came to an abrupt stop, and I watched the shadows around it swirl back into Malek. Oh, he was controlling it! He shucked open the gates, an effort born from practice, in one swift motion.

Cells lined the walls of this hallway marked floor sixty-four. Some were larger than the main dining area. Some were small, no taller than my knee. There seemed to be more creatures down here than fae. And I knew I was in the Underworld where all depraved souls go when they die, but seeing the hallways full of hurting, screaming, shrieking souls was doing something to my resolve.

Something slithered out of cell 3201 across the ground and headed for Malek's heels before us, but shadows snapped at it like a whip, and the slithering thing retreated into the darkness where its master yowled in a deep guttural language I'd never heard before. Something moved in the cell to my right and without thinking, I looked. Inside was a creature bent in on itself, wrinkled and naked, lying curled on the floor. Its striking blue eyes were wider than anything I'd ever seen. The thing was petrified, scared and . . . *hurting*. A long time ago, it might have been fae even. A deep resounding need coursed through me.

A desire to help. I stopped and watched. My chest tightened and my throat clogged with saliva.

Kade's hand on my back was gentle, but firm. *You can't help them, Valentina*.

I didn't dare look into cells after that. Instead, my attention locked onto the dragging, swishing coat of the Hunter responsible for it all before me.

Until he stopped altogether, halfway through the winding hallways I'd never remember my way out from. There before us was an empty cell.

No, not empty.

Something swirled out from the darkness, achingly slow. A pale creature in a long white completely see-through gown. My face heated, and I didn't know where to look. Summerfae were anything but modest, but this was different.

"*Kaaddee*," she hissed his name intimately. "Torturous voices have screamed of the return of the Hunter. You are not well-liked down here."

"I'd imagine not."

"I thought you'd visit me sooner."

"Valentina, this is Bivanna." Kade's voice was reluctant, but he'd dropped my hand to move closer to the bars separating us. "The vampfae that bit me and turned me fae."

My breath caught in my throat. She was the reason he became stuck on Eadha Island all those centuries ago.

Bivanna sauntered, hips swaying, to the front of the cell. Her lips were blood red and her eyes that of amber. "*Valentina*," she whispered my name. "A young thing."

"Malek has already asked, many times"—her eyes moved to the ceiling, and she winced—"and in many ways, *why* I bit you."

"He tells me you've told him nothing." Kade's voice was

also a whisper I could hardly hear over the growling of a creature three cells down.

"I've been waiting for *you*." And the most peaceful sound echoed around the cell, bouncing off the walls and into my soul. A melody, unlike anything I'd heard. Soft and needy. It trailed down my spine, pulling me closer to the vampfae before me. To Bivanna.

My toes hit the metal bars and just when I was about to put my arm through to reach for the beautiful, tempting creature, shadows slunk out, pointed like knives, and jutted toward her throat.

The music paused, and I blinked, stumbling back.

"I won't fall for that again," Kaderyn growled. "Why? Why did you do it?"

She stilled a moment before sighing long and loud. "Have you asked the House of Mythros what it is I fear?"

"Zedekiel's informed me you fear being alone. Unwanted. And the darkness."

She dismissed us with a flick of her wrist, and something about her was ugly again. "I am so very alone here, Kade. More alone than I've ever been. The one who brings the nightmares"—she hissed toward Malek where he stood, still as a statue—"makes sure I feel more unwanted now than ever before."

"Then why, Bivanna? When you knew where your destiny lay, why do something as careless as break apart the Hunt?"

"You don't understand, Kaderyn. You have your brothers banded together. Forever. In castles of onyx marble and luxuries I've never known. I wanted out from the caves we were banished to. I wanted a place where I could be with others and not the dark recesses of old ogre dens where my company stretched from drooling bloodthirsty vampfaes to the same spiders that now line these cell walls. I wanted more. I wanted to be *wanted,* and . . ." She paused. "And she was going to give me that."

"Who?" I gasped, wrapping my hands around the bars.

Her eyes flicked quickly to my fingers, like a hunter spotting the weakest prey in a herd, and I released my hold on the bars.

"My sister." Her voice shook. "She promised me rooms in Scarlotta's castle. She promised me company and—"

Her eyes danced down Kade's body.

My Kade.

"Males. She promised me balls worthy of Springfae royalty, with silks from the Summer and blood from the Autumn. Secretly, of course."

Kade swore under his breath and brushed a hand down his face.

My heartbeat faster. Sister . . . Scarlotta . . . *oh gods.*

Bivanna tilted her head to the side and her amber eyes, those now so familiar to me. "Fede promised me everything. And I don't know how she did it. But she lied," she seethed, charging at the same bars that now held her hostage for eternity.

"No." I shook my head. Lady Fede couldn't be Bivanna's sister.

"Lady Fede is not vampfae," Kade reasoned.

Bivanna slumped her head against the bars. "Well, Lady Fede wasn't always a *lady,* either. As younglings, she was my sister. Our mother had a habit of . . . making good use of a male before she sank her teeth in. And that particularly strong Springfae left her with a surprise growing in her belly. And when Fede was old enough, when it was clear she was more fae and not"—she ran a tongue over her pointed teeth—"like the rest of us, she started getting restless.

"While I thirsted for blood, Fede craved power. Even as younglings, even with hardly any vampblood running through her veins. Mother thought she'd lead our clan. Turns out she had her sights on . . . windier pastures." She paused. "And I wanted to see what she saw. I wanted *more*, Kaderyn. I wanted what she had. And she promised she'd bring me to her castle if I lured and bit the leader of the Wild Hunt. She promised me riches. And instead, I am here. More alone now than I've ever been. Or ever will be. For eternity. I was quite done with the darkness but as it turns out, Fede was quite done with her family."

I looked back to Bivanna, whose red eyes now reminded me so much of my capture and trials in Spring Court. That familiar feeling of loneliness sank in my gut, and I felt *bad* for the half-naked creature locked in these cells.

But Kade didn't. "No. Bivanna, there was another. The day you turned me fae, there was another who split my shadows." His open palm smashed the bars, scaring her back. "Who was it?"

I brushed my fingers against his wrist, feeling my love's desperation.

"You're right," she sang. "It was not I. A vampfae bite can only turn a Hunter fae." She delicately traced a finger down the bar and licked her fangs. "Make you a part of the earth."

Malek didn't appreciate that, but when he stepped forward, she hissed through her fangs and slinked back into the shadows. Hiding.

Her voice came from the darkness. "I was not privy to the plans, but a mere accomplice. And I'm afraid you ripped out my throat before I noticed much else.

"Ask my dear sister. No doubt she will have a cell in the darkest depths of this place when her time is over."

And a hollow scream started in the far hallway and carried as if it was right beside me.

"Let's go," Kade said, and I didn't hesitate to quick step it to the black container that would bring us back up and out of here. The weight of the earth above us was heavy.

"Tell me, Kaderyn." Bivanna's voice carried down the corridor, through screeching, screaming things. "Did you leave any vampfae's still alive?"

Kade grew silent and closed his eyes as he laced his fingers through the metal gate of the container. His voice, no louder than the surrounding moans. "No."

He pulled it shut with us inside.

"Maybe you're on the wrong side of these bars," Bivanna sang.

And I wanted for Kaderyn to scoff; I wanted for him to counter her implications. I wanted Malek to get us the fuck out of here.

But I gasped as Kade uttered, "Maybe."

"Malek!" I urged.

He slunk out shadows, powering the contraption and the carrier moved up once more. But familiarity curled around my heart like a snake. My attempt to warn Cillian doomed Otti Theater. Bivanna's desire to belong doomed her entire kind.

Kade was solemn and quiet. And I didn't want to pull his attention back to the present until we were out of this place. How did Malek come here? How did he manage such a place? The howling, the crying, the desperation. I wanted out.

And never to return.

25

DERYN IRONSIDE

I'd returned from a long trek from Teal's port where she was recounting her travels to a group of faeless children entranced in the pixies rhyming stories as I helped them re-patch a section of docks. Teal talked of nuckelavees stuck inland by a river.

I leaned up from my hammering and interrupted. "There's no saltwater river that runs in through Kingswood Forest."

And she took a great deal of pride in telling me I was wrong. She crossed the river herself, she said. Even stood outside the rank-smelling nuckelavee cave as Valentina and Kaderyn entered to get his shadows.

I mumbled a thank you to her and retreated to my tower. Or at least tried to, but zipping back across my tracks, Avika came out to snarl insults at me. And I hid low in my cart as I passed the rest of the valley and Brendan below.

Adrian looped my legs up onto his lap from where we sat on the daybed and began unstrapping the leather bands around the stump just above the knee. I pushed too hard at the docks and the blisters were my evidence. I tugged at the stitching on a frayed blanket. "Do you think I'm a coward, Adrian?"

His hands stilled briefly before he shucked off the iron leg and tossed it to the short table in front of us. Nearly knocking his wine goblet. "I think you worry too much about what others think."

I turned slightly, glaring but guarded. "Not everyone sweats confidence like you."

His fingers pressed along the knots of muscles in my thigh, and I moaned. "It's a gift, really."

"You don't care what anyone thinks of you."

He ran a thumb up the side of a muscle, and I drooled. I couldn't push that hard again.

"I care what you think," he said softly.

A weight sunk on us. Pieces of information I ignored before were clicking, and I didn't want them to. I didn't want my life, my little life hiding from Lady Fede here to change. With occasional nights with Rhett and all my days with Adrian, my best friend. But I had questions to ask him, and I didn't know if I wanted the answer. "Do you remember when I asked you to move the river for me?"

"Ah," he scoffed and continued his pressing and kneading, "a mighty large task. I show up tangled in brambles and blackberry stalks, prickly bastards, to find you squatting on the edge of that bloody river."

"And I asked if you'd move the river closer to the tower, so I didn't have to travel as far to collect water for my smelting."

"Mmmm," was all he said.

"And you moved it, brought it right to my doorstep." The air grew heavy. "Adrian?"

His hands stilled on my leg.

"Was that the only river you've ever moved?"

DERYN

A LONG, LONG TIME AGO

"What in all graces are we doing out here?" Adrian appeared out of fine salty mist beside me. He swiveled around dramatically at the waist with his hands on his hips. He kicked a bramble of blackberry bush as he made his way over to the rock I was sitting at. Iron leg propped up on the shoreline of a river.

"I need your help," I said, tossing a stone into the bubbling waters.

"Clearly. You're way too far from your tower."

"I need this river to divert this way." I gestured toward the very tower he spoke of.

He looked at the river before us—all fifty feet wide across. It snaked on down, past the old ruins, and to the shore on the east side of the Mainland. It was a runoff stream of freshwater from the Twin Peak Mountains. "Oh, just a small favor, then," he said, and I raised an eyebrow at his sarcasm. "What on this forsaken, prickly land for?" he continued, kicking the runners of fat blackberries that clung to his pants.

"It takes me hours every day walking fresh water to the barrels for my forging. If the river was closer, say, beside the tower. I'd build in half the time."

"Rhett's convinced you to fight for this war, hasn't he? What makes you think I can move an entire river, anyway? You think I'm a god or something?" He winked.

"Please."

"I've never been busier since I pulled you out of my seas, dearest Deryn." He absently brushed pollen off his navy tunic.

"I worry about what you do when you're bored." I smiled a wide smile at him and pushed the hair behind my ears before clapping him on the arm, found solid footing, and started my trek back to my iron tower.

He gave a shout from behind me, but I didn't bother turning around. "Hold on, what in bloody hell is wrong with the water from my strait?" He was talking of the Galeairy, the one directly below the tower. The one he found me floating half-dead in.

"The salt corrodes my metals," I shouted back.

And he spent some time after that mumbling to the brambles about me.

26

VALENTINA

Returning to Eadha required only Deathmarch and ten thousand pestering questions to Zedekiel on whether I would arrive in one piece.

"She's a Siphon, as you say," he'd said. "Let her take your shadows the same way as she got down here. If she's enough of them, and enough of earth, then she should move through the veils as easily as you."

But it worked, and I was up walking the streets of Auris hours later. After a solid hour alone with Kade in our castle's rooms, working off the discharge of energy moving between worlds gave.

I was alone, on my way to see Teal while Kade dealt with some pressing matter Oir shoved into his hands. Something had needed Kade's attention, and a pixie somewhere needed mine.

What happened here? I asked him through mindspeak. *The ground looks like an open wound.* The ground down Auris' Main street looked split, like a sword wound healing, puckered and solid, but scarred. It stretched from to edge of the welcome sign to The Malt Seas to three shops down. Shadowfae mostly avoided stepping on it, but I couldn't stop staring.

I broke the world for you, Valentina. Never underestimate your place in my life. I'll destroy it all for you. Are you with Teal yet?

Tears flooded my eyes, but Teal's squealing at the port sobered me quickly. She'd likely ask if I was crying and thwart Kade for making me do so.

"Your eyes are puffy.
They're red-ringed.
Point me to the sorry cod who needs their ass singed."

Cocking her arm toward the sky, she charged the iron limb with blue pixie magic.

"I'm happy to see you, Teal," I said, bopping my forehead into hers. "It's quite the outfit you've established here. I'm sorry it's taken me so long to come visit."

"Oh, this is nothing.
A second-tier liner." She jutted out her foot and kicked the side of the ship.
"Come see Fillagree Fen
A ship docks in port that's much finer."

"Teal! Teal! Don't ya dare fly away on me again. I'll send the shadowgulls after ya. Don't think I won't." Trudging down the steep hill was a female clad in baggy pants in a size meant for males twice hers and thick black suspenders holding them up. It dawned on me I might have seen her before when Jair first brought me to Auris. A small orb floated around her before it popped into her front pocket. She held a scowl, and something scrunched in her fist.

Teal cursed mightily harshly and tried to hide. When it was clear, she had nowhere to go. She buzzed to my shoulder and landed like I would protect her.

"Who'd you piss off now?" I muttered. My fingers itched for the gods' daggers on my back.

"Greetings, Juniper Hatch
How lovely to see you at port.
Are you interested in an escort—"

"Stop stealing my order pads for drawing up your recruitment posters. It takes a fair bit of dimas to have these made up for The Malt Seas." She tossed the flyer between us and it fluttered to the ground.

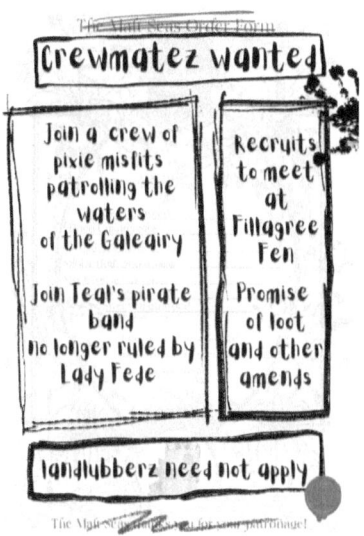

Teal gave up her innocent act.

"I was in need of recruits

Besides, it was only one or two.
I haven't yet reached Kinswood.
There are pixies that might like
To not wash dishes at night
For Spring's rulers
Those awful tyrants.
Here they can rebuild with me at the helm
To join a dynasty of pixie pirates."

"That's all well and good. I wish you the very best of successes in this particular endeavor, but stop. Using. My Order Forms."

"And what do you suggest I use instead?" Her fuming body did a backflip to expel extra energy.

It grew silent as the Shadowfae contemplated this. The orb, no bigger than a cherry tomato, sprung out of her pocket, whispered something in her ear, and zoomed back into her shirt with force. "Three dimas says you use The Lucky Owl Tearoom's napkins instead," Juniper Hatch said as her eyes flicked to me, a little in worry, but she jutted out her chin and continued, "they're embossed with gold bordering—a fine substitution."

Teal scrunched up her nose. And without the knife in her hand and the black-folded hat on her head, she might have looked cute. Her eyes flicked up toward Auris' Main street.

"Deal."

Juniper Hatch tossed coins up into the air that Teal flew to catch. And Teal said something about treasure or bounty.

Valentina, Kade's voice boomed inside my head, overtop

the daily noise of Auris' midday market. *There is someone at Shadow Court's gates.*

"Teal?" I shouted to her quickly. "I'll have to catch a ride to the Mainland another time." I wanted to meet Deryn officially, but this was a threat to Kade's court.

Teal grumbled a bit but buzzed up the street and disappeared into the crack of an open window of a shop that smelt like tea leaves and chocolate.

I met Kade's gaze above the crowd as I worked my way back to him, but his face was unreadable. *Who is it?*

General Helle of Winter Court.

I stopped briefly and someone's bag bumped into me as I stalled the flow of foot traffic.

And she's asking for you, he continued.

I'm coming. I answered him by mindspeak quickly, stomping all over that fissured crack in the middle of the street.

Should I shred her to pieces? he asked, eyes dark as night, and a vein pulsed near his jaw.

No, I practically yelped. *At least not yet. She helped me in Winter.*

We met Rhett and Jairek at Auris' city gates and walked out together to the edge of Gillies Forest from there, heading toward the singular female easy to spot against the backdrop of a black forest by her stark white hair. She was further in Kade's court than I expected his shadows to let her go.

"Knock, knock," she said, teasing with a voice filled with so much humor and malice that if I didn't know better, I'd think a female version of Adrian was beckoning us.

And when we were far enough away from any surprises but close enough that I could feel her stare on Jairek, Helle flicked down a 15-inch black dagger into the ground between us. Rhett braced to take to the air and shift, but Jair motioned to stand down.

"Found this knife in an Aileen den," she said with a sniff of her nose.

I balked. If I thought the bravest fae on Eadha was the lion-shifter beside me, I was wrong. It was this tiny black scale-clad white-haired fae before me now. She stayed unglamoured, with scars visible along her cheekbone and hairline.

Helle's eyes danced across my party. Watching. And I understood that ice magic she carried. The strong, calculating ice magic that made even the weak feel brave. It tried to pull to me now though, and I pushed it away, focussing on Kaderyn's shadows.

Kade crossed his arms and laced shadows between her feet and around her neck like a noose. "Could be anyone's." He shrugged. "Use your magic here and I'll rip your head from your body. First and last warning, Helle."

But I recognized that dagger. Last I saw it, it was lodged in an Aileen, a massive three-headed bird, in the Winter Islands when we released his shadows from the second and final chest.

Helle didn't register his threat or care if shadows were ready to coil around her like a python and squeeze. "I've come to offer a truce."

"You lie," Rhett fumed.

"I'm fae," she said, more annoyed than anything.

"Prove it."

"And break your first order that using my magic means a swift death? I'm too old for your tricks, hawkshifter. Besides, I don't take commands from seconds." She stared down Jair.

"You're in Shadow Court. Lord Kaderyn could kill you now," Jairek said more inquisitively.

"I know."

Helle and Kade stood at a standoff. The air grew stifling. She was asking for mercy, but I could feel through our bond that he wanted revenge.

"Your father held my world captive," Kade accused.

"I'm not asking for you to hold off your retaliation forever. I'm just asking you to wait."

"For what?"

"To see if I can stop The War of Many. Let me try to save the faeless. That's what you want, isn't it?"

I gasped.

"And why would a ruthless general want to stop a war she had such a hand in causing?" Rhett asked. "You've been hunting down the faeless for centuries. Even just now, a town thick with faeless near Kinswood Forest was found frozen. Their bodies no different from statues. You're saying you had no part in it?"

"My second leads them. I've long since ceased those raids."

Jair frowned. "Didn't fucking feel like it in Blackwater."

"The Lord of Shadows and King of the Courtless near my court lines and it piques my interest enough to draw my swords."

"What do you want?" Kade growled.

Sky-blue eyes stared him down. "Atonement."

What does this mean, Kade? I asked, not risking voicing it aloud.

She knows where her soul is headed when she dies, he mind-spoke. *She wishes to change her fate.*

"And maybe because there's an eighty-foot canyon stretching across the island now. I'm realizing I might be on the wrong side."

"I'll never trust you," Rhett snapped. "Kade, I say we toss her back to Winter in pieces."

Sour memories churned. But Rhett was growing increasingly agitated. "She helped me in Winter," I defended.

"What's changed? Why do you want a truce now?" Jairek

asked and, my god, the tone he spoke sounded different. Smoother. I looked between the two of them.

"Because I am Helle, General of Winter Court's vast and ruthless army, daughter to Lord Aborys." She winced, then she held Jair's stare. "And I do not want to have to harm you."

"Kill your father," Rhett said.

She sneered. "Where do you think I learned my ruthlessness? Who do you think taught me how to fight?"

"Then, the Frost Witches," Kade said bluntly.

Her attention shifted. Waiting.

"I want them gone," he finished. "I never want your father to wish her gone from me again."

And something about this felt too far. They were living creatures. It wasn't their fault, either.

"Kade, no—" I started.

"Done," Helle promised.

Kade released her from shadows. "Fight with us against your father. When the hammer falls and the war starts, give us ice magic on our side."

"I'll be in touch." She turned slowly and started limping parallel to Gillies Forest toward the Courtless instead of back up through Summer.

"You're headed the wrong way," Rhett called. He watched the way she favored the foot.

Like wounded prey before its predator, Helle'd hid the pain tormenting her. "Summer has a new lord," she shouted over her shoulder as she focussed on keeping a steady footing. She winced as her hurt ankle rolled in the grasses. "Ouch, fuck! They call this one *The Star*. No fucking clue what that means, but he's promised me that the next time Father sees me it will be in a tomb, and I believe him." She tsked and shook her head. "Not like Summer's last lord."

Jairek turned to us, rubbing his jaw. "Did Lord Grigory

have any second in commands that would overthrow him like this?"

I started shaking my head before the words came out. "I don't know. Oir mentioned a new lord bleeding us dry on market trades."

We'll pay him a visit when this is all over, Kade promised, brushing his hands down my shoulders, watching to make sure the white-haired female left his court for good.

"I'll trail her. Make sure she clears the courts." Jair shifted in seconds into a golden lion, gave a loud growl that quaked the ground across the meadow, and stalked behind General Helle along Gillies Forest's edge.

She didn't so much as flinch.

"What does this mean? If even Winter's general is wary of this *Star* in Summer?" Rhett asked.

"How mad do you think he is that we dropped half his court in on itself?" I turned on Kade, too.

"It's a crock of pixie shit. A shoe would have been a better leader than Lord Grigory. Let this *Star* lead Summer how it wants for now. Charge us more for trades, so long as he or she stays on their court lines until we negotiate alliances for the war. If he hasn't come to our doors, then we don't go to his until we need to. At least with Lord Grigory we knew where he stood."

"With his head in the sand," Rhett finished.

Kade nodded. "Spring needs my attention more. I need to know who else was involved. I need to know who else to keep an eye on."

"Will you kill them?" I asked. "For what they did to you?"

He looked at me dead on. Black eyes swallowing me whole. Rhett might as well have left because all I saw was my Kade and his impossible resolve as he said, "I might."

"I'm coming with you." I swallowed.

He clapped the hawkshifter on the shoulder. "Rhett, go.

Thank you for all you've done for the Courtless and Shadows, but go rest with Deryn. Take some time to recover. I'll go to Spring and have a talk with Lady Fede. Oir sent her notice last week to expect our visit. I'll shadowfade us back if she tries to start a war."

"Why announce it? Why not just go in swords slashing?"

"Because this is what lords do. Shadowfae's army is not near big enough, and Jair needs more time before he's ready to lead the Courtless in battle."

"But I can," Rhett fumed.

"Soon," Kade promised, and Rhett took to the skies when he knew he would not get further with Kaderyn. When Rhett's brown wings were far enough away, Kade turned to me. "It's too dangerous for you to come with me. I feel like we've just made progress with you."

"I don't want to leave you again. We really aren't bringing weapons?"

"No," he conceded. "We'll look like a threat."

"Fine, but I'm not wearing a dress."

27

VALENTINA

"Leave the daggers," Kade said as I sheathed the red one on my back.

I hesitated. "I don't think that's a good idea."

"She's asked for us unarmed."

I ran my hands down my sides, pulled out three small knives, and tossed them to the table in the foyer of Auris' castle. "Of course she did."

It was days after seeing Helle at our gates, and we were more desperate than ever to find out who was capable of organizing Kade's demise.

"We'll see what she has to say, then leave. If Spring is really with Winter, then her court is under his command. I'm not ready to put the Shadowfae through war until Deryn figures out this new metal coming from the mines. And until I know my Hunters can't be destroyed up here."

I tucked my arms under Kade's as shadows increased into a ferocious inky mass swirling around us. "And if she attacks?"

"I'll shadowfade you home," he answered into my hair.

"Us. You shadowfade *us* home." I grew severe, but we were off, fading across shadow fields, over Gillies Forests, across a deep channel created by Faemech that the sea was trying to claim, over Robinswallow River, and—

"What's that?" I asked seconds too late.

Because suddenly, we were falling . . . and drowning. *Kade!* I screamed as shadows caught me, dropped me, and then caught me again. Hard castle walls came into view below us as another tidal wave soaked our slow progress down and crashed us onto a sparkling castle courtyard.

I spit out water and Kade immediately sent shadows to block off the dozens of purple-and-gold-clothed soldiers marching out around us, screaming commands at us to stand down.

My hair draped in front of my face as I scrambled to see Summer's army.

"You've been summoned, Lord Kaderyn of The Court of Shadows"—the soldier speaking looked down to his order—"four times as per the Star's request."

"Yeah, I've been a little busy," Kade answered, giving the speaker his back.

"It's discourteous to—"

"So is washing me from his skies." Kade flicked out an arm, shaking off the water. "If he feels it so rude, he can come tell me his fucking self."

The soldier slammed the letter closed. "You'll go to him."

I could feel Kade's irritation, but Hawrenthia was not as I'd imagined. The eternal sun now burned my eyes and the flow of water magic in my veins brought up sharp memories. Memories of wisteria vines, sandy toes, and the incense burning at Otti theater.

Nerves stiffened my walk and Kade stayed silent as he stuck

close to my side. Would this new lord know about Elaria? That I was the reason Mohr targeted it?

A massive white staircase stood before us in both height and width. Butterflies swooped in and out, kissing our cheeks, then returning to the potted plants along the edges of the stairway. I didn't know what I'd find up at the top of the throne. Who had the power to rally a war cry and throw out Lord Grigory? A lump choked my throat and sweat dripped to my brow as the stairs petered out and we came to a large open-air throne room.

This was it.

"Valentina," Kade said low. "Whoever this new lord is, you don't have to say anything. You don't have to—"

"Roshan!" I yelled as my old friend from Elaria stood next to a throne adorned with sparkling seashells, white silks, and crystal blades spearing the air above. Relief rushed through me, and I wanted to run to the curly-haired Summerfae I used to save from a magog's fist ages ago. But Kade held on tight to my wrist and drops of water splashed to the ground from my fingertips.

"Valentina?" Roshan's eyebrows drew down as he rushed to me, caught in the same nostalgia that had my chest sinking in. "You're alive? Thank, Angus."

His arms crashed around my shoulders, and the smell of the sea enveloped me.

"Oh, thank the gods you're here!" My voice was muffled by his bicep. "You have no idea how good it is to see your face. In the throne room, no less." I wasn't going to be the first to let go. "Are you this *Star* we heard about?"

Shadows clung to my legs and wrapped around my waist. They were lazy, but I knew better. Kade was on edge. Watchful.

"Are you this fae that can control the island's magic?" Roshan's tone was sharp and his eyes distrustful.

Like I'd hurt him. Like I'd kept it from him.

"My soldiers said they saw shadows moving through our skies. I'm surprised to see you with him even though your wrist is free." He turned to Kade. "I've been asking for an audience with yourself for weeks now. In particular, to a new development that has my court marked by a deep canyon running through its lower court line that Rhion is filling with seawater."

Rhion, God of the Sea? I swallowed.

To me, he mindspoke back, *He never comes down here don't worry what this 'Star' says.* To Roshan, he said, "We both know no one lived near the edge of Gillies Forest. Besides, I needed a bit of a breathing room from your incessant requests for court."

Roshan scoffed. His smile washed away, and he dropped his arms from around me when shadows swirled up into our faces. "You could have put the chasm on *your* court lines. We thought the gods were dropping the island into the sea."

Nope, just a one-legged metal forger, I thought.

Kade had less tact. "To be honest, I didn't think Lord Grigory would untuck himself from his cowering corner to care."

"It's not Lord Grigory anymore," Roshan snapped.

"Clearly."

Kade's irritation made the back of my neck sweat.

Thank gods, Roshan had more decorum. "I never thought this Siphon would be the little fae who used to save my neck in . . ." he stopped and flinched. "Did you hear of Elaria? Did you hear what Autumn did?"

I placed a hand on my stomach, trying to hold down the nausea. "I tried to go back. I tried to save everyone."

"Me too," he said. "Once Autumn came to Elaria, once we knew we couldn't beat them, maybe against their magic but not against their weapons. Have you seen these new swords they have? A few of us grabbed what we could and took off toward Hawrenthia." I saw it now. Dark rings circled both his eyes.

"And Lord Grigory?" I looked around.

"And when that fool said nothing, when he *did* nothing, we led a revolt. I rallied the fae and faeless of Hawrenthia against him. Took his throne."

He was taller suddenly. Larger.

"It didn't even have to be me, Val. Anyone could have taken his place. But now that I'm leading? They'll have to pry the throne from my fingers."

"Who came with you?" But I swallowed down the lump in my throat because I knew he wasn't talking about Daria, Petri, and Sisaria.

"Myself and Braeth."

Shock had me blinking, thinking I was seeing things because out of the shadows near a circular, flowing fountain stepped the giant magog from Otti Theater. The one I spent a good chunk of my nights keeping away from walloping the now ruler of Summer Court. Their *Star*. Braeth's lumbering presence was welcoming.

"You put aside your differences, I see," I said, giving a pained smile.

He brushed a finger down his cheek. "War will do that to you."

"And your brothers and sisters?"

"All safe. We tried to clear out Otti but—" he choked. "It burned there the hottest, Val."

"Miss Valentina, 'ey burned down the theater. All of it. 'ere was too many." Scars littered one side of Braeth's face. Magog's were immune to fae magic, but fire melted their skin all the same.

"I pulled out as many dancers as I could, but I couldn't find

Miss Daria." Distraught racked his eyes. He was always so careful with Daria. Always so protective. And he'd failed.

"You're a hero, Braeth," I said with tears in my eyes.

Kade shifted his feet once on the marble. Like he was cleaning horse poop from his shoe, and I didn't know if he was uncomfortable with these creatures from my previous life. The only ones still left alive.

"I've sent soldiers out every night since I took the throne, searching for Sisaria. She wasn't at the theater. I know she wasn't. I ran through its hallways, checking as it burned to the ground. I've sent soldiers across to Autumn, even. Those brave enough to go, at least. But Summer's army had been stagnant too long and more than I needed were champing at the bit to do *something*. Anything."

Tears blurred my eyes.

You don't have to say anything, Valentina. You were a victim as much as they were, Kaderyn said through our mindspeak.

The tears overflowed. "Roshan." I sniffled. "Sisaria . . . " I shook my head when the words wouldn't come.

He advanced, grabbing hold of my forearm. "Do you know where she is? Who took her? By all of Summer's army, I will drown the island to get her back."

My body trembled harder and I scrunched my eyes closed. When I opened them again, water mixed with black shadows, and they dripped off my skin like liquid to the ground. "She was taken by Winter. Just before I was. And he made me . . . I killed them. All of them." I was heaving with my heart in my throat, confessing my crimes. "Roshan, I killed Sisaria."

"What?" He blinked at me. Before his head shook slowly and his grip on my arm bore down. "That makes no sense. Why would you . . . "

But anger and sadness had a way of blending and mixing, and when that happened, anger *always* won.

So he raged as he said, "How could you? She was your friend! They all were!"

I shook my head. He didn't understand the power of the north. My foot slid in inky black water on the ground as I tried to pull out of my best friend's grasp.

"Lord Aborys used a Frost Witch on her. Wiped her memory. Tried to make her his. He made her do it, Roshan." Kade's shadows enveloped me, pulling me back.

"It's *Lord* Roshan, Hunter," Roshan spit. "Fuck's sake, Valentina, look at you. You're falling apart."

I couldn't control it. The shadows I always pulled from Kade mixed with water, the familiar water I'd grown up with, and were dripping like ink off a pen tip. Onto everything. Me, the floor, our feet. Pools of black water spread across the white flooring coating everything it touched. Like a disease.

Kaderyn stepped between us. "We all have scars from the tyrants of Autumn and Winter. Don't forget who your enemy is."

"Oh, you do not know my scars."

Suddenly Roshan dropped his glamour and instead of his face, the beautiful smiling, laughing face I always remembered as Roshan, there was a puckered and scarred *form*, a mass of tissue and flesh where young vulnerable wide eyes once were. I could hardly see where his nose was over the scar tissue and only the left half of his mouth moved when he spoke.

"I fought against the firefae." He took a step forward, muscles bulging through fine silk shirts. The water from the fountain rose at once and created an arch above us, spinning, churning. Threatening. "I dragged as many as I could out of that blazing firestorm. Kaderyn! I *rummaged* through infernos for *her*!"

I couldn't move. I couldn't breathe. I deserved his wrath.

But Kaderyn didn't think so. "Then do something about it,

side with Shadows and the Courtless when the War of Many draws to a peak. Whose side will you stand on when it all comes crashing down?"

He nudged me back out from under Roshan's threat.

"Not a fucking traitor! That's whose," Roshan roared like I'd never seen him before. "You dared come here looking for Summer's alliance," he sneered. "You killed the one I love, Valentina. How can you stand there and face me now?"

"Wait, Roshan. Wait—" I tried.

"Winter killed her, Roshan. Don't be blinded by your pain. But I will warn you, if your mangled mouth continues, no magog will stop me from the pain I'll put you in."

Braeth stepped forward with a growl.

And I cursed the seas, the winds, the earth as my heart shattered in my chest. I called him friend. Once. But moonlit nights of escaping out back theater doors were over. Evenings of convincing Braeth to drop Roshan's neck so I could hide him in wisteria vines were long gone. We'd been forced to trade a theater's auditorium for war's doorstep and it wasn't fair. The island and her troubles drove us apart to become no better than strangers. Dare I say enemies.

"Roshan," I pleaded, wiping my nose with the back of my hand.

"Get out of my court."

"Rosh—"

"Shadowfading across my skies will be classified as spying, and I will treat it as an act of war," he continued. "You plummeted the southern edge of my court into oblivion with magic I have not seen, and that fact is the only thing stopping me from throwing you both into my prisons right now. Until I know how you did it, at least."

"You threaten our freedom with conch shell walls and starfish locks. I thought you'd be smarter. Fucking insulting, really. You forget who I am. You remember our plea for Summer when your soul is in my halls." Kaderyn's fist balled at his sides.

The corner of Roshan's lip twitched. "Don't try to deceive me, Hunter. I am not among the monsters"—his eyes, swollen and half closed, flicked to me—"headed to your halls. You will not rule over my soul when I die."

"Maybe not now," Kade growled, ushering me out of the chamber and back to the stairs. "But by the time this is over, we'll see where it is you're headed."

"Is this the eloquence of Shadow Court?" Roshan called and his glamour once again blanketed his face, back to the face I knew, and his stare was so much worse. He scoffed as if he couldn't bear to look at me.

"No, it's the fucking promise of the leader of the Wild Hunt. If you choose to side against Shadows and the Courtless, I'll run my Hunters twice through your halls and I'll have no mercy for who I pull into my shadows."

"That's not how growing alliances work, *Lord* Kaderyn." He spit the title.

"I'm first a Hunter before a lord, and I'll rain shadows on your palace for no other reason than your treatment of Valentina now."

Horrified at my admission to Roshan and the horror he'd faced, I skidded down the stairs blurry-eyed on the balls of my feet before I gasped once and gripped the railing tight, whipping around.

Because I remembered something.

I craned my neck up at the awning where a magog, my old protector, stood watching us leave. At one time it was to watch my back, and now it was to make sure I didn't return.

I swallowed thickly, but I couldn't meet his gaze. "Braeth, did Avril ever make it back?"

His eyebrows crinkled, and I almost worried he'd ignore me, but after a long silence he grunted, "Avril?"

"Redhead. Danced after Sis—" I couldn't finish. "She was taken with me. Autumn's soldiers cast her out into the middle of a sandstorm in the Glenora Desert days after we were taken."

Braeth's colossal head lumbered from side to side. "No one survives the Glenora alone. Lord Roshan increased it even 'ore so. If firefae step even one foot in it, our army will know. The Star is doing everythin' Grigory should 'ave."

A black trail oozed down the stairs in my wake like slug secretions. Water and Shadows flowed off my hands. Uncontrollable.

Avril's dead. Another life on my hands.

"Come on, Valentina. We'll return to Auris. Regroup before going to Spring. Maybe grab Jairek." *I'll run this blistering Court into the ground*, he growled into my mind.

And I didn't think I was supposed to hear that through his mindspeak.

No part of me wanted to see Lady Fede now. I saw in a passing polished vase my face, swollen and snot-soaked. How could I present myself? My limbs felt heavy and tired. But as I nodded, a piercing whistle clawed at the air and vibrated through my eardrums. I clapped my hands over my ears, but it didn't help.

"Kade!" I shrieked, but he was already moving his shadows to protect us.

Through wisping shadows, up on the cliffside that divided Spring and Summer, I saw two massive wooden reeds protruding out of the ground. The Aeolian Flutes. Beside them stood Lady Fede in an elegant white dress, one arm outstretched, sending howling wind magic through the holes, making the air scream.

I collapsed to my knees, trying to buffer myself against the onslaught of wailing, like nuckelavee claws were scratching my brain. Kade looked panicked briefly as he grimaced against the noise, no doubt worse for the two of us.

"I think that's for you!" Roshan bellowed above the noise, hands covering his own ears. Below us, Summerfae ran for cover, smothering their ears with their hands, scooping up faelings, and bolting doors behind them.

These flutes, which were once so peaceful, were weapons and I'd forgotten. I'd felt safe from them in Summer, and now I was standing in front of a lord who was ushering me toward them.

"Start climbing," Roshan yelled again, then retreated behind the slam of a door.

Could we just leave her well enough alone? Surely shadow-fading would cripple any alliance Shadows had of Summer joining our side. Roshan had laid out his threat, and it seemed Lady Fede had one of her own to make.

I turned to Kade for answers. His face twisted in pain like my own. Would retreating from Lady Fede just postpone the inevitable? I nodded once to Kade, whose face turned stony and determined. He pushed to his feet and held out a hand for me. I released an ear in favor of my love's hand.

We'd do this together.

28

VALENTINA

As soon as Lady Fede noticed our approach to the base of the cliffside, the Aeolian Flutes dulled to a manageable decibel. A ringing stayed, and I feared it would for a while yet. But climbing the cliff was another thing entirely, and I worried how much Spring and Summer were in cahoots. Occasional grasses poked out of a straight vertical dirt wall. The only saving grace was that it wasn't as tall as it looked from afar.

"Stay behind me. All we're doing is talking to Fede. Find out who her accomplices were in splitting the Hunt and get the fuck out. We can't let the Hunt fall again," Kade growled.

"And if Cillian comes?"

"Leave him to me."

Kade waited for me to catch up and we breached the cliff edge at the same time. I couldn't find a place to look that had my heartbeat steady. Sweat soaked my hairline and dirt pierced my nail beds, and seeing the smile on her face, I knew she did this on purpose. Dirty and degraded, we crawled into her court. Exactly how she wanted.

"Oh, Lady Fede." Kade sighed. "I much prefer the ringing of a dinner bell than that wailing from your *things* there."

"They're Flutes, Kaderyn. It's merely music. Besides, you looked locked in a standoff with Summer's new ruler. I would have hated for you to run away without saying hello first. Since you so kindly and forcibly beckoned a meeting."

Run away. I thought over what she said and gasped. *Kade, I think she knows the repercussions if we shadowfade over Summer.*

I heard it, too. Now might not be the best time to rid Spring of its lady. No matter how much I want to see her cell in the Underworld occupied, Kade answered.

"Fine enough time to ask where all my pixies have gone," Lady Fede said, ceasing the Flute's hum altogether. Like she was mad they competed with her voice. "I rang for more tea this morning and only one little pipsqueak of a pixie came. Useless thing spilled it all over me. I almost ripped off its arms, but settled on its wings instead. Can't very well carry tea without arms."

"Things are changing across the island, Fede." Kade's shadows licked the air. "Nothing is going to be the same as it was."

"We'll see about that." She crossed her arms across her chest.

"You know, when I first saw you in your halls, I knew you looked familiar to me. Though, I admit, I never thought your bloodline would trace back to the vampfaes. I suppose that might make you the last of your kind."

"Oh," she said as her eyebrows raised and her eyes flashed once. "And how is my sister doing? I assume you've chatted with her in that Underworld of yours."

"She's keeping your cell warm."

"You have no self-preservation at all, do you? Don't

threaten me in my court." A ringing came from the Flutes again.

"You made your sister bite me. Consider us even. I want to know why."

"Is that all you know? Interesting. You're showing your hand, Kaderyn. I'd be careful."

"It was never a secret. Whoever broke my Hunt had to know I'd come for them."

Lady Fede sighed. "I told my sister that if she lured and bit the Leader of the Underworld, I would place her high in my league of advisors. I promised her riches."

"You lied to her," I said.

"I cannot lie," she spit. Insulted. "I have no need to. She didn't survive your lover's anger."

"Did you think she would?" Kade asked.

"Of course not, but Bivanna didn't ask *my* opinion on it, did she? She was blinded by what I could give her. But I worked hard for what I have, and she was going to have to, too. You have no clue what I've done to get here, Kaderyn. What I've sacrificed."

"I'm getting an idea," Kade drawled. "Lord Brexton?"

"Was in my way," she seethed slowly as the surrounding air became thin. "We thought you'd be dead, and instead you became a *lord* and a fly in my chardonnay."

Suddenly a snarl shook the ground so loud it dulled the Flutes entirely.

"What is this, Fede?" Kade growled as a massive black beast, a cross between a wolf and a bear came charging across the fields.

The Berserker.

Cillian.

Kade? I cried through mindspeak.

"We're invited guests. Tell him to stand down!" Kade swirled shadows around us.

"Why would I do that?" Fede sang with a hand on her hip. "You invited yourselves. Besides, you know my dirty little secrets and I don't want to sleep with one eye open for the rest of my days."

Suddenly, the piercing scream of the Aeolian Flutes picked up again, and I dropped to my knees with the beast pounding the ground toward me.

I sent shadows out as best I could for the wooden reed, snaked them around it, and pulled tight.

"Kade!" I yelled, unsure if my voice carried.

I felt him pull his shadows back and a crack echoed over the canyon as the massive Flute snapped into two pieces down the middle with Kade's force. Kade's shadows picked them up and tossed them into the sea like they were toothpicks.

"How dare you!" Lady Fede screeched.

One down, one to go.

But before his shadows reached out again, Lady Fede had him on his back, arms thrust down, sucking the air from my love's lungs. I ran forward, hand outstretched, pulling what I could of the air from hers and sending shadows down to replace it. Cillian barreled closer.

But fae like Fede did this for fun and she pulled a sword from her side hidden under layers of dresses and slashed it out, cutting my arm before I reached her.

Kade twisted shadows around her neck as a gurgled gasp came from her mouth. "Goodbye, Fede," Kade growled.

But thundering stomps had us looking up just in time.

"Fuck, Valentina. Get out of here," Kade roared.

"No." I stood my ground. I wasn't leaving him.

And before Kade could rid the island of Lady Fede for good, the Berserker was upon us. Snarling.

Kade's panic filtered through our bond, and I realized it was for me. Not himself. "Go back to Summer. Let them take you. I'll get you back," Kade promised as the beast gnashed at the wall of shadows Kade made.

Lady Fede spun the earth into a swirling tornado, kicking dirt and debris into our eyes and mouths so much we choked against the onslaught. The shadows slackened from her throat. The tornado grew, spinning us up with it and tossed us across the crabgrass.

I reached for Kade, my ribs ached and only one lung worked.

"You forget I have a god's weapon and you seemed to have left yours at home." Fede's voice was ragged, like her windpipe was crushed.

Valentina, please go, Kade mindspoke.

I'm not leaving you! I screamed at him the same way.

Valentina, please.

"Kade, look out!" I cried as Cillian whipped into him with a ferocious paw outstretched, snagging the side of his shoulder. I tossed my weight at Lady Fede, bashing her to the dirt of her court below me. Her face was sharp, features pointed. Her fae glamour was spotty, and I saw the true mask behind the villain.

"Who were you working with? Who's poisoning Lord Brexton? Who split Kade's shadows?" I snared her arms to the dirt with shadows and covered her face in a thick layer. If she couldn't see us, maybe she couldn't suffocate us.

"You really don't know." She tried to laugh, but it was broken. "And she's so close to you, too."

I gasped. *Who?* I was too far now from Summer Court to feel Summerfae and the water magic that came to me easier. And I hesitated pulling on shadows because they were needed elsewhere as Cillian, in beast form, sat on top of my love, threatening to carve off his face.

Fede tried anyway with a cruel laugh to suffocate my one working lung, but I pulled on her with her own magic, holding the air inside like a bubble.

"Mmm, you learn quickly." Her knee shoved me in the chest, and I went sprawling over behind her.

"I know you sided with Winter. His city reeks of Spring's tulips." I panted into the ground.

She got to her feet, dusting off her skin. "Oh, please," she scoffed. "Who else was there? Autumn destroys my forests, even after I so graciously allowed them into my festivals. Summer is useless, though perhaps not anymore. Your lover was digging his heels into his own demise and the Courtless . . . as beautiful as they are, something has that king in a chokehold. There was only one option left. And have you met Winter's general? I'd rather be behind her than against her. Shadows and the Courtless won't stand a chance against him and his army. Lord Aborys will pull you back." Her voice, but a whisper, hissed through to me. "And you'll fight against all you love."

I charged at her, screaming. I wasn't going to lose my mind again.

"Unless, I say you slipped off the cliffs like I've done to so many others before. We'll see what Adrian's seamutts think of a lonely little Siphon." A gust of wind blew me off my feet and tumbled me to the edge where earth fell away, and sea churned below like a monster, mouth open ready to eat.

My feet dangled as she sauntered closer, fixing her white dress over her curves. She crunched her foot into my knuckles and I cried into the cliffside.

Not far away, bone broke between Cillian's teeth and Kade growled against the ground. Something was wrong. Kade couldn't move out from under him.

Kade, get up. Please get up. I begged, moving along the cliff edge dodging Fede's stomps.

"You're a baby rabbit trapped in a fox's den," Fede chided, grinding my hand into the ground again. "You're no match for the powers of Eadha."

I screamed louder than the remaining Flute making blood drip from my ears. Louder than my fear even because Cillian sat atop Kaderyn and was digging his way through him to the earth below, shredding his chest like paper.

"KADERYN!" I screamed, not believing what I was seeing as the Berserker mauled my love. Pure panic had me scrambling for purchase under Lady Fede's feet. She hissed insults at me, trying to kick my hands into the sea.

But the beast stopped suddenly and looked at the white figure above me. His yellow eyes narrowed as he dragged himself off Kaderyn.

Kade wasn't moving.

I sobbed. *Kade, please get up. Please.* But I would do anything to save Kade and I pulled on magic that felt like Jairek's.

"Tell my lovely sister I say hi," Fede hissed for the last time as I reached up with one hand, now so different from my own, black and furred, and dug Berserker-like claws into her foot, piercing her straight through to the compacted ground below.

She wailed into the air and the wind ripping through the Flute stopped its attack.

"Tell her yourself." I puffed into the dirt.

Cillian leapt, roaring as he crashed into her, soaring over me into the belly of a beast churning below.

They disappeared into the frothing, foaming waves of the sea.

"Kade," I whimpered, begging him to move. I had to get up. I had to save him. I couldn't do this without him.

I dug my feet into the sandy side of the cliff and pulled,

fingers and ribs broken, lung collapsed. I dragged my broken body to him.

"Kade, hold on to me. Hold on," I whispered.

The mangled skin on his shoulder hung on by threads. Muscle, bone, and *innards* peeked out of his chest and stomach.

I had to shadowfade us.

Screw Roshan. I wasn't letting Kade die.

I swirled shadows around us as fast as I could like I'd seen Kade do countless times.

His voice cracked above a whisper, and an eye opened slightly. "Just think of home," he said as his head lolled to the side. "Think of our bed. Our"—he blinked, trying to stay coherent for me.

"Okay, okay, Kade. Hold on. I've got you." My tears splashed against his cheeks.

With the last of my strength and the dwindling shadows of Kade, I shadowfaded us home.

But there, fading over Summer on Hawrenthia's palace balcony, was Roshan watching me as we spottily flashed in and out of shadows—falling then catching—slowly and painfully across southern Eadha.

But I clung shadows to Kade. If he fell, I fell. "Don't leave me, Kade," I cried. "Please don't leave me." And I worked all the magic I knew how to do—all the magic I was best at.

We smashed hard into the ground, and my vision blurred.

We're here, Kade. Hold on.

But he was barely breathing. The shadows had all but left him.

And as all went black, I wanted to die.

29

DERYN IRONSIDE

"Avika, not right now," I begged, retreating from her through the valley below my tracks.

I was racing down my tracks not a hundred feet from the mountain when I saw the flailing arms of my sister beckoning me down. And like a chump, I fell for it.

"When is a good time for you? You don't want me working with Carmen. You still haven't told me what that earthquake was, or if it'll happen again."

"It won't happen again," I answered, limping back for the nearest support beam. I'd rather climb it and tightrope walk down my tracks to the cart than face her berating now.

"Damn it, Deryn! We don't have Shifterfae dropping us food and demigods whisking us away whenever we want to travel more than ten feet—"

I spun around, facing the hurricane head-on. "What are you insinuating? I've worked for everything I've built."

"Me too, Deryn! Except I had all of them to lead too." She thrust a hand back at Brendan, the town in the valley. "I had other faeless' pain to carry, not just my own, while you abandoned us. While you abandoned me."

"I couldn't, Avika!" I screamed. Rage crashed into a violent meadow fire inside me.

But she didn't back down. *God's, why did she never back down?* "Those HorCains keep leaving paw prints on our porches. An ewe went missing three nights ago. When are you and your *friends* going to do something about it? What are you waiting for? Us to be slaughtered in our sleep?"

"I'll handle it."

"When? In another couple of centuries?"

"I couldn't come back to you, Avika. No matter how hard I tried. I was too scared of the fae." And if I thought my admission would grant me grace, I was wrong.

Her voice quieted, and I knew better than to think it wasn't still laced with vitriol. "We were all scared, Deryn. But you ran and hid in *that*."

I was an eddying fire, caught in a raging cycle of being fueled by fury, destroyed by my shame, and yet I'd been built anew from ashes of molten iron ore. I *created* something.

A home.

A castle of iron.

"Stop insulting my tower," I warned, hands shaking.

"Or what?" Her eyes narrowed.

We were screaming, shrieking no better than banshees. Perhaps we understood one another because we were sisters, though long since called each other that. And maybe I'd always know what she was saying when she was angry, and she'd hear me through my gnashing teeth and tear-soaked face. But it was a lost cause. We'd spent too long apart.

Half of Brendan stared at us like we were a two-headed flying beast ready to light their town on fire.

Staring at *me*.

I turned away from my sister, hair frazzled, nerves even more so, and limped for my tracks, wiping my face as I went.

Criticizing her in front of her settlement surely undermined her leadership, and I had enough sympathy left after the blazing inferno inside me to walk away first. Maybe I was really retreating from battle, and I was lying to myself, too.

But compassion?

I didn't think Avika had any at all.

I cranked the cart, pushing the lever down as far as it would go, and let the wind force the rest of the tears off my face. It was too fast. I knew this, but I needed the safety of my tower. Now.

Jerking the lever back long before I met the edge of my tower, I eased the cart into its cradle and kicked a loose iron beam left on the floor behind a wheel so it wouldn't disappear down the tracks. I had a system, an intricate system of latches and locks, but I couldn't think straight to do them now. Not with her words still ringing through my head.

Leaving Avika's company left me blistered like molten sparks were constantly landing on my skin. She kept throwing my heart into a hearth like kindling for a fire.

Shuffling sounded from up in my rooms and I pulled too hard when my leg got caught on something metal trying to get to my stairs. My pants shredded near the ankle.

There, around the corner, pacing in my bedrooms, was Rhett.

"Rhett," I sobbed. "You won't believe what Av—"

"It's not enough, Deryn," he interrupted with dark circles around his eyes so black they looked bruised. He paced again. "The firefae are trying to build bridges across. They're even launching flaming bundles of tar-soaked wicker across the canyon." He pulled at his already spiked hair. "They won't give up. I was wrong. Kaderyn and Jairek won't ever be able to avenge my father's death. I've been doing all this work for them for nothing."

"Don't say that." I moved for him, but he pushed my hands away when I got close.

"Lord Ohrem trots around his court with my father's feathers on his cloak and all Jairek and Kade tell me to do is stand down. Kade's waiting and Jairek's still stuck in his head." He paused and the light of the night and my own grief cast his face in shadows. "Give me the Faemech, Deryn."

"What?" I recoiled.

"Give me the whole bag or box or whatever you have, and I'll fly it over Autumn *fucking* Court. I'll blow the entire court away."

"Rhett," I said slowly, so I didn't startle him. This wasn't like him. "There's faeless and faelings and fae that aren't Lord Ohrem . . ." And I shouldn't have said his name.

Rhett lunged for me. "They're slaughtering my court! No one fucking cares, Deryn. Not even you."

I flinched as his face scrunched up with an anger I thought I had left in the valley. "I care, of course, I care."

"Then fight with me. Use your Faemech and destroy Winter and Autumn Court."

My stomach turned sour, and I drifted out of his grasp. "Hundreds of thousands of deaths would be on my hands. Is that what you want?"

"You sit here with all this metal and do nothing about it."

"Rhett—"

"No, I'm sick of everyone telling me to wait. To hold off. To stand down. To let my father's death go!"

"I did what you and Kaderyn asked of me. I gave space between the courts and the Courtless and Shadows."

"It's not enough," he roared and slapped a hand against the open wall of my tower. His hand sizzled and burned.

"What do you mean?" I stilled with my hands splayed open, wishing this was a dream, wishing he wouldn't hurt himself on my iron.

He launched forward, arms flying. "I mean, we are still hiding! This isn't just for the faeless, Deryn, like Valentina wants. This is the Courtless' chance to destroy Autumn Court for good."

"A war won't right their wrongs," I said softer, reaching for him.

He dropped his head back. "It's a start. Tell me you'll build more weapons for the war. Build iron to carve Autumnfae out from their eternal fire."

"Out of the very metal that harms you?" I scoffed. "In the wrong hands, it'll be the death of you. What then? Huh?" I shrieked. "You come to me next, floating on your back, wings outstretched, no breath left in you at all, with my own metal sticking out of your chest. Is that what you want?"

"At least I won't be hiding!" He roared into the night.

He roared into my soul.

I stopped dead. Tears filled my eyes. Because he knew. He *knew* why I hid. He knew I feared the Lady of Spring. Tension in the air released like the dropping of a bit of a horse.

Rhett had made his true feelings known. "Deryn, I'm sorry. I—"

"Get out," I spit. Tears funneled down my face in streams.

He stepped forward to grab me, but I scrambled out of his hold and over to the side of the bedroom without Faebric covering my metal.

He took one barefoot step on the raw iron. "I won't leave you like this." His skin scorched.

But I couldn't be responsible for his pain right now. Mine felt too big. And with one last glance, I retreated to the iron workroom below—to the innards of the tower where iron was thickest, and I pretended it was an iron cage around my heart. *Nothing could reach me here.*

I picked up my hammer and relit the forge. Smashing cold iron did nothing but rattle my bones, and *by my iron ore*, I needed the ache. I needed the echoing clash to drown out the hawkshifter upstairs in my rooms calling my name. A name I winced at. I reached my arm back and before I cracked it on the anvil, a caw pierced through the open window.

Rhett left.

I smashed down harder as tears fell to my shirt, but my grief weakened the hold on my hammer, and it clattered past the anvil and banged against my leg. My metals were my own, something I built, a shell of protection, but the dishes I made, the trinket boxes with iron stretched almost as thin as Teal's arm were because I *liked* what I did. It brought me joy. And now my sister seeing my creations caused me a shame I couldn't hide from because my iron was all over the Mainland and Rhett wanted more of it. Wanted more of *me* out there.

I smashed my fist against the shelf of trinkets, sending iron crashing against iron. An echoing *clank* reverberated around the workshop as they fell to the floor. The things that once gave me purpose, and gave me my sense of pride, were tainted by Avika's observations.

Gaudy, she'd said. That *thing*.

I crumpled into a heap beside my destruction and sobbed.

"Dearest Deryn," came Adrian's voice, sounding unsure, like a crack of thunder waiting for lightning. As he knelt beside me, his body heat and the smell of the sea consumed me. "What has that cantankerous sister of yours said now?"

I tried to give a lighthearted laugh, but it turned into heaving. Adrian pulled my hands from my face, scooped under my legs, and carried me to the broken daybed on the other side of my workshop.

"What is it?" he prodded. "Shall I flood the valley?"

I gave him a look, I think, but I still couldn't speak.

"What's happened? You seem to have all your pieces." He tapped each leg and arm. Like that was all that was important and not my heart breaking for Rhett and his need for revenge.

Eventually, I choked out the words. "He wants me to join the war. He thinks I'm weak. And he's right."

"This tower is proof of your strength. It's been forged and fought for. He's a fool not to see it."

"He has reason to be angry."

"He does not have reason to pull you into his bitterness." And with a sigh, he said, "You're a magpie, dearest Deryn. A collector of broken shiny things. The most broken of all being that hawkshifter you love."

I turned into his shoulder. "What is the purpose of the faeless? What am I meant for, Adrian? What is the purpose of *me*?"

"Oh, dearest Deryn." He pulled me tighter to his chest as some realization hit him with a sigh. "I found you floating in the reeds in boggy waters. Chased off seamutts foaming at the mouth to get another bite of you." A tender hand brushed away the hair stuck to my cheek.

My breath caught in my chest as his forehead came to rest on mine. Adrian was pure power, and we spent so much time together that I sometimes forgot what he was. But now, chaos was rolling off him, uncontrolled, and I didn't know what to do. The fights with Avika and Rhett left me emotionally drained.

"The gods are selfish and unforgiving, but they did not make mistakes when creating the faeless and they definitely did not make a mistake when they created you." He tipped my head up to look up at him.

I'd never seen my best friend as distraught as I did then. I wanted to close the distance between us, press into the comfort and warmth of this demigod who kept me company for almost two centuries at no perceivable benefit to himself. But what would that change? There was too much at stake. I was too alone to lose Adrian too.

He leaned back. Eyes as wet as mine. A slender finger rose and brushed flakes of iron off my cheek. His skin didn't burn. It didn't sizzle. His deep dark brown gaze stayed on mine and his voice was barely over a whisper, but he might as well have screamed it, "You're more godlike than I am."

I wanted to reach for him.

"Adrian . . ." I whispered, begging him.

His raw voice cracked. "Call to the waters if you need me."

I fluttered my eyes closed and my body softly met cushions as Adrian misted away. The spray danced across my face, and I pressed my fingertips to my salt-spray-covered lips.

"Thank you, Adrian," I said to the dark of the room. My forge burned like a deep love in my chest I didn't want to admit.

I knew he'd tell me not to thank the fae.

A small metal bowl sat on the table before me, housing a batch of iron nails I kept forgetting to bring to Teal's port. It was now full to the brim with brine-smelling water. "I'm thanking a friend," I whispered to the water.

A thumping pulse sent ripples through its surface.

30

VALENTINA

A week later, Kade opened his eyes only once.

Oir had run down the steps as we crashed to the castle's foyer, dress in hand, calling for any healer upon seeing the mess of Kade and me. She had grabbed me by the chin, and I blinked up at her, begging, "Help him. Help only him."

But she'd helped me too.

I'd taken the brunt force of the fall and fractured my skull on impact. But I'd survived with three cracked ribs, a collapsed lung, and broken fingers—though now they'd already healed.

But Kade? So much worse.

"What did he go up against?" Oir had asked as they carried him away, his fingers slipping from mine.

"A Berserker," I muffled, barely breathing, then passed out entirely.

So now I sat in an uncomfortable chair waiting for Kade to wake up, holding my throbbing head in my hands, answering Oir's questions. "Lady Fede admitted to making her sister drop Kade to his knees but wouldn't confess who gave her the poison for Lord Brexton." I would not tell Oir we knew it was a female, or that Fede confessed they were close to Shadow Court. Both of which pointed my suspicions to the Shadowfae layering herbs on Kade now.

"She didn't tell you who?" Oir asked, not looking up from her task.

I bit the edge of my fingernail. "No."

Oir turned and looked out the window. Almost dramatically, because we both knew the sun wouldn't rise for a few more hours. So, it was even more redundant when she said, "You've been up late every night this week."

"I can't sleep," I answered. How could I? Kade was lying mangled in a bed so far from our rooms. Alone.

She leaned up. "I could give you something for that."

And my voice turned severe. "Your job right now is to heal Kade."

Her eyes narrowed, and I scolded myself. I was exhausted and in pain. My ailments healed except for the lingering headaches, and I refused the Virtusa Tonic from Oir countless times. Mohr used it to drug me in Spring's cellars. I could barely stand the smell of it on Kade's breath.

A low groan came from Kade. "By my fucking hounds, Oir. Whatever you're packing in there burns."

I rushed to his side.

"Well, that's what you get for almost getting yourself killed," Oir snapped.

"Hi," I whispered, choking back tears, not knowing what part of him to touch.

His foggy eyes looked muddled gray, and he frowned as he said, "You promised me you'd never do that."

"I'm sure I did no such thing," I mumbled into his knuckles, kissing each one.

You took away my pain, Valentina, he said through mindspeak.

You were dying, Kade. And we were crashing. If I killed us both trying to get back here . . . I stopped and wiped tears from my face. *It was the only thing I could do to help you.*

"Come here." He tugged me to the bed beside him and pressed his lips to my forehead, then my lips. "I don't deserve you."

I wanted to bathe him. Rinse off the blood and medicines. Take him to our rooms and heal his body with mine. Because I choked on the words that wanted to tell him I would take his pain away forever if I could. And I'd do it again right now for him, but knew he'd hide me in his Underworld forever and there was still a nagging pull that needed me to stay on this messy island.

"Are they alive? Did Cillian and Fede survive the fall?"

"Our soldiers watched a floating white dress pass by our court, being pushed by the waves south of here. By the time we got a ship out to it, it was gone." Oir cleaned up her medicines and moved toward the door. "I'm going to hire the pixies next time. I fear they're better on the seas than Shadowfae. Don't tell them I told you that."

"Thank you, Oir." Kade nodded.

She smiled back.

I didn't waste any time once the door clicked shut. "I've sent for Jair. He's going to watch over you." *Because I don't trust Oir,* I thought, but kept from him. Whoever poisoned Brexton had knowledge of herbs, and that left me few suspects.

"Where do you think you're running off to?"

I wanted the instant satisfaction of quick answers. The ones that would tell me things would get better. The promise that tomorrow wouldn't carry the weight, the same suffering, that today held, but passing through life and these hallways like a ghost wasn't moving anything forward.

If I'd said nothing to Cillian about Blackwater, Roshan would still be stealing glances at Sisaria in Otti Theater. And now look at us, Sisaria was dead. Blackwater had fled. Roshan, though he had found strength, had overthrown Lord Grigory. And hated me. Teal'd lost an arm in the northernmost reaches of Winter Court trying to get Kade's shadows back. But wallowing in my pity wasn't the way, either. I was punishing myself for not being strong enough against the Frost Witch's spells.

"I almost miss traveling the courts with Jair and Teal," I confessed.

"I don't miss nuckelavee sludge in your hair, that's for sure."

I snorted. "It seemed simpler when we were fighting Eadha's monsters in forests than monsters leading entire courts but right now, I need . . . to get a clear head."

"Are you in pain? Valen—"

"I'm not taking the damn tonic. It's not about that. I need —Kade, I need a break from the fae." Confusion racked through me, and I didn't think it had anything to do with the skull fracture.

He seemed to understand because he said, "We can go to the Underworld. Give me a day—two, tops."

"No, Kade. You're not ready to go anywhere." I was angry again and I couldn't tell him.

"Go to the Mainland," he offered. "Go see Teal and her port."

I thought this over. "There's no fae?" I asked. I wanted to meet Deryn, a proper meeting. Eventually. But I didn't think I'd be good company in this mood.

"No," he shook his head. "Just faeless, pixies, ogres—though they stay in the mountains, and Carmen."

"Carmen?"

"She keeps the ogres mining for Deryn. They've been there since before Shadow Court. They do their thing and we do ours. Though I imagine I'll have to step in in case Fillagree Fen's pixies go on a field trip through the caves."

I grimaced, leaning down near his lips. "There's a lot to worry about now."

"And here, my biggest worry before was the Summerfae who just attached a sex tie to my wrist." His hand laced through my hair, and I held back the wince at the pain it caused my head.

"Let me warn Teal for you. I haven't visited her docks yet, anyway. Nor the faeless. I want to see the town. Make sure they're all right." Maybe visit Deryn with her iron after that.

I pressed my lips to his and his shadows twirled against my skin.

The Mainland was all magicless.

Exactly what I needed.

"Keep my shadows on you, please."

"I'll be too far to siphon them." I moved away toward the door. Too scared to tell him I needed a break from shadows, too. "I can still hear you in my head, don't forget. I called to you while you rode the Wild Hunt. I can get your attention across a silly strait."

"Thank my hounds for nuckelavee sludge, then."

"Just not in my hair." I gave him a wink and closed the door.

AN HOUR LATER, AFTER I HAD A GOOD CRY BECAUSE Kade was alive and awake and maybe I was more concussed than I thought, I stepped one foot onto the ship named The Meandering Sea Mollusk. Something swept my feet out from under me instantly. The air whooshed out of my lungs and a rib re-cracked.

Large sauce eyes made me go cross-eyed, and the tip of a small button nose touched mine.

"A tongue with a twist
Yes, one such as this.
We'll take it to the shore.
You'll start with the eyes
I'll get the thighs
Until there's nothing more."

The small pixie with tattered wings had my legs bound in a dirty ship's rope in seconds.

"Get off me!" I thrust a red dagger to the tattoo on his neck. "Teal!"

Teal, in her stiff black hat, popped out from somewhere below deck and muttered something about 'not this one'.

"Some of my sparkier mates
Have taken to using force.
Their argument comes from decades of hate.
I can't say that I endorse."

The dagger sliced easily through the ropes. "You listen close-ly," I said, grabbing her by the collar. "We don't coerce the faeless or those traveling across the Galeairy. Patrol the eastern and western corridors if you must." I thought of Lady Fede at the mercy of the pixie pirates. "But no one is eating anyone's eyes!" I shrieked and side-eyed her whole operation.

"He was *joking.*"
She gave me a big guilty smile.
"*Probably*—probably joking."

"And yet, I'm on my back, Teal," I said, hefting up to my feet.

"Right, well, I suppose I can keep a closer eye."

Teal flew around masts and buzzed up to the helm, demanding compliance and yelling orders. She dressed in full black now, which was a shock from the flower petal dresses she used to wear. Even her hands had such gloves that her fingers poked out. At least, on one arm. The other was a beautiful design of iron woven to bend and move like an arm. Deryn was really something.

Lights flickered in the thick early morning fog along Filla-gree Fen's coast. Small candles sat melted in broken bowls stolen from who knew where along the dock's outer edge. Signposts stood at the apex of crossways, their signs slanted, muddy, and completely illegible. Half a dozen ships swayed in Galeairy's waves, and it was a wonder Adrian let them in at all. Fish markets created an odor across the strait that I worried would attract ogres, but apparently it just lured shadowgulls. Their tails left a trail of black shadows through the sky. 'A much more enticing delectable,' a pixie had said. Vines I recognized from

Spring weaved along the tops of shops, growing full and lush in the Mainland's late spring warmth.

I wondered who exactly had planned and built the pixie homes and huts made of crates, which were upside down, wider above than below, and looked like they'd blow over with a single breeze. Hoping it wasn't the one buzzing about in the sock.

A little pixie in a flower petal dress flung a tattered cloth off the front of her store. She sold matching flower dresses and hats and, much to my surprise, clothing for the size of a fae too. Or faeless. Pixies built a pulley system along the mountainside to catch runoff into wooden pails, and they carried it further down the waterfront from there. As we approached, the port of misshapen docks seemed strung together by small pixie hands and hopes and dreams. Which was exactly why I asked to be docked further down.

"Adrian doesn't mind you taking over his strait with a crew of pixie pirates? I mean, did you even ask him? You're building a port in his waterways," I asked Teal on one of her trips down the mast.

She scoffed.

"Meddlesome gods give and take what they please
'Call to the waters', they'll say as they leave.
But I know where their eyes go when they're quiet.
Stealing glances, *not loot*," Teal tutted.
"And they call *me* the pirate."

"Mmhm." I sent her a quizzical look without the foggiest idea of what she was talking about. "Thanks for the ride, Teal."

The ship bumped into port and pixies immediately bounced over the sides, tying us steady.

Not as terrifying as I thought it would be, I thought. "Kade wants you to watch out for the ogres, Teal. Don't let your friends stray too far from port. Make sure they know of the dangers in the mountains."

"Yes, yes, keep the pixies together.
Deryn already gave us that lecture."

"What did I do, Teal?" came a shaky voice near a patch of pixies banging at the docks with their fists. She smacked her hammer on an iron pin piercing through two planks of wood. "There, see how I did that? Now the entire dock won't fall apart the next time the faeless try to unload. Take these, and do the same along the edge of the shore. You can't charge your passengers if they end up taking an unexpected bath in the Galeairy."

The pixies grumbled.

"Hi, Valentina," she said quickly before picking up a second iron bucket of bolts and moving onto steady land. "Nice to see you."

"Deryn?" I called for her.

She froze, and her shoulders met her ears. I frowned. I'd never seen someone afraid of their own name before.

"I was coming to see you, actually." I held my hurting rib and ran to catch up with her.

"Me? Why? Does Kaderyn need something else?"

"Well, to see you and Blackwater Junction."

"Oh, they go by the name of Brendan now. Named after a faeless who passed away."

"From what?"

"Age. I think it's an isolated incident though," she said, but quickly added, "I don't think it's my metals."

I frowned. *Why was she so defensive?* "The thought never crossed my mind. They're lucky you could provide them a place to lay down their roots again."

"Be better if these damn HorCains would stop taunting

them. I'll see if Teal can bring you down to the valley. I was just heading out to the last HorCain sighting."

And I had no clue what a HorCain was, but I still asked, "Alone?"

"Adrian can't approach HorCains and Rhett . . . is busy." She sniffed and I could tell she didn't want to elaborate.

"Do you want company? Here," I said, taking the bucket from her hands. I knew under those pants she had only one working leg. "Give me this." My arm suddenly tugged down with its weight, and something strained inside my ribcage. I winced.

"It's quite all right. I'm used to the weight of iron." She took the bucket back. "Why are you holding your stomach? You're limping."

"It's fine. It *was* healed until that bumpy ride over here." I shot a parting glare at the tattooed pixie as we moved up parallel to the mountain. "Kade and I had a run-in with Lady Fede."

Deryn froze. "What happened?" Her breath came out in puffs, and it wasn't because of the iron she carried.

"We found out Lady Fede was half vampfae. She coerced her sister to lure and bite Kaderyn during the Wild Hunt. It turned him part fae. We were trying to find out who her partner was. She didn't feel inclined to tell us anything except that it's a 'she' and that she's right under Shadow's nose."

Deryn cleared her throat, and her eyes flicked to the mountains behind me.

"Don't worry, I don't think it's you," I said quickly, thinking of Oir.

She gave a startled laugh. "The Lady of Spring is responsible for this." She clunked the iron bucket against her leg. An audible *clank* rang out.

"Then you'll be happy to know Cillian dragged her and himself off the cliffside."

"The Berserker? Into the waters?"

"He hurt Kade pretty badly, but he's healing." I grimaced.

"I can't believe she's part vampfae."

"I don't know. She always seemed like a bloodsucker to me."

She smiled then. A genuine smile and I couldn't help but smile back.

31

DERYN IRONSIDE

Valentina dressed in the usual thick black Shadowfae cloth but crisscrossed yellow and red daggers holstered across her back. I'd been around Adrian and his gods' sword enough to know it was forged from metal from the Otherworld.

I kept my distance from them all the same.

I was suddenly aware of my own shirt, which I hadn't washed in three days, and of the burn holes in my pants near my thighs growing frayed enough to shove my entire hand through. But I couldn't ask Rhett for new clothes now. She'd asked if I'd be going to check out the HorCains alone and I couldn't nod quick enough. I wasn't ready to face Rhett. It still hurt, thinking about him and his words. And Adrian, well . . .

A quiet, controlled sadness lingered off Valentina and mingled with the fear I knew she could smell off me. We were quite the match.

Her gaze landed on me, and I twitched under the attention. It would be a long walk if I couldn't find something tangible to say. I wanted to say how remarkable it was that she united Kade with the Wild Hunt. It must have taken a lot of bravery. I wanted to ask what the Underworld was like and how traveling the island with Teal had been. I expected at least a few gray hairs from it. By the second time her blue eyes turned my way, my cheeks heated.

Finally, she gestured to my waist. "Something is shining from your pocket."

Glancing down, I saw the half-uncovered mirror from Rhett sliding in and out of the small pocket where I kept it with every heave of my leg. The pocket had a large hole and my cheeks heated.

"Thanks," I mumbled, shoving it down with a pointed finger. Calling him here now was the last thing I wanted. "I use the sun's rays to signal to Rhett if I need him. Three flashes toward his court and it meant come quick. Two flashes and it meant come, but there wasn't immediate danger. It's how Rhett and I communicate from so far away."

"That's very smart, a neat invention. Are those yours too?"

I bristled under her scrutiny, and my chin dipped down. I didn't know how to take a compliment, so instead, I explained the tracks and their purpose.

She stopped to admire or criticize my tracks. I didn't know which, before she said, "Teal mentioned you were a genius."

Oh, by my iron ore, change the subject, Deryn. Change the subject! I urged myself.

"Teal told me you created a magic amplifier in Summer Court?"

She cringed, and I knew I'd found the wrong question to ask. *Damn*, I scolded myself. *I should have stuck to the topics of Teal.*

"Of sorts," she answered. "It was a picture frame of mermaids near a broken chair in Otti Theater. It allowed me to take the entire theater's pain all at once." Then she laughed as she added, "It meant I could get back to eating desserts sooner."

"It was clever," I offered.

"It was self-preservation."

And I looked to my tower, and tracks because I had things built based on that as well.

The slow steady climb gave me enough time to feel completely inadequate in her company, so I filled the space explaining what a HorCain was. Not exactly vengeful creatures, but they had teeth and claws to worry the faeless all the same.

"Deryn, wait." She raised a hand.

I froze, instantly on edge, searching for the beasts lingering too close to the town. "What's wrong?"

"I feel—nothing. Sorry, never mind. Are you sure there's no fae here?"

"Positive." I nodded as the sun rose high in the sky. "Carmen's a witch. She lives in the mountains. Maybe you can feel something from her."

She gave a small laugh. "I wasn't sure if you knew who I was."

"I've been fixing Teal's shoulder when I pass by her port. It gives her time to get out some solid rhymes."

"I needed a break from fae problems." She frowned. "Being a Siphon, I need to be calm like water, passionate like fire, quick as wind, steady like ice, brave-hearted like shifters, and fluid like shadows. It's too much. Nothing roots me."

I smiled, shrugging. "Being faeless doesn't mean I don't feel water give me life with every drop, and just because I can't command fire doesn't mean I don't feel it light my soul with every swing of my hammer against metals mined from bedrock and clay. I dig my hands into the earth when I grow my crops, and I *know* I'm a part of the earth as much as any fae."

"Why—" she stopped. "How do you keep going, Deryn? When you're tired. When things get too much."

I gave her a self-deprecating smile. "I'm not as strong as you think I am."

She gestured to my leg. "You're made of metal." And more incredulously, she added, "And you blew up an island."

"Both defensive strategies," I said, shifting the bucket of bolts to my other hand. "I'm not one to go to for advice on moving on, unfortunately."

She turned to me with balled fists. "I'm so . . . so angry. All the time. How are you so calm? With how they treat the faeless, Lady Fede's treatment of you, Rhett's obsession with violence. Am I the only one who thinks he's trying to get himself killed?"

I shrugged. If only she knew about my problems with my sister. But she saw my frustrations and validation seeped into my bones. "I hammer iron, Valentina. Sometimes until it's the shape I want it, sometimes until I can't feel my fingers. And sometimes"—I looked at her, really looked at her so she felt the weight of my words—"until I can't feel anything at all."

How many times had Adrian saved me from burst blisters bleeding down my forearms? How many times had he crashed us to the daybed, pulling me away from my smashing to talk mindless chatter to me until I fell asleep?

We were around the far side of the mountain now and I scanned the dirt paths south of us, looking for tracks of large-pawed HorCains.

"You're sure there's no fae here?"

"I'm positive. Maybe you feel something different around HorCains." But then, years of living alone had improved my senses enough that I knew when I was being tailed. The hair on my neck stood on end, and my palms sweated. "Valentina, don't stop walking, but I think something's tailing us."

She whispered, "Do HorCains work together? Will they ambush?" Her fingers twitched at her side.

I could tell it was something dangerous. "They might. I'll handle it, you run—"

"The depths you are!" she snapped. "I have gods' daggers strapped to my back. On my count, you run and—"

I dropped the bucket of bolts and pulled out my hammer in one move. Valentina was fast and had a dagger thrust toward the threat when I gasped. "Valentina, no!"

Because inches from Valentina's gods' dagger was my niece. "Breena, what are you doing out here? By all my iron ore, it's not safe."

The small faeling looked up and green eyes stared back at me. But everything else about her was Avika and me.

I swallowed, falling to my butt. *If I got my niece killed . . .*

"There's HorCains out here. You shouldn't be out here at all, let alone wandering by yourself," Valentina berated, equally breathless.

"Something's wrong with her," Breena said, and my cheeks heated.

"Breena, that's not kind." I thought of a slew of excuses I could try to explain away her ill manners, but mostly I just wanted to seep into one of the rocky cracks and never come back out.

"Not Valentina." Breena shook her head. Her long, soft hair swung from side to side. She looked years older than her small stature indicated, but her eyes were scared.

"Don't worry, the HorCains won't come any closer," Valentina said, holstering her dagger. "We'll get you back to your mom." She grimaced. "Maybe avoid telling her I had a dagger to your throat, though."

Breena continued to shake her head. "I'm not afraid of

those creatures. I'm afraid of what's in there." She pointed to a crude door I'd never seen before jutting out from the mountain face of the Twin Peak Mountains.

It faced the sea instead of Adrian's Galeairy. Seawater spray rusted its entire flat surface.

"Where does that go?" Valentina asked.

"I don't know." I searched around. The ogres very well could have carved the rock out. I supposed it led to more corridors inside the mountain. I made fixings for the doors, and bolts for the beams. And hinges. But these hinges didn't have a speck of rust where they moved. And this door? It looked well used.

"Deryn! Look out!" Valentina shrieked, raising her hands to my face.

I grabbed my hammer and ducked in time as ice magic shot over my head.

Spinning, a HorCain slunk low with its claws outstretched, reaching for Breena. I smashed my hammer down on the HorCain's paw as ice magic climbed up its body, freezing it solid.

Breena stumbled back.

"Oh, by my iron ore, your mother will kill me if you get hurt. Or worse, she'll scream at me again," I puffed.

This one was different, younger.

"They aren't our enemy, Deryn," Breena said, moving closer.

The HorCain struggled to snap out of its icy cage.

"Their teeth tell me differently," Valentina said, hands still outstretched as she moved closer, inspecting. "It has odd eyes. Do you think they shift like the Courtless?"

"No, Rhett said they might have been something like fae once. I have a feeling the gods are responsible for the way they are."

"They're jealous," Breena whispered.

I blurted a laugh unexpectedly. Hardly. "We're not fae," I said slowly to the HorCain.

"Breena! Breena!" her mother shrieked from below the mountain near my tracks.

I dropped my head back. I should have let the HorCain eat me.

"By Daina, I swear you'll be the death of me!" Avika trudged up past my tracks. Any closer and she'd see the frozen HorCain.

"Go, before your mother sees and grounds you to her hip. Go!" I said, ushering her around the biggest of boulders.

"Tell her you asked me to come," Breena begged.

"What? No, that will not help matters." I got enough assault from Avika for my own actions.

"Please," she begged again.

It pulled on something. I wanted a relationship with her. I wanted to see my niece grow up.

Avika was out of breath and frantic. "What in all graces are you doing out here? I've been searching the entire valley for you. HorCains were spotted this way." Her gaze flicked to me and stayed.

Sweat dripped down my back and my cheeks pulled tight. Damn it. "I . . . I . . . told Breena to come. Avika, it's my fault." My shoulders stiffened and I prepared myself for her attack.

My sister crossed her arms. "Oh, you're still a shit liar, Deryn! And she turned on her daughter. "Don't even think about leaving Brendan again."

"It's fine. Valentina and Deryn saved me."

"From what?!" Avika screamed, dragging her daughter down the side of the mountain and to the soft valley below. "You don't think they have more important things to do than save you from your own naivety?"

"Usually it's me she's screaming at," I said, watching them leave.

Valentina gave me a look, and I didn't want to elaborate on my problems with my sister.

"What do you think?" She cocked her head near the HorCain's jaws. "Is that good? I might try to thaw him out now." Valentina raised her hands and fire blasted the ice encasing around the beast. "It feels too much like fae, this magic, Deryn."

"Maybe it's coming from him?" But I looked back at the door.

"Stay away from the faeless in the valley," Valentina warned when its jaws released from the ice, and it snarled.

I needed to solve this with the HorCains once and for all. Before I made good on my word and used Faemech on the ruins they hid out in, but it didn't sit right in my gut. I much more enjoyed creating than destroying. But it wasn't just me anymore. I had Brendan to look after—from afar, at least.

As soon as the HorCain broke fully free from Valentina's hold, it took off backward with its tail between its legs. A young one, indeed.

The lecture Breena was getting still echoed across the valley, and I somehow felt responsible. "Come, I'll take you to Brendan. I need to find a way to signal HorCain sightings near town lines. They'll need to monitor the tree line until then."

"Sure, but can we take those?" I followed her finger as it led directly to my long straight tracks that soared overtop the valley.

"You *want* to take those?"

Her hand landed on my shoulder, capturing my attention. "Absolutely."

"You made this by yourself?" she asked as we approached.

"I nodded. It's faster to move the iron to my tower. I spent my early days dragging it, but with one good foot, I was spending most of my time camping in the valley. But in the past, the HorCains came much closer to the Galeairy shores."

"Why didn't you build your tower closer to the mountain?"

"Have you tried sleeping next to ogres?" There were more reasons, mostly Carmen's desire for privacy, but this felt fun with Valentina and when she laughed. The tension left my bones. "Okay, hop in. Sorry it's small, I'll build a bigger one now that I know it works. Hold on tight. Don't lean too far one way or the other." I directed her as I pushed the lever forward, slowly.

And even with prepping, she still flailed as it started moving. It differed from anything on Eadha, that I knew for sure.

A smile spread across her lips, and I pushed it a little further, moving us away from the mountain. Once the valley spread out below us, faelings came charging out of the fields. I sometimes wondered if they waited for me to drive my tracks.

They jumped and waved, trying to get our attention.

"It feels like we're flying! I feel like a faeling. Carefree and happy," she said with her face pressed into the wind, hair pulled back, and eyes closed. "I haven't felt like this since I was six." Valentina spread her arms wide in the air before leaning over and looking down. "They're waving to you, Deryn!" she shouted over the roaring of the warm almost-summer wind. An eager smile stretched across her face.

The faelings raced below the tracks, jumping off small dunes, and a few tumbling into the grasses, laughing. Others howled up at us and I leaned down to see them better. Because they were shouting *my* name.

"Deryn! Deryn! Deryn!"

"Wave back," Valentina urged with a wink.

I started tentatively at first. In case they were just swatting flies around their heads, but when they hollered louder, my whole body swayed with the motion. A smile stretched across my face, and I feared it'd be permanent. *I was going to remember this moment for as long as I lived.*

Reluctantly, it was time to stop the cart. Or we'd miss the valley entirely.

When the cart came to a halt, and she opened her eyes, tears swelled the rims. "Thank you, Deryn."

We spent the next hour touring Brendan's settlement. They offered us free food and clothing, but both of us were stuck in the familiarity of what we liked to wear and declined their offer. But the food, oh we ate the food.

Eventually, we stopped, and she stared up at the black castle across the Galeairy.

"I don't know where I'm from," she said finally, finishing the last bite of meat a street merchant offered us.

"Then it's a perfect time to start anew."

She bit her lip.

"Don't look at the castle too long," came the voice of the street merchant. A husky big fellow who I could tell talked more than he thought. "Sometimes there's a figure, there in that window, that just stares at us from across the waters. For days on end."

The meat became hard to swallow, and I had a feeling I knew who that figure was.

Val gave a small smile as she said, "She needs to see you surviving. It'll remind her she has to, too."

I heard them talking sometimes—when my sister wasn't screaming insults at me—how a beautiful fae saved their friend's body from a block of frozen ice using rain gutters and buckets. And I really didn't know the extent of the horrors she'd faced. So I turned to possibly the strongest fae on the island and said, "Thank you."

She blinked at me with big, innocent eyes. "For what?"

"For saving Blackwater when I didn't have the courage." *When I was hiding in my tower,* I wanted to say. *When I knew where I was from and ran, anyway.*

Valentina laughed. "Kaderyn made Adrian angry, and he took away the shielding rain over the town. I hardly did anything."

"His rain left them isolated, unable to thrive. It wasn't living—not really. They were able to see what life was like outside of a god's protection. Hiding in safety isn't living. I'm seeing that now."

And as we shared a look, I hoped this Siphon would visit the Mainland more. It was nice having another female to talk to, but I didn't know how to ask her to come back, and I was too afraid of her rejecting me, that I said nothing as I walked her back to Fillagree Fen.

Maybe one day I'd have the courage to make a friend.

Until then, I had Adrian.

I SPUN AROUND, WATCHING THE DEMIGOD SWIRL HIS glass of wine, tipping it almost until its contents spilled. Whatever happened between Adrian and me, we both stuffed it down. He went back to telling me of the recent fae he played tricks on and drank his wine as he passed me tools. I went back to pretending I didn't miss his closeness almost more than Rhett's.

"Is someone . . . knocking?"

"Hmm?" Adrian shrugged. "Don't ask me, I never knock."

Minutes later, I hefted open my iron door at the base of the tower to the sight of my sister on the other side.

I'd taken so long in answering that she'd moved back toward the valley.

"I didn't know if you saw me and just . . . chose not to answer." She wrung her hands.

I cleared my throat, trying to feign my surprise. "It's noisy in my workshop—I mean, workshop. Is everything in Brendan all right?" I looked over her shoulder, but all seemed quiet and sleepy in the valley. "Is Breena safe?"

The moon was high, and I was too tired for a fight.

"Is this what your leg is made of?" she asked, poking the outer shell of my tower with a tentative finger. "It smells funny."

Here we go. I sighed. "Do you need something, Avika?"

"No, I mean, yes. The town is fine. I just wanted to thank you for looking out for Breena today."

We stared at each other in a standoff with weapons of mass destruction locked and ready. A simple sway of a breeze would change the direction of the conversation. But I had a great day with Valentina, and I didn't want to ruin it, so I leaned my head against my metal doorframe and said, "I'm sorry."

"Me too," she answered, far quicker than I expected, dropping her hands.

"Come in for a rest. It's a long walk back at this time of night."

And she gradually stepped into my tower; Apprehensive, like the entire thing was going to come down on her.

"Oh, Avika!" Adrian shouted from over the railing. "Coming for the party?"

"I used to wonder where you'd run off to," she answered with her hands on her hips. "All those times you'd come to Blackwater; you couldn't have mentioned that Deryn was alive?"

"Der-yn . . . Der-yn? Never heard of her." Adrian flashed a wide white infectious smile and disappeared above. "Now come along, my dearest Deryn, I was almost done with my story about the shrew running loose at Fillagree Fen port yesterday. You should have *seen* the pixies trying to catch it with a bucket."

I looked to Avika, regrettably, but ushered her up the stairs. "There's no stopping him."

HOURS LATER, DEEP INTO THE EARLY MORNING, AFTER she'd filled me in on the history of Blackwater I'd missed, Breena's birth, and gossip from the pixie port, she looked around the room and said, "I've never seen anything like it. This is really something, Deryn."

Bristling under the scrutiny, I didn't know how to take her praise. My nose stung and my chest hurt. "Thank you."

"Look at all this, even." She faced my wall of trinkets. "You've been busy."

I glanced at the Faemech sitting in crates behind her. "You have no idea."

"Are you joining the war?" she asked, nodding to the large wall of swords I'd been making since the faeless took to the valley.

And if she had asked me when we first took Teal's ship over here, I would have turned away, retreated at the very mention of it, but now a box of powders sat in the corner at her feet, detonators beside them. Could my inventions keep Rhett safe? It's what he wanted from me, and I feared he was going to dive in, whether anyone helped him or not.

Adrian grew quiet on the other side of the room.

"I don't know," I whispered, truthfully. Because I really was a terrible liar. "There's fae that care about the faeless. Enough to start a war with the other courts, too."

Avika frowned like she was thinking but her jaw was set. She hefted an iron sword off the wall but struggled and the tip of it banged into the floor. "They're heavy." She looked up at me, eyes wide, then to my shoulders and arms, which I knew were twice the size of hers.

There was nothing dainty about iron-wielding.

"They have to be to break those bronze daggers at your waist." An insignia of a howling wolf's head in an outline of a beast's paw was stamped into their handles.

"I didn't understand before. Not really," Avika said, nodding down to my iron foot.

I skidded it behind me.

"Thank the gods you're alive."

"Yes," I said, looking at the demigod lounging on my daybed, with his damn legs on my table. "Thank the gods."

Adrian's eyes sparkled, and he tipped his glass up.

I shuttled Avika down my tracks to the valley, stopping halfway so she could climb down the support beam. I waited in the early morning light until she reached the edge of town before cranking the cart toward the Twin Peak Mountains. Because I knew what iron looked like when it rusted shut and that door Breena found was not it. Something was still nagging in my gut.

What was hidden behind the door in the mountain?

32

VALENTINA

"What do you mean you're going to Summer?" Kade growled from the hallway.

Visiting the town of Brendan and riding on Deryn's tracks reminded me to move forward. I had gotten stuck in my head with all that had happened, and it reminded me I was still alive. Still able to make forward progress. "You have your truths you need to find out, Kaderyn. I have mine."

Kaderyn limped into view, smelling of herbs. "I'm not letting you go alone. Especially if you're going to Summer *fucking* Court. Roshan could have helped us up on that cliffside and he didn't."

"I know," I breathed.

"They have a fire lit under their asses, Valentina. They have centuries to make up for being the weakest court. They will not be lenient on trespassers."

"Does this mean you're not coming?" I asked, strapping on my boots.

Shadows pulled my laces out of my hands and finished the ties I'd started. "I can't fade us there. Roshan will know."

I nodded. "Then we'll ride. I'll get the horses ready."

"Listen, little lion. I love that you're feeling better and more like yourself. Just hold on until I can arrange for Jairek's to come. I don't trust these lords and ladys."

"It's almost summer solstice," I shouted from the hallway. "I want to be there and gone before the sun hits its position in the sky. I don't want Summer stronger than they need to be."

You're sexy when you're bossy, Kade mindspoke, because I left him brooding in our rooms.

You have an hour to get Jairek here before I leave by myself, I mindspoke back. There was something I had to do.

I was returning to Willowspeak. Where it all started.

I held the reins of two horses as they ate meadowgrass at my feet, a black stallion and a brown mare that reminded me so much of Malvasia I couldn't rightly look at her for any length of time.

Kade had three minutes to appear before I left without him. I bit my lip and lay a hand on my uneasy stomach. I wanted company, but I worried if Kade had healed enough. *Damn,* I thought. *I should have gone to Oir and told her my plans. She'd command Kaderyn not to come.*

Maybe I could just grab Jairek . . . I thought as Kaderyn rounded the side of the gardens atop Deathmarch flanked by the golden shifter in lion form.

"She's going to cause a scene." I nodded to the massive black mare with shadows dancing off her but then looked to Kade, who, at all times, had shadows swirling close to his body and Jair, shaking out his golden mane. "Never mind, let's go."

Not half a day's ride and we rode into the square courtyard of Willowspeak in Summer Court. Shadows helped us move across the deep canyon between the courts, now with a rushing river down as far as the eye could see.

I pressed a hand to my chest, willing my heart to settle itself. Everything was exactly the same. *Gods, why did it have to look the same?* I avoided the sight of Ms. Multhorn's alderwood porch. My stomach threatened to heave, even thinking about it. A part of me knew I wouldn't still see the frozen bodies huddled there with my father's hand reaching to the sun, to Angus, but I wasn't risking it.

Angus, I scowled.

There, in the center of the courtyard, looking no worse for wear, was the statue of Summer's revered god, Angus, the God of Love. Sculpted from white marble, he sparkled gloriously in the bright sun.

I hopped off the black stallion as Jair shifted into fae form. Kade circled us on Deathmarch, warning anyone from getting too close.

"What's the plan here, Valentina?" Jair asked, lighthearted, but his back stayed to mine. Watching. I pulled on his lion-hearted bravery and pressed my hands to the cobblestone at my feet. It was heated by the sun. And it was as if I could see little six-year-old me's hands outlined on my now larger ones, eternally glamoured to hide the scars from my travels.

The townsfae watched us warily and with good reason. How could a fae like me now have ever come from this small town?

I stood and brushed a fallen mango tree leaf from the statue of Angus's toe. The ones I pressed myself upon when I was six . . .

I turned briefly, looking for Kaderyn, hoping I would find the strength to hold back my tears. To hold back my anger. But in turning around, I faced Ms. Multhorn's porch. The railing. The vine-lined wall. The corner that Winter Court sectioned off the faeless and froze them solid. Roshan's parents and sister. My father.

Anger bloomed like the rising sun. I turned and harnessed the magic in the courtyard. Kade's shadows, Jair's shifter magic, and the water magic from the crowds. I hooked my hands around the statue's calves and shoved violently backward. Water and shadows leaked off my hands like I was bleeding black and, with one last push, the statue smashed to the ground, scattering chunks of marble to the cobblestoned courtyard.

And if the fae of Willowspeak avoided us before, they sure couldn't now.

A few fae came out, hands raised, magic pulsing off them.

"Why'd you come here?"

"Who are you?"

"Look, it's the King!"

"He's shadows."

"It's the Wild Hunt."

Whispers threaded the air.

"Send for the army. This won't stand anymore."

"The Star will do something about this."

Kaderyn hopped down off Deathmarch as if he wasn't recently mauled by Cillian. The air charged with magic, but I didn't want to fight Willowspeak.

"I expected that behavior from him," came a smooth voice from behind us, "but not you."

Through the growing hostile crowd came a male in gold

clothing. His honeyed hair flipped around itself like waves at the shore. Something about him was off. Godlike.

His statue did not do him justice.

"Angus, that's about far enough," Kaderyn warned, materializing his shadowsword. Careful to stand before me and hide his limp when he moved.

"Oh, you'll give me lessons on going too far?" Angus chuckled, so good-naturedly in the moment's tension that it bloomed anger in my chest. "How's the Underworld these days? Rumors say there's a massive crack running through it. Broke the barrier between this world and yours for her."

"And I'll break the one between yours and this one if you come any closer," Kade threatened.

Angus shoved his hands in white-lined pockets and squinted up into the sun.

"You won't take her from me," Kade growled, but even I heard the desperation.

Angus laughed again. "Why would I go and do something like that? I *made* her for you."

My head grew dizzy.

Kade looked at me, eyes wide, then back to Angus, before dropping his head and his defensive stance. His sword dematerialized. "Oh, for *fuck's sake*, Angus. What did you do?"

Angus hopped up on the statue's base, the one smashed to pieces at our feet. Townsfolk bowed down at him as he sat on the pedestal. "Valentina is godborn. She was created, sparked into existence. Like you and I, Kaderyn."

My throat closed, and my neck burned. "No, I'm not. I had a father."

"Oh sure, I gave your tiny body to him to look after. To hide in this small riverside town."

"But why *him*?" I cried. "Mrs. Treelear lived next door. She was the strongest fae in town. She could have protected me. She could have saved me from so much pain." Not begged a six-year-old to take away his pain as he died. "Why him?" I cried again and slashed at the tears on my cheeks. "Why did you give me to Father?"

Angus's voice was soft and slow as he said, "You needed to love a faeless."

"But it broke my heart," I confessed, black tears ran down my face and fell to the sun-heated cobblestone.

"I know," Angus said with such sincerity that I dropped to my knees and cuddled my stomach. "I placed a Siphon on Eadha. One who could use all the magic the island had to offer. Or none, if that was the company she chose."

"Why?" Jair snapped.

"Because the faeless were dying, and they needed"—Angus peered down at me, eyes shining—"*help*," he finished.

I heaved into the ground, forehead pressing down. Some vague realization that it might have looked like I was praying. And maybe I was. Not to Angus, but to the truth being revealed.

Because I was the help.

"The faeless were dying," Angus repeated. "The Hunt was broken. The Hunter was losing hope, and no one was challenging it because no one cared."

"I care," I whispered, sand blowing out from my words.

"I know, *sweetheart*." Angus's words were soothing like the river, easing through the parts of me that felt broken. "I know."

And I didn't know how long we stayed like that with Willowspeak townsfolk gawking, Kade with his head tipped back, Jair laying in the sun like he was sunbathing, Angus sitting on his broken pedestal and me . . . surrendering to the truth about what I was and what my purpose was for.

The sun rippled off Jairek's hair and we all watched as he turned his face up to the bright beams.

"Summer looks good on you, Jairek," Angus beamed, prideful.

"Yet, it's Winter that's on my mind," Jairek answered, refusing to look at Kaderyn and me.

Eventually, I leaned up. "But how did you know I would warn Cillian about Autumn attacking Blackwater? Nothing would have changed if I hadn't said something to him."

A large bumblebee landed on Angus's shoulder. "Because that is who you are."

"You knew Valentina and I would cross paths?" Kade growled. "How did you know I would save her from Mohr?"

To this, Angus' eyes turned hard as he looked at Kade. "I didn't. You're a stubborn, unpredictable bastard." He gave a small smile. "But the island was deteriorating, and I was out of options. Lord Aborys was hunting down faeless. He calls them a blight when they are simply—*next*. Some of the other gods wanted to wipe the island clean of faeless and fae altogether. Start over. But I had faith."

"In what?" Kade scoffed.

"In her," Angus drawled, pointing at me.

The faeless, though beautiful, were not like the stars in the sky or the crystals of the earth like the way the fae were. There was nothing sharp and jagged about their features. Or Otherworldly. Instead, they looked of the earth itself. Like windswept wanderers, with hands deep in dirt. Broken nailed. Freckled. Sunkissed and flawed. The gods wanted this. The faeless were meant to survive.

"You are not *alone*, Valentina. You are Summerfae, clearly," Angus said to the black water pooling around me. "You are shadows, and fire, and wind and ice. Perhaps shifter, if the desperation calls for it. Even faeless, around the right company. You can choose when all this is over, what you want to be. Not what's needed of you."

"But until then?" I asked.

"Until then—"

But, *oh gods*, his eyes grew wide, more vulnerable than Kade's.

"—I'm going to ask you to be brave."

And I picked myself up; up out of a puddle of black shadow-soaked water, up out of my despair at the death on my hands, and I sucked in a deep breath for what I still had to do.

Kade loomed close.

I felt it now. That deep-seated desire to help others was not my weakness. Taking away others' pain did not make me frail. It made me strong.

"Power comes from belief," Angus added with parting words before he dissolved in beams of scorching hot sunlight.

"In which god?" Jair demanded now by my side, chest puffed and desperate.

"In yourself," came a whisper.

33

DERYN IRONSIDE

If this was just an ogre trail for them to pee in the sea . . . I swear, Deryn, I berated myself. But I had to find out what that door was for. Having an escape route was smart, but it was clear that those hinges had been well used. And the path from the waters—well worn.

I ducked around.

But *by my iron ore*, I wanted it to be stuck. I wanted this to be nothing more than a random door in a random mountain, but I was old, and I knew better. Lady Fede told Valentina that it was a female who organized Kade's demise. And that she was right under Shadow's noses. Valentina thought it was Oir, and I had a sinking feeling it wasn't herbs keeping Lord Brexton under.

But a spell.

So I wanted the door to be rusted shut from sea and metal. I wanted to apologize to Carmen for prying the next time I saw her.

I moved a hefty rock wedged near the base of the door aside

and my heart sunk when it swung with ease and banged against the mountainside.

Empty tunnels spewed out like tines on a fork. Black iron support beams held up the cave roof, dented with ogre fists like the rest. But these beams didn't have my brackets or my bolts. She didn't risk me knowing about this place to install them.

"Help me! Help!"

I froze, my guiding palm flat against the cool damp stone, and clenched my hammer in the other hand. I didn't want to look. My heart rattled against my ribs like it wanted to burst right through.

But I turned. There, in cages lining the back wall of a cavernous opening, were fae locked in chains.

"Oh, by my iron ore, Carmen, what have you done?" I covered my mouth with my hand, trying to block out the stench. I blinked then blinked again, desperate to shun away the sight now.

Each cubed iron cell held a fae from a different court. Summerfae lay in a puddle of water, pooling in the stone crevices below her, shackled to the wall with iron chains corroding her skin. The Springfae with matted streaks of silver hair, no longer able to glamour it away, looked up at me with a vacant glance. The telltale golden eyes from Autumn, perhaps the most lively of them all. And the last, the farthest cage, an aged Winterfae with white hair and features so slight it made my eyes water, lay motionless.

They were rotting away down here, surrounded by iron.

I stumbled backward, tripping on a jagged rock. My iron tower was designed to keep the fae out. Carmen used iron to keep the fae *in*.

"Get me out, you dumb female." The Autumnfae coughed, spitting blood against the ground.

I pulled the pieces of myself back together and lumbered to his cage.

"Hurry up, before they come back," he urged.

Why would she do this? I pulled my hammer and bashed at the lock. The crashing of iron on iron was never subtle, and I cursed when it bent but didn't break. *I need the key . . . or fire.* "You need to melt the lock. Hey, look at me. You can melt this."

"She steals our magic! Iron cripples us. Don't you think I tried it? Go find someone more useful."

But my mind was mush, and I would not be yelled at anymore. *How could she do this?* I pressed a hand to my chest. *This wasn't real. This couldn't be real.* "Shut. Up. I can't think straight when you keep opening your mouth." He was bound to call all kinds of things down.

And sure enough, footsteps echoed down the far tunnel.

"Shh. Quiet. Don't say I'm here," I whispered. Hoping I could put my trust in a loud-mouthed firefae, I lunged around a fallen beam and rock debris. But my heart fell to my knees when I heard the slight accent of Springfae. I knew that voice.

It haunted my every waking moment.

"That bitch clawed my foot, then Cillian pushed us out into the waters. Ouch! Not so hard," Lady Fede said from somewhere down the back tunnel. Her voice bounced off the walls. Sheer panic made me bolt for the door, willing to swim across Galeairy just to escape her.

"The irony of this situation is not lost on me," I heard Carmen say. "It's completely gone, Fede. Let me stitch it properly."

I froze and ducked down around the corner, cursing the iron door when it banged against the mountainside. *But could I leave the fae to die in their cells?* It was the pixies all over again.

"If you leave me here," hissed the Autumnfae, "I'll scream for them. I'll call them right to you."

I grunted, cursing the mouths on Autumnfae.

Lady Fede snapped, "Cillian fought me the whole way down the fucking cliffside, too."

Uncontrollable trembling racked through my body, and I bit the soft skin of my hand to stop my teeth from clattering together.

Carmen's voice jeered. "I warned you. I said that dog would turn on you, didn't I?"

"But for her?! Some damn gods' gift he is."

"He doesn't know what he does in Berserker form. He'd slaughter his mother if he had one," Carmen said, and the gentle clinking of metal against metal echoed out.

"Speaking of mothers, stop taking Spring Court's fae. It's making me look incompetent. At least take one with no family to whine to me about and rally the swine in the streets."

"It takes a lot of magic to sneak into fae courts, Fede. The stronger the fae, the longer they last in my cells. Not just any old vagabond will do!"

The door banged again in a passing breeze, and I missed part of their conversation.

"And my damn pixies have fluttered away. The Hunt is back, Carmen, and he knows I was involved. He knows what I did."

"You didn't mention me, did you? Fede, did you tell him what I've done?"

"Oh, stop. They don't suspect you. There's a benefit to being alone, I suppose. But what about the Hunt? We need to break it again."

"I cannot change that Bivanna's bite only dropped Kaderyn fae and not dead. I cannot change that *he* only split and hid his shadows."

"You'd do well to share my fear of the Underworld, witch. There is no rest in the next life for creatures like us."

"I'm not fae, Fede. I've seen things even death will retreat from. I've done things to earn my swift placement in the worst of the depths, and the things I've yet to do will not grant me any favors."

"I say we kill them all," Fede snarled. "Anyone who knows it was us. Kaderyn can't have our souls if we don't die."

The door banged again.

"I need to cauterize this wound. It's too large."

"Do it," Lady Fede said.

And the caves erupted with her screams and an acrid fleshy smell seeped through the tunnels. I sobbed into the dirt, covering my ears as her shrieks echoed off the rock face and screeched into my soul. The firefae writhed on the ground behind the iron bars.

"There. Done. Now get off my Mainland and don't let anyone see you. I don't want anyone snooping around."

"You're always so pleasant, Carmen." Lady Fede's voice was out of breath.

A distant door swung against the frame, and I froze for longer than I needed to. I needed to get the fae out without them knowing. Maybe I could get Teal and her pirates? Or signal to Rhett?

I spent a good deal of time crouched down while the Autumnfae hurled insults at me before I felt it safe to move again. But I was only one faeless.

"I'm going to get help," I hissed to the firefae and headed the way I came. The sunlight shone through the doorway like a beacon.

He started his insults again. "You cowardly useless—"

"This is truly unfortunate," Carmen said, darkening my path.

My stomach fell, my heart smashed against my ribs. I pressed a hand against my satchel. *My hammer.*

"See, Deryn? You must place the rock behind the door, or it thumps loudly against the mountainside. It turns out I do not share your skills as an iron welder and my measurements were slightly off when I built it. But you can see why I couldn't exactly let you do it for me. Don't you?"

"How could you do this, Carmen?" I slowly backed up, shuffling my iron leg.

"I am a witch, Deryn. We don't get by with friends and siblings. I was skewering rats for food, my body broken, until luck fell onto the shoreline in the form of a broken faeless from Spring."

"You and Lady Fede broke the Wild Hunt. Why?"

"I tried, foolish female. I tried to abide by earthly rules. But there are places that scare even me, and the Hunter's Underworld is one of them."

"You're afraid of death?"

"There is a Hunter there, the one who brings the nightmares, and I am not naive enough to believe he won't do his worst with me. I had to break the Hunt. I'd rather my soul languish for eternity in the earth's soil than in the Hunter's halls."

"But you're killing those fae, Carmen. They're dying!" Snot ran down my nose. I backed up again.

"Once my days were no longer numbered, once Kaderyn fell from the skies, once I had the freedom to live as I chose, I learned I could sustain my life on the essence of fae. Iron made their magic leach from them, and I figured out how to absorb it."

"You sent me away to the far side of the island. You wanted privacy to do this." I pointed to the cages now behind me.

"Yes, but it wasn't on purpose, Deryn. Once I had you

huddled safe far away from me, that's when the first Summerfae came to our shores. They bathed in the shallows, trying to get a glimpse of the newly formed Shadow Court, I think. And I gave them fair warning, Deryn. I warned them that the Mainland was not safe, and I tried to tell the sweet Summerfae to go, but at the end of the day . . ." She opened her arms wide. "I am what I am. I could feel her magic dripping off her near our iron rich mountain. I wanted to capture it. So, I chained her in here."

"Summerfae was the first to go missing?" I looked back at the water pooling under the fae now.

"A sweet thing, too. Water magic was the first I learned to use. But they die quickly if they aren't strong enough and she only lasted a month. When one dies off, I capture another."

"How did you break the Hunt?"

"I didn't. I just needed to find the ones that could. I kept up my end of the bargain with *him* and Fede. I made a spell so strong, old Lord Brexton's mind went to mush. All she needed to do was to go back to her roots, convince her sister to start the events. Lure and bite the Hunter."

"Carmen, you don't understand. Lord Aborys thinks the other fae are doing it. He's slaughtered faeless for centuries because they couldn't save the Lady of Winter."

Carmen moved to the last cell, to the white-haired fae barely breathing on its floor. "Embee was so strong for so long. I've never captured a fae like her since. Say hi, Embee."

"Who else? You said, *him*?"

She smiled then. "*I* needed the Hunt broken, and *he* needed a safe haven for a mangled faeless. When Kaderyn was laying there, sightless and broken after Bivanna bit him, *he* tore his shadows apart. I wasn't planning on Kaderyn becoming fae for good, though. If I had *his* strength, I would have torn Kaderyn's physical body to shreds. It's what I asked of *him*, but he does what he wants. Comes and goes as he pleases, as you know. I should have known he'd make a game of it. A foolery of my situation. When I found out what he had done, that he'd only split and hid Kaderyn's shadows and not killed the Hunter for good, I almost strangled the one-legged fae at my doorstep."

Me.

"But your quick creation of iron from ore became too great. Became a great way to keep the fae away. Even as I stole them for their usefulness."

"Get away from me!" I screamed, and the trapped fae in the cells retreated from the sound. Beat and broken.

A caw of a hawk outside filled me with hope. Rhett was here. I scrambled out of her grasp, smashing my hammer against her staff. I needed to break it, rid her of her magic.

She followed me as I ran.

"Your unagreeable lover came snooping around. Really tested the limits of my walking stick. Afraid I pulled too much magic from the Springfae trying to subdue him."

I ran faster, whipped around sharp corners, heart racing in my ears. If I could just get to Rhett . . .

"I think all those visits to your tower make him more immune to iron than the rest," she called.

I strapped the harness on tighter across my chest. He'd take us out of here. I had to tell Kaderyn it was Carmen who broke the Wild Hunt.

"Come here, Deryn," Carmen sang as we neared the iron door. "Don't make this more difficult. I warned you not to go snooping around in my caves."

Wrinkled eyes looked up over an outcrop of rock, and she blasted fire at the stone. "You think you're safe out there? Subduing Rhett with fae's magic was not so hard, but pouring the Citrine Tonic into his mouth was another matter entirely."

I burst through the rusted iron door and froze. *What did*

she say about Citrine Tonic? I craned my neck to search the skies for Rhett.

Her voice grew louder. "Spring uses citrine to succumb fae to their very basic of instincts, I hear Shadowfae drink small bits of it like an alcohol, but I wonder what a gallon of citrine poured down a hawk's mouth will do when he sees a juicy *rabbit*."

Suddenly, a blast of water blew me out the door and to the hard ground. Carmen's grayed and wrinkled face stood over me and I crawled backward.

"But you're so much meeker than that, so how about . . . *a mouse*." Her deranged eyes shot wide.

I screamed and dove over the rock edge as magic hit me.

"You should have stayed to your side of the Mainland, Deryn."

I tumbled, arms tingling, legs shrinking, head pounding. The taste of blood coated my tongue as I bit my lip with pointed incisors and looked down the bridge of a nose not my own.

"I gave you everything you asked for. Ore-mined and space. But you saw too much. I'll tell Adrian his pinning was for nothing. I'll tell him you finally agreed to run away to the Courtless with your hawkshifter."

I scrambled out of drapings of cloth, knocking free the mirror I used to signal to Rhett. I caught a brief glance at my reflection in the tumbling dirty lens and scampered back through the armhole of my shirt. My harness was now twenty sizes too big and meant for a faeless, not a . . . not a . . .

"And your hawk will drive a sword through himself when he realizes that the tasty mouse he snacked on was his cowardly lonely little faeless, Deryn Ironside."

A boot smashed down, and I bolted, rolling as fast as I

could. I scrambled out of the neck hole. Carmen's foot came down again.

"Run, little mouse. Don't keep your lover waiting," she taunted.

A gust of wind smelling like Springfae magic blew across the mountainside, blowing the mirror and me down again. We bounced off rocks and through meadow weeds.

A caw echoed across the skies.

Hide! Hide!

With no way to signal to Teal, no way to let Kaderyn know who broke the Hunt, no way to tell Adrian. . . *oh*, Adrian.

Claws snapped shut, pulling up tuffs of grass around me. I scrambled again, through crevices, through mole holes and ones made by creatures bigger than me, but the hawk didn't relent.

Rhett was going to eat me.

34

VALENTINA

"Valentina, there's a pressing matter"—Oir burst into the library, hair untucked from her braid—"I need you to come with me."

I closed the book I was reading on Eadha's artifacts and quickly met her at the door. But could I trust her? She'd never given me a reason not to, but . . . "Where's Kade?"

"He'll meet up with us shortly."

I turned back to where I was sitting and clicked my tongue, calling the three hounds to my sides. "I'm ready now." I sent her a look of warning.

Lady Fede said her other accomplice in splitting the Hunt was close to Shadow Court. Just how *close* was close? Oir and Juniper Hatch were most skilled in deadly plants, being a healer and a spice runner, and now this one was beckoning me away with her.

Oir raised an eyebrow at Dormar behind me. "My shoes were found buried in the gardens. Do I even have to ask which one of you it was?"

Dormar wagged his tail.

Oir's eyes narrowed. "I thought so."

We headed for the side door that attached Auris' tavern to the castle. Which wasn't so bad except that through the tavern, you could exit into Auris and travel to the docks and beyond. If she was trying to lure me away, it was the perfect getaway.

"Where are we going?" I paused just before the tavern door. It was completely dark. But I knew Kaderyn, and he'd never let the tavern close down.

She ushered me in. "Almost there, after you."

We stared each other down.

Kade trusted her, but I didn't know her. The only maternal figure I ever knew used me. "Heel," I commanded to Gal and Lolo and kept Dormar at my back.

But if stubbornness was a full hand of matching shadowanimals, Oir would have me beat.

I sighed, but locked up my senses and pulled her shadows to me. Leaving her but with wisps. The corners of her mouth upturned, but she stood defiant, holding the door.

I took one step into the dark tavern, my senses on edge, ready to pull my daggers when—

Things exploded overtop my head. I pulled my daggers in half a second, ready to thrust into the closest enemy as the lights flicked on.

"Surprise! Happy birthday, Valentina." But Jairek's voice was half-strangled from the shadows I had laced tight around his throat.

I halted the gods' dagger inches from Kade's neck. Teal tossed another bucket of shredded napkins overtop my head like confetti. And I cursed at Kade profusely. "Has your brain been minced? I almost killed you!"

The shadows I sent out around Jairek's neck loosened as he said, "Oir, you were supposed to take her daggers."

Kade, with one finger, pushed the dagger down and retreated the shadows into him.

"She was ready to use them on me. I wasn't touching them." Oir raised her hands and backed away. "If you need anything else, I'm in the back. Happy Birthday, Valentina. I thank Angus for bringing you to us." She smiled.

"It was me. I brought her to us," Kade growled, ushering me into a booth.

But I was smiling, and the adrenaline fizzled from my body.

Fwoof! Fwoof! Teal danced in the air around us, tossing more confetti until Kade confiscated her bucket of shredded paper.

"What's going on?" I asked.

Big loopy smiles graced the lot of them.

"We're celebrating your birthday."

"But I don't . . . I don't even know when my birthday is."

"I know, but it's the first day of Summer's reign and though you are shadows, it is without a doubt that you—with your warmth and big heart and love—came from Angus." But even as he said so, a ring of shadows stayed locked around my wrist.

I raised an eyebrow at Kade.

If he's seeing this, I don't want him getting any ideas, he mindspoke to me.

The bartender brought out a cake and a raw chunk of meat for Teal.

And I looked at the three of them—my family.

We all bore scars of our travels; Kade's had nail marks on his chest from when he tried to claw out his beating heart, claw marks from a Berserker, and welts on his hand when he tried to pick up the iron key. All hidden under glamour. Jairek's back, minced by me and a whip, and a scar on his stomach from Helle's holly wood arrow hid under his clothing. Teal's scars the most visible of all, with an intricately decorated metal arm.

And me; my insides like glass were slowly coming together again.

"Thank you. Not just for this, but for saving me in Autumn Court. For taking me in."

Shadows slunk out, carrying a tray of something from the back, and my mouth watered. I knew that smell anywhere across Eadha.

Honey pastries!

I licked my lips. "How much extra did this cost you? I'm surprised the *Star* let you buy them at all." I cringed.

"Now's not the time
to query stolen desserts from Summer's lord.
And do please ignore the wanted posters
From our neighbors seeking a reward
For the ship that sailed into their port
And stole sweets like these sorts
Leaving their shores in proper discord."

"You stole them, Teal?" I dropped a half-eaten dessert to the plate.

She looked me dead in the eyes with no remorse as she snapped, "You're welcome."

I laughed as her pirate hat fell over her eyes. We were lucky Teal, and her bandits were on our side.

"I still can't believe Lady Fede and Bivanna were sisters," Jair said, shoving the empty plate away. "And Lady Fede promised Bivanna a place in her court if she bit Kaderyn?"

"Yes."

"But why would Lady Fede want the Hunt disbanded?"

"She didn't seem to care, to be honest. She wanted something from whoever did, though. Lord Brexton seems to be under some type of . . . something. Medicine? Wish? Who knows, no one's seen him since he fell ill. He could be dead for all we know."

"You think an herb from our court? The young Shadowfae have taken a liking to Citrine Tonic from Spring. They take it in small doses, eases their worries, they say."

"Oh, Oir must love that. Young Shadowfae trading with Spring."

"What are they trading?" I asked. "What are they giving from our court?"

"I don't know, but the Hunt gets broken and Lord Brexton of Spring falls ill. It can't be coincidence. Lord Aborys accused me of as much in Blackwater."

"You think someone from Shadow Court helped?"

Oir was the oldest, wisest, and it turned my gut to ask, but I thought Kade too blinded to see it. "What was Oir doing in the fields the day you fell, Kade?"

He shut me down quickly. "It's not Oir. She pulled me from the caves and took care of me when I couldn't look after myself."

My trust in others had disintegrated. In myself, even more so. Though I was learning to trust myself again. "Your spice runner?" I offered.

"Juniper Hatch is perfectly harmless," Jair answered, shoveling half of Teal's untouched cake into his mouth.

"She'd have enough stock to warrant a trade with Spring. She could've given Lady Fede something to poison Lord Brexton." Kade contemplated this. "She keeps a boat, *The Sea Barrel 2* in the shallows of the Galeairy Strait east of here. If she's not at her store, she'll be there."

"Juniper Hatch is more concerned with the dwindling numbers of Lunatillos in the Courtless' mandrake leaves than any kind of poison or even court proceedings. Plus, you still haven't apologized for stealing her boat, the *Sea Barrel 1*, and leaving it in a nuckelavee den. She needs an apology from you before an accusation," Jair defended.

"I'll go visit her," Kade promised. "But first I must return to the Underworld. Something has my Hunters in a mess. Zedekiel keeps sighing through our bond, telling me to come as soon as I can." Kade swallowed a mouthful of Solanci.

I knocked him with the back of my hand. "What are you doing sitting here eating cake?! They need you."

Celebrating you is important to me, Val, he said through mindspeak but to the table, he said, "They aren't in danger. They just feel . . . confused. Maybe one of them wished a baliroq into the castle grounds."

I laughed. "They'd be more confused by a cute little pixie than a baliroq." They'd know just what to do with a beast like a baliroq. A small, blue-skinned rhyming pixie, though? I didn't think so.

Not long later, something bad must have happened in the Underworld because Kade grew motionless, black eyes unfocused, and we urged him to go. Teal raced off to the docks with cake stuffed into her pockets, saying she was going fishing. And Jairek returned to the Courtless as he was spending more time there since Kade got hurt. Something seemed to shift in him and the Shadowfae of Auris whispered behind their hands about the return of the King of the Courtless. In the meantime, I was going to find this *Sea Barrel 2*. I sure didn't owe Juniper Hatch any apology.

I followed the shoreline along toward the mountains that separated the Courtless and Shadow Court when there, below the steep incline, was a small wooden boat identical to the one we used in Spring Court's nuckelavee cave. *Sea Barrel 2,* it said scrawled on the side as it bobbed in the small wake of the shallows tied to a stake on shore.

Damn, she wasn't here. I sat down in a patch of weeds, cursing myself for not checking her store first. Despite feeling like myself again, I didn't want to walk through Auris with the constant stares.

I squinted out over the Galeairy to the growing town. I couldn't make out who was who, but a big sign *The Sunny Bramble* could be seen as the bright summer sun stayed longer in the sky during Summer's cycle. It was Glynnera's shop, the seamstress from Blackwater Junction who helped Kade and me before Winter rode in. But now the word *Sunny* was visible, the wooden plank that once covered it had been removed. I smiled.

They really were thriving.

Deryn's tower sat near the shore, straight across from where I rested. Smoke rose from behind it, and I wondered if she was smelting iron.

Further along, Teal's Fillagree Fen port lit up with movement. The pixies appeared like fruit flies from here, but my gods, they were busy and determined little things.

Then there were the Twin Peak Mountains, where the witch commanded the ogres.

Something shone brightly down along the far mountain face. Something brief but blinding and when I blinked, it was gone.

I stood up, squinting. *What was that?*

There it was again! A flash of light shining off the sun's rays.

Deryn told me she'd signal to Rhett across to the Courtless with a small pocket mirror attached to a string. That was how she got his attention.

My spine tingled. It could be nothing. But Oir had told us Lady Fede was last seen in the mountain waters. And when I squinted really hard, a hawk was diving into the rocks near the flashing mirror.

Another flash.

Something was wrong.

My feet thudded against the soft ground as I took off running back toward Auris. Once I felt even the slight fog of Shadowfae magic, I pulled as much as I could until I had enough to shadowfade to Inkravere Port, hoping Teal was still fishing with cake.

It was spotty, and I crashed to my knees on waterlogged docks, scaring a pair of shadowgulls up into the sky. Within seconds, small pixie-sized daggers were at my throat.

I pulled the red dagger from my back. "Bring me to Teal."

She must have heard us because she popped up from below the docks and shoved a fish into her pocket.

"Teal, I need a ride across to the mountains. Fast."

"Stand down ya scallywags.
A ride to the mountains, you say?
Get aboard, oh don't bother her with pay."

"But around the backside, Teal. I don't want to be seen." I sheathed the dagger and pushed strands of hair out of my face. "I think Deryn's in trouble."

35

VALENTINA

The Mountain loomed overhead. *Why did it look larger than normal?*

Teal spewed off a rhyme about coming with me, but the last thing I wanted was her near ogres.

"Stay with the ship, Teal! We might need a quick getaway."

I flew up a well-used set of stairs behind the Twin Peak Mountains, two at a time, red and yellow dagger at the ready. Until before me was the door we'd seen chasing off the HorCain. The one Breena felt uneasy about. I felt magic run through my bones again and gripped the daggers harder. Something wasn't right. I cursed myself. I should have investigated it sooner.

Did I risk calling out for Deryn?

"Deryn!" I whisper-hissed.

Something about this door felt like a trap. I circled back around to where I saw the mirror tumbling down the mountainside. Clawing through grasses, I searched for it, but fire magic returned to my chest and wind magic gave that breath-lessness.

"Deryn!" I hissed louder, but stopped when something crunched under my black knee-high boot.

Scraping my foot away, chunks of broken glass and a gold frame on a chain remained.

Deryn's mirror.

Faster, Val! I chided myself, ducking behind boulders and ripping around to the iron door. It banged against its frame with each passing breeze. A pile of clothing lay just before it with a leather harness I recognized as Deryn's.

Something was very very wrong. And when I went to call her name again, a long painful moan vibrated out the door. I slunk inside, using the tip of a dagger to ease the door open. I could sense the fae magic stronger. Fire roared in my veins, water magic kept me calm, and wind fluttered in my belly.

Another moan.

I followed it down a narrow passage to the right and stopped abruptly when I met the sound of the moan.

A firefae, with gold eyes shining in the cave's darkness, was chained to the cave wall, slumped over. His brown hair hung in strands together.

"Oh gods," I whimpered. His skin was gray, and the iron burned straight through to the bone where it touched. One more step and I saw the rest. Cells lined the back wall: a fae from Autumn, Spring, and Summer and Winter lay in each. Propped up or chained by iron metal, they were slowly being killed. *Used*.

The Winterfae didn't move, and I feared she was in the worst condition as barely any ice magic flowed from the white-haired female fully slumped down on the ground.

I had to get the rest out of here.

"Help me," the firefae choked out. "Help me first."

I moved to the waterfae who was nearest. "Who did this to you?" But I knew. My basic instincts, now honed by the battles of the fae, knew something was off that day Deryn and I sought out the HorCain. I rolled my knuckles around the iron cell bars. "I'm going to save you."

Could I pull on their magic and not kill them? I didn't know. I slammed a dagger down against the iron padlock and it crumbled into pieces at my feet. The crashing echoed around the vaulted room. I fell at the waterfae's feet. "I'm going to take this off. Then you need to get out of here." Tears ran down my cheeks. "There's a ship down this side of the mountain. With pixies."

Her wrists were wilted to the bone, and the chains burned through her red summer dress and slowly burned away at her chest. I smashed down through the chains against the walls, and she fell into me with an *oomph*. Blood coated me where she tried to brace herself. Her cheeks sunk in, hollow. If she survived, she'd never be the same.

I crawled out from under her. "Get up, get outside to the pixies. Please." But I knew it was futile. She wheezed with every breath. "Get up, please. I'm trying to save you."

I went to the next cage and wiped my wet face. The firefae who pleaded earlier looked in better condition. I broke through the iron containing him with my daggers and slipped them back on my back.

He grabbed my arms forcibly. "It's the witch. The witch is coming. Save me. She burns me with iron."

"Take her." I pointed to the Summerfae slumped, crawling toward the light of the tunnel. "Go. Get outside! Get both of you to Teal's ship."

But he clung to me and kept hollering for me to save him.

A moan came from the Springfae and frustration at the

firefae fastened to me was bubbling. I was *trying* to save him. "I have to save the others. Take her and go!"

But just as I went to push him away, something skittered up my leg and through the narrow opening at my waist and into my shirt.

Its claws scraped and dug into me as it climbed up, up, up. I hopelessly swatted every place I felt the pinching of tiny claws.

"What the—" I shrieked, pushing the firefae away. When there, popping out of the collar near my breasts, was a dirty brown mouse no bigger than my palm. *Gross*! I yelped as it scratched at my neck. I grabbed for it quickly and went to toss it away, but something in the low light, with the insane pandering of the firefae, caught my attention.

It had three legs.

The back one, missing.

I loosened my grip, allowing the small creature to breathe.

It sucked in a breath and chittered again.

I was losing my mind. I was no doubt as crazy as the male clinging to my ankles because I cocked my head and whispered, "Deryn Ironside?"

It pipped and peeped and chittered again.

"What. Happened," I said ever so slowly.

"The witch knows you're here," came the Springfae still locked in the cage.

Suddenly a blast of water shot out, flushing down my legs, and the firefae at my feet went limp. The waterfae curled in on herself into the dirty cave floor.

Out walked a frazzled-haired female with a tall staff.

I shoved mouse-Deryn into my shirt and whipped around a cave wall, putting space between me and the newcomer.

"I tried so hard to keep others from my caves, but she had to go and invite an entire colony of faeless to my valley."

"I take it you're Carmen. Want to tell me why I am in the middle of a dungeon of dying fae?"

"I didn't want to kill them. The Winterfae lasted so long. It's not my fault they weren't all as strong as her." She squinted at me, scrutinizing, then smiled a wicked thing as she said, "You have a darkness in you I can see. Honed by the horrors of the island. We aren't so different."

Sweat ran down my back. "You and I are nothing alike."

I bolted for the door. I couldn't very well save the fae if I was dead. A massive wave splashed up, wetting the rocks, taking Deryn's clothes with it out to sea. All that lay behind was a heavy iron leg. I leapt over it and a caw pierced the air above me.

"Deryn, thank the gods. Look it's Rhett!" I shouted and waved my hands for the hawkshifter.

He circled overhead, casting a looming shadow on the ground as I ran down the mountainside.

"Rhett! Rhett!"

Here's a battle he can gladly fight, I thought, but mouse-Deryn bit down near my collarbone. *Hard.*

"Ouch!" I pressed where she bit and jumped over another large boulder, landing hard on my butt. "What was that for?"

She chittered and zipped further into my clothes.

My spine tingled and the shadow of Rhett above us increased as he dove, beak wide, claws ready.

I didn't have a harness. How was he going to—was he trying to—

His claws snapped on the rock behind me as I twisted out of the way, but I wasn't fast enough, and his claw snagged on my daggers' holster. I felt a tug, then release as my daggers ripped from my back. Twelve-inch-long scars scraped through the red rock where my back had been.

I shook flat on my back, my heart in my throat, because he

wasn't trying to save us at all. He swooped away, shaking off my holster like it was a nuisance and my daggers fell to the valley far below.

He circled again.

Shit! "Deryn, what's wrong with him?" I scrambled to my feet. I thought of sending fire out to scare him off, but I would be siphoning magic from a half-dead fae in the caves. And I was afraid of killing them.

Deryn shook against my chest, unable to tell me anything.

Running was good, I decided. We *needed to run to Teal.*

"Come on." I cupped her near my neck under my clothes and ran along a gaming trail back around to the south side of the mountain, eyes to the sky, watching for the claws of a hawk-shifter.

When suddenly out of the iron cave door stood Carmen and Lady Fede. I dove as a gust of wind whipped the hairs around my face, skinning my knees against bare rock.

"That's the Siphon I warned you of," I heard on the breeze. "You called me back for Cillian's plaything?"

I grumbled some swear words I'd only heard Kade utter. I couldn't very well lead a malicious witch, a half-vampfae, and a crazed hawkshifter to Teal, or the settlement of Brendan in the valley on the other side. Lady Fede would kill them all.

"Now what, Deryn?" I muttered to the mouse, who couldn't answer me, let alone tell me a plan.

She jumped from my shirt to the rock we hid behind and skittered as fast as a three-legged mouse could go toward her iron tracks and her cart. It sat there, patiently waiting.

"I can't drive that!" I hissed.

But she was relentless, scampering toward it and then back to me.

A blast of fire singed the rock she stood on as the witch and Fede started coming our way.

"Fine." I'd rather die crashing in a rubble of iron than make Deryn face Lady Fede.

I snatched mouse-Deryn and ran, blocking their attacks with what magic I could pull from the fae. Carmen shot a fireball again. Gods, I worried about the condition of the firefae, and I quenched it with water before it hit my feet. Lady Fede tried to pull wind magic and suck the air from my lungs, but I blocked it with a wall of water, panting anyway because she was strong, and her magic tightened my airways.

Faster, faster!

I dove the last five feet into the hard, unforgiving metal base of the cart, cradling Deryn like a faeling into my neck.

"We're here, Deryn! Now what?" I looked at the gears. Which one meant . . . go? "Oh, for fuck's sake, we don't have time." I kicked out a foot against the solid mountainside behind me and held on to the edges of the cart for dear life as we shot forward along the tracks.

Deryn jumped on the control panel and hopped to the top of a lever, pawing at the air with one small, clawed hand.

"That one?" I asked, dodging a blast of water. I grabbed Deryn before she fell and cranked that damn lever halfway forward.

The cart tipped on its back two wheels and my heart fell out of my ass as I slammed a foot down near the front to balance it out. Suddenly Rhett landed on the gearbox, and the weight of him crashed the cart down, finding balance on four wheels again.

He pecked the air, seeking Deryn out. I pulled Fede's magic to me and blew a large gust of wind at him and he fell, dropping ten feet before finding his wings and righting himself.

The cart raced now toward the obsidian tower, even faster than Deryn had us go before.

Oh gods, this was a terrible idea.

36

VALENTINA

Little lion, Kade said down the bond. *Why does it feel like you're flying?*

Kade! It was Carmen, the witch on the Mainland. She's the reason the Hunt broke.

Deadly silence echoed back. *Where are you?*

Rhett swooped down, beak open, reaching for the mouse clawing up my chest. *Deryn's tower!* I narrowly ducked, banging my elbows on the bottom of the cart. *Kaderyn, something is wrong with Rhett.*

I'm coming, Kade raged through our bond.

A blast of fire scorched the front of the cart, heating the metal. Sweat traced my temples. Faster, we needed to go faster. "What do I do, Deryn?" I looked at the gears and metal levers. "Make this thing go full speed!"

She leapt out of my collar and onto a lever like before, but immediately squeaked and danced her little paws across the panel. The metal had turned bright red. I scooped her up as fast as I could and tucked her back in. Small heat spots where her paws touched my skin made my heart crack in two.

But Carmen wasn't relenting, Rhett was banking, coming back, and Lady Fede was nowhere to be seen. I tucked my hand in my sleeve and cranked that lever down slightly. The cart jutted once and . . . slowed down.

I turned in time to dodge Rhett's talons. They banged off the side of the cart and sent it rocking. Carmen's fire blast ceased. I looked back at her as she jumped down the side of the mountain, tracking us.

Below in the valley, faelings played while their parents tended the fields. Glynnera's hands were nimbly sewing a white fabric on a wooded porch facing the forest, watching a few faelings kick a ball in the dirt.

"Get inside!" I screamed, waving. "Get away from the tracks!"

Faelings looked up and waved back. They didn't know they were in danger.

"Go inside!" my voice cracked. "Glynnera, get them out of here."

Glynnera's rocking stopped, and she stood. Placing down the fabric on her vacated chair, she cupped her hands to her face, blocking the sun. She must have seen my distress because she started yelling for the other faeless. They looked up from their laboring and I screamed some more. I screamed until my voice grew hoarse, banging my fists on the scolding metal.

Then, when I saw them running away, I slammed that damn lever forward. We lurched on two back wheels again and my ribs crushed against the back of the cart.

Scratch marks down my neck told me I was doing this whole fucking thing wrong.

"Okay, Deryn. Okay." I leaned forward, but the cart jutted down suddenly, and we slammed into the molten heated panel.

I recoiled, dropping to the floor. Skin scorched, frustrated, and terrified for everyone in our wake.

We sped across the tracks. Wobbling too far to the sides if I moved any which way. But I peeked to see the faeless had gathered their young and ran from the fields. Relief sagged my shoulders, but was met with regret. The amount of trouble Deryn had gone to protect them, and I just brought a witch to their door.

"Do you know what happens when you cool metal? I bet that mouse in your pocket does," Carmen yelled. Somehow, she'd gotten in front of us as she stood twenty feet below the iron tracks, with her staff pointed up. She sent ice magic, Winter's magic, and ice crusted along the iron control panel. It sizzled and hissed.

But the ice magic was a reminder. *I* was made for this.

"Oh, by all the gods. Screw this." I pulled the magic to me and froze her hands down the staff.

Momentarily, Carmen panicked, and tried to drop her weapon, shaking off the chunks of ice clinging to her. I gathered fire magic and shot a blast at her head. She turned in time and the back of her head lit on fire.

She squawked and patted it out with ice-block hands.

Once she was free, she returned her blast of ice magic to the front of the cart. Missing me entirely.

"What's her plan, Deryn?" I didn't get it. Didn't . . . ice strengthen it? My hair bristled.

Deryn squeaked and ducked down further into my clothing. Frustration at talking to a mouse made me let out a growl before the screech of a hawk drowned it out. I looked just in time as Rhett's talons landed and he perched on the front ice-covered section, pecking for his prey. The weight of a massive hawkshifter bearing down on the cart slowed it down. He snapped for my neck, and I moved just in time and when he went to do it again, I blasted him in the face with fire.

He recoiled, swooping down below the tracks, but the front of the cart gave a loud *CRACK* and gave way, snapping off where the rapidly heated and cooled metal panel had been. It tumbled to the meadow below. I fell to my butt, shuffling as far back in the small cart as I could, and pushed my arms against the sides.

"Fire! Don't stop! Keep targeting the hawk!" The faeless of Brendan smacked Rhett in the side of the head with rocks on his return trip.

They were *helping*.

But we were now on a broken speeding cart, gears gone, with momentum launching us forward, and the unforgiving iron tower coming in way too fast. A wheel rattled, bouncing on and off the track.

"Oh, Deryn, how I wish you could tell me what to do."

She poked her head up out of my collar, squeaked loudly, and ducked back down.

"Yeah, I know. Hold on." I braced myself. A thick iron wall marked the end of the track. I had to leap and not crush my friend curled in the frays of my shirt. Fear and bile choked my throat.

Deryn bit as a warning and I vaulted out over the edge of the broken cart.

We landed hard, rolling in the nearby grasses at the base of the tower, and ducked as an ear-splitting *KABOOM* reverberated around us. Pieces of metal and earth exploded, scattering the air with shrapnel. I bent low, not wanting to lose my head.

I curled wheezing in tall grass that tickled my ankles through torn boots, feeling rattled, burned, cut, and unable to hear anything with one ear. Acrid smoke filled the air as flames flickered from a small fire nearby.

"Perhaps install a safety break," I muttered to the mouse, who jumped out of my shirt, climbed over broken metal, and up a railing, disappearing inside her tower. I groaned, lifting my aching body, and crawled to follow. I might as well have had my head chewed off and spit out by an Aileen.

Double vision blinded me, but magic swelled in my bones again.

Carmen was near.

I scrambled up the iron stairs, following the squeaking of the three-footed mouse. "A weapon, Deryn. I need a weapon."

I whipped to the second floor of her tower and against a wall, near a flaming forge, were a dozen swords meticulously lined up along a wooden rack. Dozens of tools I didn't know the names of marked the other wall.

"This will do just fine," I said, grabbing a heavy iron sword, recently polished. Then I gave the little mouse a sharp look. "Not bad for 'not a fighter'."

Deryn pipped once in response.

"Oh, come out, come out, wherever you are," came the sing-song voice of Lady Fede.

I froze, trying to decipher where she was. Deryn scurried for cover up the sleeve of a navy and silver tunic left lying on the edge of a daybed.

"You really think you can hide from me?" Fede taunted, closer to the south side of the tower. "This iron might keep me out, but wind carries *life* on its breeze, and I can take it away, little mousy."

A gust of wind burst through the glass panes, spraying thick shards across the room. I screamed and ducked, but the wind didn't break. It pushed so hard that my feet slid against the cool iron, pushing everything in the room out the floor-to-ceiling bay window to the east. I grabbed the edge of the daybed as glass peppered my skin. The tunic Deryn hid in tumbled around itself, dancing on the wind like attached to a clothesline blowing across the room before snagging on the splintered edge of a broom handle. Half the shirt hung like a flag out the window, threatening to drop Deryn down to Lady Fede.

"Deryn!" I cried, jumping into the onslaught of gale-force winds roaring through the tower. Sheets and debris flew like ghosts, blinding me. Iron hammers and small heavy dishes banged into my legs, bruising my thighs as I grabbed what I could to get to Deryn before she fell.

"When that blubbering scared faeless showed up at my castle asking for help for a town I couldn't give a pixie's ass about, I should have sucked the air from her lungs right then and there," Lady Fede roared over the wind.

And I had half a second to dive for the tunic before she sent a second burst of wind through the tower, this one so strong that full iron swords flew out the window and to the ground two stories below.

I grabbed for it, but my nails dug into my empty palm. The tunic was gone. It was all gone. Shirt. Broken broom handle. Her.

Shit, shit, shit, I cursed myself.

Pushing off debris, I leaned upright just in time to see a maniacal face through the stair banisters. I ducked as a blast of fire from Carmen's staff exploded inches above me.

Carmen's face peeked between the iron rails of the stairs. "What are you going to do, Valentina? I am hundreds of years old. You're a mere stain ready to be smudged out. They can't know what we've done."

"But did you know I can do this?" I said, creating a spinning tornado of fire and air like I had in Scarlotta's castle before the Spring Festival.

Carmen panicked as she tripped down the stairs, fighting off tendrils of fire licking her sleeves. But maneuvering the tornado was tricky, and it fizzled out when I couldn't get it down the winding stairs. I grabbed for a sword that lay at my feet.

Carmen was up again, blasting the room with ice, freezing the air, and I started laughing.

I pulled as much ice magic to me as I could, no longer fearing it. It quickened my senses, strengthening me. "Wrong move, Carmen. You don't know what I've been through."

But something—something familiar—calmed my mind, and it wasn't any ice magic from the north.

Something better.

Thick black shadows slunk up around Carmen, surprising us both.

"But—but how did Kaderyn know? I watched you the entire time. You didn't send for help," Carmen asked, wide-eyed as shadows snaked up her entire body. The sheer power of them left it to be only one Shadowfae. The very same one I was able to mindspeak to all because Kade used his magic in a nuckelavee den.

"That's the magic of nuckelavee sludge, bitch," I said as Kaderyn, from somewhere down the stairs, pulled his shadows tight, and drew a terrified screaming Carmen to him. Her glass staff lodged itself between the rails.

I bolted back to the window. With Kade able to fend off Carmen, Deryn was going to need my help with Lady Fede.

Lady Fede sifted through loose belongings, scattered clothing, and broken furniture, stomping her boot every so often and laughing in her horrific singsong voice. "Little pest," she cooed. "You know, I haven't thought twice about the terrified faeless I shoved off the Aeolian Cliffs all those years ago. Never crossed my mind that you were the one building all Carmen's metals."

"Hey!" I said, jumping out the second-story window to the debris below. "We have some unfinished business."

In a split second, I created and shot an icicle straight for the Springfae's heart. But she moved in time, and it sliced the loose arm of her dress. The same white ballgown, though now muddy and bloodstained, I last saw her in when she tipped over the cliff with Cillian.

"You're in over your head," she scowled.

And I really *looked at* her. The sleeve was loose because there was no arm beneath it. "Oh, Fede. Did you have a run-in with the seamutts?" I mocked, then held her eye. "Or was that your pet, the Berserker?"

"You mean your lover? Tell me, Valentina. Who was the *pet* in that relationship? He caged you and used you for tricks and company. Ah, there you are!" She reached down as mouse-Deryn inched out of a broken wooden drawer. Fede snatched her violently into her fist.

Deryn skittered in her hand, her little paws flailing to scramble out of her hold.

"So many bones to break." Lady Fede smiled.

"Let her go!" I pulled fire to me.

Fede snuffed it out with air magic. "You think I haven't fought firefae before?"

Deryn's nose sniffed once, then chomped down on the curve of her thumb.

Lady Fede screamed, cursed something awful, and threw Deryn as hard as she could at the iron tower. My heart stopped and fire burned through my veins. She'd die if she hit the unforgiving iron wall.

But the three-legged mouse soared through the open window, and a small plunk reached our ears.

"Deryn!" I cried, forcing a blazing rage of fire at Fede.

Fuck! I ran.

Back through the destroyed first floor, past the simmering fire from the crashed cart, and to the stairs, taking them two at a time. I unhooked Carmen's staff when it blocked my way and tossed it to the floor. "Deryn! Oh gods, Deryn, where are you?"

The heat of the forge raged behind me, fueled by Fede's air magic. *Please be alive, please be alive.*

Lady Fede's snarling round face appeared over the iron railing as a blustering gust of wind lifted her up and over the balcony. But there was no Faebric here anymore. No barrier between her skin and the iron.

I grabbed for a loose hammer where it was wedged near the forge and grabbed for Carmen's staff in the other.

Deryn scampered out of nowhere and ran as fast as she could up Carmen's staff in my grasp. I tried to shake her off. I tried to pluck her from its glass orb and hide her behind me. But it was too distracting, and Lady Fede stretched out a hand and *pulled*, sucking the air from my lungs.

I grappled to hold on to enough air magic to breathe, sending out slinking shadows to pull at Fede, but Deryn wouldn't get off the end of the staff.

She wouldn't run! Why wouldn't she run?

Frustration and desperation bubbled up and melded into one. I dropped the staff and focussed on breathing. The brown mouse ran up *again* to the glass ball on the end and jumped up and down. Trying to . . . trying to . . .

Oh.

Deryn was trying to break it! Spots dotted my vision and blood pumped to my ears so loudly I couldn't hear the shit Lady Fede was saying, but my fingertips met the last six inches of the staff. And with one strangled gulp, I swung it as hard as I could against the raging forge. Immediately an explosion blew hot coals into my face, and I ducked and turned as they singed my back. A crash trembled the tower as the force broke the iron flooring and the forge smashed through below.

A shrieking scream shook the air and suddenly every magic left me but that belly-flopping air magic and the steady magic of shadows. I gasped and choked as air returned to me, and unleashed shadow magic, blinding Fede standing overtop me. But a breeze, too strong, blew and dissipated my shadows. I crawled backward until my palms edged over the hole in the iron floor.

Suffocating.

"You underestimate how far I'll go to get what I want. There's nothing you can do." But with no Faebric between her and the immense iron, flecks of blood seeped from her pores. "There's no magic you can use that I haven't fought before." She laughed. "There's no magic you can possess that I have not seen."

A raspy voice echoed in the rambled iron chamber. "How about this one?" Just then, Deryn sprang up behind Lady Fede and pulled her trusty iron hammer tight around her neck.

A blood-curdling scream parted the Springfae's lips and echoed inside the now hollow tower like a clapper inside a bell. Her fair skin instantly bubbled and started to split. I covered my ears, but Deryn, naked with her brows touching, and bared teeth, hung on to the slight fae's neck from behind. And even with a Springfae's strength, the sheer muscle from Deryn, an iron forger, kept her on her back.

Eventually, Lady Fede's knees buckled, and her eyes floated up, showing their whites. The hammer burned away her throat, leaving it raw, gaping open like a fish as Lady Fede gasped for air. Deryn dropped off her back and crashed to the ground. Her hammer embedded in Fede's throat. She fell face-first against the iron flooring of Deryn's tower. The skin of her cheek sizzled like water in a hot frying pan.

I collapsed, sucking in air. "Oh, thank gods, that's over."

Deryn looked back toward me, and with eyes wide, she sniffed her nose. "Do you smell that?"

But all I smelt was burnt flesh, debris, and open air. I tossed a loose hand up. Whatever it was, it had to be fine because Spring's queen bee was dead.

Deryn didn't carry the same sentiment because her eyes turned to saucers, and she beckoned me to her. "Come on, we have to get out of here!" She scrambled around the sizzling body and headed for the stairs.

"It's okay. Kade's somewhere with Carmen—" I choked. A smell was blooming from below.

"Get out of the tower!" she growled again. "Valentina, I stored the Faemech below." She pointed behind me to the hole in the floor where the forge fell through. On a small shelf through thick smoke, I saw the iron box marked *Faemech*, the very substance that split an entire island in half.

"The river," I grunted, scrambling to my feet as I pulled her away from the stairs and to the far north window with the large balcony railing.

Deryn pulled out of my hands and shook her head incessantly. "No, I can't. You don't understand. Please, not the waters."

"Yes, Deryn. You can, and you have to." I gripped her head, pulling her frantic stare to me and not the simmering waters below. "We'll do it together."

I hefted her up, naked and trembling, onto the railing and climbed beside her.

"Adrian," she whispered as sea spray hit our faces.

"Jump!" I commanded and pulled her with me as we hurled into the Galeairy Strait.

Caws of a hawkshifter sounded overhead just as our feet plunged into the cool waters.

Frothy bubbles danced up my skin as I sank. Deryn's hand was suddenly ripped out of mine and I scrambled to find her under the crystal blue waters. My heart raced and I couldn't think straight. If I saved her just to have her killed by the seamutts . . .

Bubbling fish tickled my legs as I kicked the final time to the surface.

Immediately spotting them.

Adrian, fully clothed and submerged in his waters, cuddled a very naked Deryn to his chest. "I've got you, dearest Deryn. I've got you." He brushed wet hair off her face. "I'll always have you."

Despite his cooing, she was hysterical and attempted to crawl over him out of the water. But eventually, she relented, clung to him, and sobbed into his shoulder.

Adrian's brutal eyes met mine, daring me to say something.

And it all clicked.

But I had a love of my own to worry about. "Kaderyn!" I screamed in absolute terror, swimming as fast as I could around the far side of the tower. He gripped Carmen, or what was left of Carmen, in his massive fists and seethed down at her. With my call, he looked over.

"It's going to explode!" Waves knocked water into my mouth, and I choked.

He took one look at the tower and a last parting look at Carmen before holding her at arm's length and kicked out his foot, meeting her chest. She flew backward as the tower ignited and exploding metal shards ripped through the air.

KABOOM.

I ducked under the bright blue water just in time to see Kade shadowfade into nothingness.

Everything shook as the tower blew to pieces.

I came up again as Adrian's eyes met mine and I knew for sure anything coming near Deryn was dead.

A seething pixie's voice screeched over the waters.

"Hurry forward
Steer shoreward
Pull them from the waters.
Get the thorns out
That means you, Scout
Or I'll be takin' back your coffers."

The Sinking Albatross sliced through the waters, passing cheering faeless on the shores. There at the front, miles closer to the tower, was an out-of-breath Avika, with her hands cupped to her eyes, looking for her sister. The waves bouncing water against Teal's ship battered me against it and twice almost pulled me under but, *by the gods*, it was good to be back in the waters.

I closed my eyes to its serenity.

Lady Fede was dead.

The witch was dead.

It was over.

"Do I need to pat you down again and make sure you didn't grow a tail?"

I smiled before peeking open my eyes and there on the deck of Teal's ship was Kaderyn, leaning down, holding a hand out for me. Shadows swirled around him like a welcome party.

"You have a much bigger boat this time," I said, spitting out a wave of water.

"It's a *ship*." Teal winced.

Adrian pushed Deryn into Kade's arms and Teal spun around her naked body with a large tunic.

But something in Kade's stare toward Adrian told me he would not be allowed to board. Kade used shadows to lace around me and hefted me in one go onto the deck. Exhausted and worn, I fell to the soggy, broken wood. Kade crashed down not seconds later, wrapping me in his arms.

"Are you hurt?" His hands roamed, despite our audience.

I shook my head. "Are you? Carmen was ruthless."

He leaned his head on the ship's side. "Onward, Teal. Take us home."

Deryn looked back at her tower. A hawk squawked overhead, and she scooted under the mast.

I shot up a cover of shadows above us.

"What's his deal?" I fumed.

"He's under Citrine Tonic. Carmen spelled him to target me once she turned me into a mouse," she said.

"Tasty little morsels," came a remark from the pixie covered in tattoos and patched wings I'd met earlier.

Those two were going to have a lot of explaining to do.

When the ship sailed by the faeless, they cheered and hollered louder, screaming Deryn's name again and again. Avika's black hair whipped in the wind as she ran parallel to the ship along the shore.

"That's for you, Deryn," I said, bumping her foot with mine. Too tired to move.

For a moment, she glanced away from her sister. Long enough to give me a smile. "That's for us."

"Yes, cheer for me!
Love me!
Pay me!" Teel chirped from the helm, and she shot a

blast from her arm up into the open sky, narrowly missing the circling hawk.

"Put it away, Teal!" Deryn scolded, and a meek apology returned on the salty air. "Will the faeless be safe?"

"Not yet," Kade said.

"What happens now?" I asked, because there was a haunted look in his eyes.

"Now," he said, rubbing my knee, "we go get patched up from Oir. Eat until we can't move. Sleep until even blinking isn't too much effort."

"Then?"

"Then," he growled, looking at me and the full heat of Kaderyn's black stare moves straight through me. "Then, we go to war."

37

KADERYN

Some creatures on Eadha come into your life and become a part of you. Sometimes without you noticing. They grow between the cracks of your mistakes, your flaws. Valentina was like this, sprouting tenderness and hope, laughter and lightness. That, though I carried heavy burdens, it didn't have to feel like it. Days weren't chores to get through anymore with her. Some creatures pry their way into your heart with bloodied fingers cursing. This was Artos. Whereas Jairek's pain saw mine and we threaded together on a mutual ache and disdain for the island. And Teal? Well, she was small enough to fit into even the tiniest of cracks in my heart.

Teal dropped the two of us off behind the Twin Peak Mountains. To the same old gaming trail Valentina used to find the captive fae. I returned the Springfae, Autumnfae, and Summerfae back to their courts, but I'm sure it did nothing to solidify my innocence in this entire fucking mess.

Carmen sat right under my nose the entire time.

"After you," I said, ushering Winter's general through the

thick iron doorway that led to the cave's tunnels. I ripped the door straight off its hinges the last time I was here.

Helle moved now through the cave systems, pensive but steady. Her steps were slow, and I couldn't blame her. Fae had a natural repulsion to iron and had avoided the rich mountain for that reason. Too much of it burnt the air like a poison.

And it turned out Lord Brexton hadn't been poisoned at all. He was under a spell from a witch. I felt like a fool for not seeing it. Carmen was one creature; how could she have caused so much destruction?

I couldn't voice that now as we rounded a corner to the lineup of cages where she held a fae from each court captive, pulled out their magic, and used it to build her iron castle beneath the mountain.

A strangled gasp escaped Helle's mouth.

We left her mother here for her to see. For her to mourn. It felt right considering she helped Valentina and Jairek in Winter. And we weren't sure she'd believe it if she didn't see it for herself.

"Killing the faeless had no bearing on fae being stolen from the courts. Carmen only took one Winterfae, not because she feared your father, but because of your mother's strength. Carmen didn't need to kidnap any others. Embee survived right until the very end, Helle." I'd unhooked Embee from the iron chains and Val arranged her so that her worst wounds were hidden.

But Helle grabbed for her mother and pulled her into her chest, heaving iron-laced air, rocking back and forth. "Where is she? The one responsible. Where is Carmen?"

"I killed her. Blown to pieces with Deryn's iron."

Helle snapped, "Did the Ironside know? Did she know my mother was here?"

"No."

"How could she not know? She was right here! Kaderyn, all this time! How did you not find her?"

Her shoulders shook as she sobbed and raged at me. And what good answer was there to give her other than my own fucking problems had consumed me until all I saw was my pain and it blinded me to the trials of the island for far too long. Deryn too. So, all I could say was, "I'm sorry."

We stayed like that until the sun switched positions in the sky.

"Tell me, Kaderyn, that I am released from your halls when I die," she sniffed. "Tell me I've earned my repentance. I want to see her again in the Otherworld." She smoothed down her mother's hair along her ear.

I sucked in a deep breath through my nose. "I can't do that, Helle."

The piercing blue eyes and disheveled white hair of the fae before me sent a shiver down my spine. Despite my hardened nature, it made me instinctively reach for my sword.

"I did as you asked," she roared. "I got rid of the Frost Witches. I buried your mare through snow and ice. Fuck, Kaderyn! I gave Val the bow in the tundras, I took my army out of Silvermere for Jairek's escape. You're telling me none of it mattered?"

"I'm sorry, Helle." And I really fucking was. "Every time I check, every time I look close to see where your soul goes, it's always with me, in my halls, in my Underworld."

"Fuck you, Kade!" she roared.

And if she wanted to use ice magic on me, I thought I might even have let her. Maybe once, because when I returned to my Underworld last, I had Zedekiel check too, but it was clear:

Helle was meant for the Underworld.

A web swept out from the Winterfae, spreading, crawling, and coating every iron surface in that degrading cell until all was white, sparkling, and frozen, without an inch of black to be seen.

Helle was strong, and I didn't know where her heart lay regarding her offer to fight against her father now that her mother had been found. "Helle, I have to ask," I spoke slowly, afraid she'd run me through. "Does this change where you stand in the War of Many? Can I still count on you joining my army?"

With one last kiss to her mother's forehead, she stood, fists clenched and faced me. This tiny, scarred fae who could make my strongest Hunter hesitate said, "I'm not joining your army, Kaderyn."

She walked out of her mother's crystalline tomb, tossing her words back with a promise full of spit and violence. "I'm going to lead it."

38

DERYN IRONSIDE

Auris' library was a multi-leveled sprawling cathedral with shelves upon shelves of books, maps, and archives. A purple glow shifted through the library with the passing clouds from above.

But the hidden meeting room off to its right, behind a moving bookshelf marked:

Pixie Earwax and All its Magnificent Colors:
The Complete Collection

was nothing short of stifling.

Especially with the company it held now.

We'd spent the last half hour listening to Rhett tell us why it was a bad idea to have Helle know our plans. " . . . as she sits there mocking us in a beast's skin."

And though I was still unsure what she was doing here,

Helle, Winter's general, cocked an eyebrow and said, "Would you rather I wear nothing at all?"

The room exploded again, and my shoulders hit my ears. Avika was more suited for these situations in both volume and tact.

Helle'd brought her mother's body back to Silvermere City for Winterfae to mourn. The pixies swore they heard crying from across the island. But it didn't change Lord Aborys' mind. If anything, it solidified his obsession with ruling the island. "The last thing I'm doing is mocking you. Baliroqs kill for sport. They're vile creatures and often massacre towns in my tundra. But dead, their scales become malleable and just as strong. Or almost." Blue eyes met Jair's.

"We cannot fight Autumn, Spring, and Winter," Oir said, and I was happy with the subject change.

A little pixie in a flower petal dress scribbled notes in a ledger in the center of the room.

Oir continued, "No offense, Jair, but the Courtless is disorganized and in disarray and Shadow Court is centuries younger than its neighbors. We've had to spend our days building a self-sustaining city instead of armies like the rest."

"We fight them all." Rhett thumped his fist on the desk.

I chewed my lip.

"Did the Citrine Tonic melt your brain? We'll be outnumbered," Oir snapped, unhappy with his outbursts.

"I'll try talking to Roshan," Valentina offered.

"He's too young to lead and has no experience managing an army. If he keeps sending his soldiers out, he'll have none left," Jair said, rubbing a hand down his face. He faced General Helle, leaning on the edge of a desk with his legs kicked out. "Autumn has all the weapons and they've found a way to forge them stronger. They break the bronze we have."

"But it doesn't break Deryn's," Rhett said.

I didn't cringe at the sound of my name.

"She can make more iron weapons," he finished.

"Don't drag her into this. She's done her part, blew apart the island even. Use that beak for something other than throwing her into a war!" Adrian snapped from beside me.

Rhett pushed off from his chair, one of the few in the room, and stalked closer. "And what have you done, Adrian? Whose side are you on?"

"I'll do it," I said, but it came out meek, barely above a whisper.

They roared at each other.

"I'll do it!" I repeated louder, stepping between my first love and him.

The room grew quiet, and the heat of the attention pulled my shoulders to my ears again. I continued, "I'll make enough iron weapons for this war."

Adrian laughed, but there was no humor in it, and he moved back to his original position, holding up the wall beside me.

"You lot have issues," Helle muttered.

But I wasn't giving up. "I'm going to build you enough weapons for your army, Kade, and enough for every faeless who wants to fight."

"Deryn, I like the sentiment, but they'll be slaughtered before they step even one foot near Winter," Kade piped up for the first time since we entered the room. Valentina says he hears his Hunters through something like mindspeak sometimes, so it keeps him quiet. He swears far more now though.

"They deserve to fight," Valentina added, and I relaxed a bit, knowing she had my back. "It's their war too."

"How are we going to touch iron weapons, dear?" Oir asked.

I held my breath because I was showing them a creation and

it always caught me around the throat. I tossed down a hammer, and it thunked to the table. "I melted down the wrist bindings Jairek brought back from Winter for the handle. The mallet, well, you won't want to touch that part."

Rhett picked it up, twisting it in his hands.

"I'll build every sword like it," I finished, stepping back to the safety of the wall and Adrian's side.

"Who's going to mine your ore, Deryn? Marcus is fae and has Gael's hammer. You're only one faeless," Helle asked. Her sky-blue eyes met mine, and I looked at the floor. She'd never directly addressed me before.

I didn't even know she knew my name.

Without Carmen, the ogres left their mines and terrorized Fillagree Fen but only for less than a handful of minutes. Luckily, their docks weren't meant for the blustering weight of an ogre, and they fell through into the Galeairy. A passing pod of seamutts made sure they didn't resurface.

Later, Kade and Jairek chased the rest out of the caves, scattering them thousands of miles south, and Adrian was kind enough to take the Horn of Bran for safekeeping.

The pixie scribbled away, and I swallowed. "I have someone in mind."

The room grew silent. Which I knew for some, was hard to do. But some manner of finality passed over the eight of us. A merger. A promise. It laced through us more than Kade's lingering shadows.

"The War of Many is the at the closest it's ever been," Oir said.

"Will we win?" Valentina asked, big-eyed up to Kade.

The room grew silent once more except for the scribbling of a pen.

"Ah," Helle said with a shrug, pushing nimbly off from

where she took up an entire couch to herself. "I'm not worried."

"And why the fuck not?" Rhett yelled.

Helle, in armor of a beast's skin, created an icicle out of thin air and stabbed it through the carefully curated plans penned down by the pixie scribe. She patted the terrified pixie gently on the head before sauntering through the room of once-enemies to the door.

"Because you have me." She winked to Rhett.

Jairek smirked and trailed behind.

But if Helle was standing against her father, then she wanted something, and I felt she'd show us just how far she was willing to go to get it.

LATER, AFTER SETTLING THE PLANS AND CALMING down the pixie, I came across Adrian in the recently emptied hallway of Auris.

"Are you going to live in Illediff with your bird lover?" he asked.

"No, the faeless helped me lug my iron smelting tools to the valley, at least the ones that survived the Faemech. I'll be staying with my sister and my niece."

Adrian nodded, and I felt sea spray on my skin. He was leaving.

"Adrian?" I called. "Will you still visit me in Brendan?"

"I will visit you in Brendan, dearest Deryn. I will visit you in your bird lover's nest. I will visit you whenever you call—"

"—to the waters," I finished.

He smiled and gave a small wave while I mustered the

courage. "Adrian, wait!" I closed the distance between us. "I don't know why you did it," I said, shaking my head, "but I know what you did."

Warm brown eyes locked on mine, swimming with galaxies he'd seen before in worlds so far away from my iron tower.

I didn't tell anyone. And maybe I should have, but also, maybe I was selfish like Rhett and his obsession with war. I wanted my Adrian to stay with me and I worried he'd leave if Kaderyn knew. If he found out.

"Do you regret it?" I asked.

The room chilled, and he gave me a pained smile. "Never in all my millennia had I had a more worthy cause."

And he misted away.

I WAS GOING TO BUILD THE ENTIRE DAMN PORT OUT of iron if it meant I could stop rebuilding joints glued together with sticky fingers and pixie spit.

"Deryn?"

"One second," I called, hammering the last nail through the uneven driftwood, and looked up at my sister.

It'd been a week after I told Kade I'd build his metals, and I would, but until then I was using spare iron fragments from my collapsed tower to patch Teal's sub-standard work.

"Sorry to bother you. I know you're busy."

I pushed up out of the knee-deep waters. "Is everything all right?"

"I'm hosting a meeting. I have an announcement for the faeless. Teal's bringing her crew. I was wondering if you'd mind being there. You don't have to. I know you're busy with the War starting. But just, maybe, as a favor to me?"

I told her of my plans to build the weapons for Kaderyn's army and for any faeless who felt able to fight. Valentina was right, this was their—no, *our*— war, too.

"When?" I asked.

Avika glanced up to Fillagree Fen's sundial made from a fork and a dirty dish. I made a mental note to get Teal a clock because I couldn't give her mine; she broke it with her iron arm.

"When I've convinced you to come with me." Her face scrunched up into a cringe.

That meant now, the gathering was happening right now.

I wiped wet hands on my dirty shirt and grabbed my satchel of tools. "Lead the way."

But she took the satchel from me and snapped it around her waist. "I've got this."

"It's heavy," I warned.

She glanced back over her shoulder. "I need the practice."

We walked in silence down from the port to Brendan to a small raised wooden platform near the strait. I looked to the waters, and they pulsed once, sending ripples across its surface. I smiled.

Adrian was nearby.

Brendan remained untouched through the fight with Carmen and Lady Fede. Valentina and I were much of a distraction.

I tucked my hands in my pockets, feeling naked without my bag, and leaned against the support beam of the podium Avika climbed. Flocks of faeless stood down at her feet, chattering.

She gave me a hard stare, and I shifted the weight off my iron leg.

"Town of Brendan!" she called. "No one knows what we've

been through. No fae could have guessed we'd survive as long as we have. Things have changed so much for us, but our fight does not end just because we've left their shores. We need to fight to make sure the fae don't come to ours.

"And we can do it if we band together. Because we're not faeless. We are not *less* of anything. Like the ground, the very humus we go back to, we are humans. We will adapt and survive. We're a product of this earth as much as any other fae and we will defend our right to live.

"I am Avika *Ironside*"—gray eyes shot to mine and tears blurred my vision— "and I will lead us into a new age. My sister, Deryn Ironside, turns ore into metal. She's brilliant. We see every day what she's able to create. We see the usefulness at the port."

The pixies cheered, and I rubbed my arm across my leaky face.

"We see the usefulness across our skies." She pointed to my tracks and the cart I used to hide in. "She's going to build us weapons, so we never feel as helpless as we did in Blackwater Junction ever again."

Applauds charged the air.

"But the ogres of the mountains are gone, and she's only one *human*," she continued and with a chest full of bravado and courage she yelled with a fist to the air, "And we're going to mine it for her!"

Cheers exploded from the pixies and the faeless from one end of the crowd to the other for what felt like hours. There was no hiding anymore. I was going to do this, and they were going to help.

"Now a few words from our neighbors in Fillagree Fen from Teal." Avika stepped down, but before she made it the entire way off the podium, she turned back to Teal, who had a ruthless look on her face. "Keep it clean, Teal," came her warning.

Teal nodded once, eyes bugging. She thrust a little sword up as she paced the air above the podium. She fired off a blast of pixie magic from her iron arm. "Listen up ya, scoundrels." And she went on to pitch the usefulness of Fillagree Fen and her pixie pirates.

A few hours later, I pulled the singular muddy-colored sword out from between broken chunks of metal. The one Rhett brought me from between the ogre's shoulder blades. The wreckage of my tower was immense. I was going to need a new forge, but my anvil survived, and most of my tools.

I held the pommel, spun it once, then laid it down on a broken panel of wall that was once my bedroom.

The War of Many was going to start.

I pulled my trusty hammer out from my satchel, the one of full iron, and smashed it down, imploding the peaceful bliss of the meadow surrounding me. The glinting sword shattered into shards at my feet.

And I was going to build weapons for us all.

39

VALENTINA

I found him at the entrance to the small cave on the west side of The Court of Shadows. At the place where it all started. The place he banned all Shadowfae.

Even me.

Overgrown riddenweeds blocked its entrance and the clouds overhead rumbled like they were ready to fall. I was on my way to bring Deryn back her fused hammer, and to congratulate the faeless—I meant, *humans*—on relighting the forges in the mines, but Kaderyn's shadows led me out here instead. It didn't take any fae or soothsayer to know something unforgivable happened here.

Something catastrophic.

Kade's strong back hulked in the small entrance as he stared into the cave's core. I dropped Deryn's hammer into the weeds and looped my fingers into his.

Startled, like he hadn't heard me coming, he looked down to where our hands joined. "This was where it happened, Valentina. Where the Hunt fell."

I swallowed thickly. I wanted to tell him he was safe and we were going to get through this together. But there were no words to comfort the Hunter who had been torn from his brothers and forced to face the emotions of earth alone. So, I followed his gaze into the musty, humid black heart of the thing. "You want to do this?"

"I have to."

We walked in, over the rocky, unmanaged pathway. An echoing in my ears like someone screaming made water flood my eyes because I was sure it was Kaderyn from so long ago. *My* Kaderyn.

"I was lured by Bivanna, called by the vampfae's song. It pulled me from my Hunt, pulled me away from my Hunters," he said, his voice hollow and haunted. "Deathmarch waited outside the cave while the hounds and I entered. They yipped at my heels, they pulled at my clothes. They knew. *They knew.*"

We stopped in the center where the ceiling was highest. It just skimmed Kade's head.

"And she bit me," he continued.

"What did you do?" I whispered.

He looked down at me, his usual black eyes sparkled with emotion. "I ripped out her throat."

I held my breath.

"Then, while we lay, both destroyed in our own ways. The footsteps started."

And as if I could hear them, the slow *clop, clop* methodical rhythm of a confident swagger bounced against the walls. Wait, I really was hearing it. "Kaderyn!" I hissed. "I can hear it."

Someone was coming.

Kade sucked in a breath through his nose. "You know, in my gut, I *knew* it was you who split my shadows," Kaderyn said, still staring off at the bloodstains on the cave floor.

I spun around and gasped.

"Don't take it personally, Kaderyn," Adrian said, sauntering into the cave, hands tugging on his navy and silver tunic with a large white smile plastered on his face.

Kade turned to him now, but not in anger. Not with the same anger I held. A solemnness graced his usual gruff tone as Kade said in awe, "All because a god fell in love with a human."

Adrian's smile faltered, and he gave the briefest wince and shake of his head. "It was the only way to keep her safe. Carmen promised to protect her while I was in the Otherworld. She demanded the Hunt to fall."

The more I thought about Adrian's involvement, the more it rattled my brain. The chests had Adrian written all over them; the sea river inland and the freshwater runoff that trapped the nuckelavees. Adrian could do all of it.

"With help, you could've gotten them back centuries ago. How was I supposed to know you'd become a miserable recluse, brooding about in your castle instead of across the island, playing my games? But no matter how much I hate you and think your hair is stupid, the balance was off. The dead were trapped for too long. It's for the best you returned to the Wild Hunt."

"You're a god," I scoffed. "You should have known better. You knew what would happen to the island."

"Carmen wanted him dead for good. Break the Hunt forever. Instead, Bivanna made you fae, which was the only way I could steal your shadows from you—"

"When I was broken and bleeding," Kade scoffed.

"It was supposed to be temporary. There was no other way, Kaderyn, I hope you see it. And if it eases your mind, be sure I paid dearly for it." But softer, almost at a whisper, he said, "She doesn't know."

"You won't tell her?" Kade's shoulders fell.

Why was he softening? I thought I'd be holding him back. I

thought I'd be saving this damn demigod from the wrath of Kade's impulsive anger.

Her, I repeated in my head and gasped.

"The bird-lover is more suited." Adrian tugged on his tunic, straightening it out like it would straighten out the mess he made of the island.

Deryn Ironside.

Kade's shadows flicked slowly. "Gael said he was being punished, forced to stay at the Fortress."

"The reason for the chests and key, I'm afraid."

"What was in it for him?" I asked.

"They're gods, Valentina. They don't need a motive. He's a boastful idiot. I simply asked if he could."

"Call Gael," Kade demanded.

"Oh, must I?" Adrian grimaced and flopped his head to the side. "Autumn's god is brash and crude. But he's always down for a good time. So, there is that."

And when neither of us moved, Adrian sighed and grabbed the hammer I dropped at the cave's entrance. "Avert your gazes unless you can stand for the rest of your days to be jealous of my size," he said over his shoulder as he reached down and undid his pants.

"Oh gods," I muttered, scoffing up to the cave roof. "And you say Autumn's god is brash?"

We silently stood for a moment listening to the sound of Adrian pee on Deryn's metals as I thought of a dozen different places I'd rather be.

"There is no wonder the others banished you from the Otherworld," came a thick-accented voice from deeper in the cave. One I heard in Autumn's Fortress so long ago. "I was on your damn side to let you back up to the Otherworld. Until now! Stop pissing on my metals, half-god."

"Gael," Kaderyn said, drawing his attention.

"Hunter, I congratulate you on your return." He winked and looked at me. "Nice to see you again."

Kade's hand tightened in mine. "Even when you had such a hand in causing it?"

"Eh? Oh, the iron chests, ya mean? A simple deterrent. Your shadows were not gone forever. I thought it was quite clever until the other gods exiled me to my Fortress for it. Seems they didn't think it was quite as funny.

"I think we all but gave up on you, Hunter, until iron-abled Valentina stumbled your way. Then she chained you with the Caterina del Aamod ties and I swear I heard them howling in the Otherworld."

Adrian took a step forward. "For the record, Kade. Since we're friends—"

Kade groaned.

"—I never gave up on you," he finished.

"Oh, stop kissing his arse. I'd like to see someone kick some sense into ya. Going and fallin' in love with a faeless? What were you thinking?"

"Erm, they're called humans now." My words came out pedantic, and I cringed. "Gael, how is Marcus making a stronger metal?"

"Oh, you know about that, eh? Seems you left somethin' in my court, Valentina."

"I didn't." I was tied to Kade wearing Autumn's furs. "I *had* nothing to leave."

"Something came across that desert with you. Something Marcus won't give up without a fight."

I racked my brain. There was nothing! Slippers, maybe? Even the broken Caterina del Aamod ties came back with us.

The air grew tense and thick, waiting for Kaderyn's next move. We had a war with other fae at hand. Was he going to start one with the gods too?

"Are you going to kill me, Kaderyn?" Adrian asked, breaking the silence like his fate rested in the next few moments.

"No."

"Bloody hell, why not?" Gael roared. "There's no fun in the lot of ya." He disappeared in a puff of acrid-smelling smoke.

Because I fell in love with a Siphon, and I would do anything to make sure she was safe, he mindspoke to me. *I understand why he did it.*

I could feel his mind wander to his Hunters and the wrath he unleashed breaking the veil between worlds.

For me.

"So what happens now?" I asked.

Kaderyn looked down and locked me with his beautiful black eyes. "Angus believes in you. I believe in you. It's time to make the earth shake, Siphon. We have a war to win."

"Valentina?" Adrian called from the mouth of the cave with a wicked sparkle in his eye as Kade and I made our way back to Auris, hand in hand. "How did it feel?"

And I wasn't the same Valentina from Otti Theater, not even the same one who survived Mohr. I was stronger.

Frost quieted my mind.

Ice had hardened my soul.

I was going to persevere.

"Cold," I answered.

"I'm not talking about my waters."

I shook my head. "Neither am I."

Adrian's smile curved up into a delectable thing. "Then you're ready for war, Valentina."

"I'm ready for it all to end."

Stick around for King of the Courtless, the last and final book in the Wild Hunt Series

WANT TO READ THE SHORT STORY OF HOW KADERYN saved Teal and Jairek? **Skies of Onyx** can be downloaded here through bookfunnel. (Or copy and paste this https://BookHip. com/PQCTCAW)

Want to know how Deryn Ironside made the Fabric? Meet the iron-wielding inventor in **Haven of Feathers and Ore.** It can be downloaded here. (Or copy and paste this - https://Book Hip.com/LMDPWJJ)

And finally **Origins of Shadowfae**, here, (or copy and paste here- https://BookHip.com/PRDBVKG) depicting the details of Kaderyn's fall from the Wild Hunt.

The best reading order for these short stories are:

1. Origins of Shadowfae
2. Haven of Feathers and Ore
3. Skies of Onyx

FOR INFORMATION ON UPCOMING RELEASES COME visit www.hjreese.com and join my newsletter.

ACKNOWLEDGMENTS

This book would not be possible without you, dear reader, emailing me and messaging me on my almost non-existent instagram account (I'm sorry) telling me how much you loved following Val, Kade, Teal and Jair. Without you I'm not sure this would be in the world today. I want you to know that every time you sent me a message, or tagged me in a post, (or even just followed me, read my newsletters etc.—you silent readers, I see you too) you made this little writer fall to the floor in gratitude, and I'd peep out a *thanks*, days late because I had convinced myself that there was no way you were talking to me about my books.

Thanks to all the moms in my life who keep me organized and motivated, specifically; Cheri, Lidia, Rosa, Karen, Marie and Maria.

Special thanks to Stacy Jane, I hope I did you justice with this one. Your support means the world to me. And the writers of NAU, for making the writing world a little less lonely.

And thanks to everyone on my newsletter who reads them and the absolute ridiculousness sometimes contained inside.

Lastly, I wanted to share a conversation I had once with a coworker who I greatly admire. She is one of those people who just rocks at life, you know? The ones who just intuitively figure things out without even breaking a sweat. This conversation was pretty frustrating at the time but it honestly lives rent free in my head. And now I hope yours too.

HJ (me): Carla, can I ask you a question?

Carla: Go ahead.

HJ: *really nervous at this point because the profession I was in was chockfull of personalities that didn't understand creatives* What happens when you've tried your hardest, when you've exhausted all your resources, and you still can't do it?

Carla: *without hesitation* You keep going.

HJ: *blinking profusely at her* No, no. *Haw. Haw.* No, no. I mean, you can't keep going. Your best wasn't good enough.

Carla: *annoyingly more confident and matching my blinking now* Keep. Going.

HJ: *wanting to throw my shoe at her* I mean, when you've tried your hardest, but your best didn't get you where you want to go.

Carla: *speaking slowly, no doubt questioning my intellect* Whether you think you can or you think you can't, you're right.

HJ: *unties shoelace*

And we've all heard that saying before but the masterclass she was teaching me was to not give up. So please, if there's something you desperately want and it really doesn't look like it's going to happen. Just keep going. Keep trying. You only fail when you give up.

Last lastly, King of the Courtless is coming.

You can count on me.

I gotchu.

But pre-orders make me want to stick my head in a nuckelavee's mouth and for my mental health, physical health and the health of my neighbourhood, we shan't be doing it again until the book is done.

Join my newsletter for updates on a timeline. I update there first.

ALSO BY H J REESE

Dancing With Darkness

Shadows of Solace

Rise of a Huntress

King of the Courtless

(Pre-order TBD)

<u>Short Stories on Eadha Island</u>

Available for free if you're on my newsletter or for purchase in paperback (bundled as a collection) here

Sign up for my newsletter here https://hjreese.com/newsletter/

Haven of Feathers and Ore

Skies of Onyx

Origins of Shadowfae

ABOUT THE AUTHOR

H J Reese is a left-handed, second-born, Sagittarius, who often falls into all the stereotypes these represent. She lives in a small town in Ontario, Canada but her dreams take her around the world. She is the author of the Wild Hunt books. Visit her website at www.hjreese.com for more information.

www.ingramcontent.com/pod-product-compliance
Lightning Source LLC
Chambersburg PA
CBHW032232010726
47494CB00002B/459